NADINE LITTLE

Soulblind

An Urban Fantasy Romance

LITTLE PUBLISHING

Sign up to my mailing list to get exclusive stuff, free advanced review copies of my books before they're published, and exciting news on what I'm up to.

Choose your free sign-up gift from one of the options below (either type this address into the internet browser on your phone or computer or flip to the back of the book for the QR codes):

1. An explosive prequel to my dystopian Scotland series: https://nadinelittle.com/sign-up/
2. A character sheet from my dragon shapeshifter romance: https://nadinelittle.com/character-sheet/
3. A bonus epilogue from my angel apocalypse trilogy: https://nadinelittle.com/bonus-epilogue/
4. A bonus scene from my demon romance: https://nadine little.com/bonus-scene/

Happy reading!

'You cannot love a person fully
without knowing the darkness
etched into their soul.'
Sav R. Miller, *Promises and Pomegranates*

'A man without reason
is no better than a mad dog,
and mad dogs must be put down.'
James L. Sutter

1

I've been in love with my brother's best friend since I was four-teen. Xander featured in every teenage fantasy. Hell, in every adult fantasy. I pictured him when I lost my virginity, though even that struggled to improve the awkward experience. I still picture him when I'm touching myself. I swore the next man I had sex with would be Xander and no one else, even if I became an old spinster. You'd think I'd get bored after thirteen years, but the ache is always there. The yearning for him to see me as more than his best friend's sister. The flutters and tingles and throbbing in the pit of my stomach. None of that shit has faded.

Which is making it especially hard to kill him.

"Do it, Q-tip!" he yells at me. "Quinn, *please!*"

He fights the grip of his captors as they wrestle him towards an unmarked van, his heels kicking divots in the grass. The shot is already tricky with the third wave of Revenants between us.

Q-tip—the completely unsexy nickname Xander gave me. Before I hit puberty, I was tall and skinny, with a mess of strawberry-blonde hair. He said I looked like a used cotton bud.

He pleaded with Olly to kill him first, earning a punch in the mouth from one of the enemy grunts manhandling him. My brother gritted his teeth and emptied his rifle into the horde shambling across the lawn. At seven hundred and fifty rounds a minute, it cleared quite a swathe.

But they keep coming. I've never seen so many. Zombie-apocalypse many.

My vision wavers, misted by rain and tears and mud. The strap of my helmet digs into my jaw. I'm kneeling in a puddle behind one of our metal barricades, watching the love of my life being dragged away. The drum of footsteps vibrates into my kneecaps as the Revenants advance, the bodies of the first two waves barely slowing them down.

An Anima mystic controls them. Maybe more than one. Agents of our evil overlords, protected somewhere in the palatial building of the independent school that was our target, the Pentland Hills a blurry backdrop in the grey drizzle. It's all imposing columns and Latin-inscribed stone. A front for training bad little mystics, Anima or otherwise. A place to gather their Revenant horde.

Bullets zing into our barrier.

Fucking soulblind grunts. I'm one myself, but at least I'm on the right side. The side of the plucky underdogs who refused to join the coup.

A minute, maybe less, and we'll be overwhelmed by the Revenants the grunts are guarding, the rest of our army already scattered in the woods behind us after *El Capitan* ordered the retreat. It's just me and Olly, shoulder to shoulder. And Xander, begging me to shoot him.

I slot the retractable buttstock of my HK G37 rifle into my shoulder. I hold my breath because my lungs want to hitch, and peer around the dented edge of metal. Various shoes squelch and stomp. Some Revenants are barefoot, little holding their ragged clothes together except threads. They are a wall of bared teeth and howling gullets. Liquefied dirt splatters in their wake.

We were told the school was empty. Abandoned. Xavier, Xander's older brother, was his usual snooty and arrogant self as he briefed us. But this whole operation has been a clusterfuck. We arrived with the usual complement of Anima mystics as backup, but when it all went to hell, there were too many Revenants for them to lay their souls to rest even as we shot the shit out of the meat puppets at the same time.

I see it in flashes—the bodies churned as much as the grass, the unexpected appearance of a second wave, never mind the first. Chaos. Xander trying to rescue a guy when the Revenants broke through our line. Both of them on the ground. Two of our Anima mystics falling victim to teeth and hands. The order to retreat. Xander already taken, the third wave parting around him.

We'll be blamed for this—the Unbound. Distorted to look like the bad guys. Not the ten thousand other arseholes and their deluded minions who are *actually* the bad guys, controlling the mainstream media and every other body of power across the globe.

The *Guild*. The polite name for the arsehole majority. Not as cool as our moniker, obviously.

I squint through the mechanical sights. The disjointed gaps in the wall of stampeding Revenants let me see the blood on Xander's mouth. Beneath his helmet, his black hair is damp and flopping over his forehead like it always does. Panic makes his lime-green eyes brighter, like sunshine through a beech leaf. If I were closer, I'd notice the forest green bordering his irises and the thick, dark lashes accentuated by the eyeliner he wears to piss off his brother.

A bullet whispers of death as it whines past my ear, the enemy grunts still taking pot-shots at us from their ambush position behind the pediment of the central portico. My breath trickles out. My aim steadies. The cacophony of battle dims to a gentle hum. I focus on the spot between Xander's beautiful eyes. Wait for the perfect opening.

One heartbeat. Two.

Relief floods Xander's face and his lids flutter shut.

I squeeze the trigger.

Olly slaps my gun and it jerks to the side. My bullet catches a Revenant in the throat, spinning him around, gouting red. He trips, lost in the mob, but will keep crawling, even if every bone in his body is crushed. Unless the brain is destroyed or the soul is returned, they always keep coming.

Three heartbeats. Four—and it's too late.

The Revenants swarm towards us. Xander disappears into the back of the van. A barrage of rounds squeals into our barrier, forcing us to duck.

"How could you do that?" Olly pants at me. "You love him."

He has the same strawberry-blond hair as me, though shorter and mostly hidden by his helmet. Same hazel eyes and scattering of freckles across his pert little nose.

I tell my brother everything. There are no secrets between us and that includes my ridiculous infatuation with his best friend who, sadly, also happens to be *my* best friend.

Happened to be.

"I could do it *because* I love him," I sob, my fingers blanched and wrinkled on my gun. "You know what they'll do to him. I can't spend my nights imagining it."

"Well, I'd rather Xander was alive. If he's alive, there's hope."

Olly sniffs hard, swiping a hand under his dripping nose. He rests the barrel of his rifle on the top of our barricade and looses a burst. The roar batters my ears.

"He's not alive," I say. "Not anymore. He was as good as dead the second they shoved him in their vehicle."

"He could escape."

"No one escapes."

"We might see him again."

I look Olly square in the eye and say, "I pray we don't."

Pain and denial twist his face. My heart feels shattered. Cold. As dead as I wish Xander to be.

"We have to go," Olly says, his voice strangled.

I shake my head. "I'll cover you."

"Don't you fucking dare, Quinn. I loved him like a brother. I'm not… I'm not losing my sister, too."

Fingers manacle my bicep. Olly's gun coughs in his other hand. He yanks me upright and we stumble into a bent and zig-zagging run. My rifle jumps against my thigh, having slipped from my hands, forgotten. I strain my neck to glance over my shoulder. The vehicle holding Xander pulls away beyond the ragged line of Revenants. Bullets patter into the forest.

A wet fern slaps me in the face when I whip my head back around, my soul as leaden as my feet. My arm goes numb under the press of Olly's fingers. I choke on the scent of mulch and mould and pine.

As we melt into the woods, I can still hear Xander shouting my name.

2

I remember the moment I fell in love with Xander, like I'm still the same gawky and ungraceful teenager I was when it happened. He was the outcast of his family. Literally. An unwanted pregnancy, then a failed abortion. They already had one perfect son. One more could never live up to expectations.

And he didn't.

The difference in his appearance to his parents and older brother made it worse—black hair, green eyes, and a slender build to their blond and blue-eyed loveliness, the father and number-one son as muscled as rugby players. All of them Anima mystics, the most powerful of the three levels of soulkinetics. Self-appointed, of course. Sure, Anima mystics can rip out your soul and turn you into a slavering meat puppet, but Terra mystics can manipulate the soul of the earth. They can literally get the dirt to open up and swallow you whole. Okay, so they can't move mountains or anything so grand, but the strongest can cause earthquakes and avalanches.

We can protect our souls from being yanked out, but try stopping a giant hunk of rock zooming for your face.

Still, the Dawsons were rolling in it—huge mansion on a private parcel of land, expensive cars, good standing in the community. And Xander, the soulblind disappointment.

Xavier was doted on. He was awarded every opportunity whereas Xander got leftovers and hand-me-downs. They didn't even celebrate his birthday. No wonder he rebelled just to get some attention.

He spent most of his childhood at our house. There's barely a memory of my life without him in it—a gorgeous, tousle-headed boy with a quick grin and a mischievous twinkle in his eye once my parents coaxed him out of his sullen shell. I remember the day he started at our primary school in Melrose. He was in Primary 7 with my brother while I was in Primary 5. Xavier attended the fancy St Mary's Prep, but came over at lunchtime to taunt him. Olly pushed Xavier in a puddle, and he and Xander became best friends. I may have also jumped in the puddle while Xavier was splashing around like a dying pelican and squawking just as loud.

Xander told me and Olly about soulkinetics long before their presence became public. We didn't believe him at first. He showed us videos—people and animals acting like zombies. Lights on but no one home, their souls yanked from their bodies by Anima mystics. Terra mystics changing the course of rivers. Plants behaving very unplant-like, moving and grabbing people, their souls controlled by Essentia mystics.

Xander's parents, naturally, were high up in the mystical hierarchy, perpetuating a system that had been operating for hundreds of years throughout the highest level of human society. They were responsible for teams who tracked down mystics at risk of exposing their existence to the general masses. The minority who used their gifts for evil.

Shame they were never really the minority.

At sixteen, Xander got red highlights in his hair and wore eyeliner and dark clothes. He painted his nails black. I redid them after he got most of the varnish on his fingers. My parents complimented his new look at dinner, then sent him off home. A few hours later, I was about to go to bed in my favourite pink camo pyjamas, the trousers flashing my ankles due to an unwelcome growth spurt, when I spied movement in our treehouse. A flicker of candle flame through the pouring rain.

Xander liked to hide there when his parents had been particularly cruel.

I dashed outside. Fat drops of water darkened my t-shirt and slicked it to my flat chest. My hair was its usual frizzy cloud.

I may have grown in to my long legs, tamed my hair, and developed a decent pair of boobs, but I still feel—*felt*—gawky and flat-chested around Xander, and I'm almost bloody thirty.

Fourteen-year-old me climbed the wooden ladder smoothed by our hands, and crawled through the door of the treehouse. Xander sat on the rug, hugging his knees to his chest.

"Hey, Q-tip," he said.

A bruise swelled the corner of his mouth, a fresh bead of blood oozing on his lip. His eyeliner had run in black streaks, as if the hair sticking to his cheekbones was leaking dye. His jeans and t-shirt—borrowed from Olly—were sodden.

I mirrored him, my knees almost reaching my ears. "You can come inside, you know."

"I know," he said, his voice cracking. "I wanted to listen to the rain."

"Your mum and dad not like the new look?"

He attempted a smile, but it wobbled. "Nope. Maybe tomorrow I'll get my tongue pierced and really piss them off."

He dropped his forehead on his knees. I shuffled next to

him, pressed hip to shoulder, and cuddled his trembling body while he cried.

And that's when my heart both broke and sang for him.

He did get his tongue pierced. It was the object of many a fantasy—what it would be like to kiss him. That hard metal ball he clicked on his teeth when he was concentrating. What would it feel like in my mouth? What would he taste like?

I saw him with a girl not long after. He had her pressed to the wall of the high school gymnasium, out of sight of the main building. Acid churned in my stomach—a hot flash of jealousy—but I couldn't tear myself away. I watched them from the trees lining the playing field, my heart hammering while teenage rage and angst scorched my gut. His hands slid under the girl's top, stroking up her sides and sliding round to cup her boobs. Ridiculously gigantic boobs for a sixteen year old. One hand delved lower to disappear up her skirt.

It made me hot. Squirmy. I scuttled home and touched myself for the first, but definitely not the last, time.

Xander had a string of girls from then on, but never the same one for more than a few months. I couldn't help feeling smug when they inevitably cried and begged him to take them back, even though he was always honest about not wanting anything serious. I might only be his friend—practically his sister—but he never left me. I had him. Always.

At seventeen, he experimented with bisexuality, partly because he was curious, but also as a giant 'fuck you' to his parents. He didn't rub it in their faces, though one of their conservative friends saw him with a boy and gleefully tattled to his family. He was disowned and thrown out of the house. My parents took him in, no questions asked, and treated him like their own until he was eighteen, and he and Olly moved to uni, where they roomed together.

Hell, did that feel like the end of my world.

Of course, this was all before the world *really* went to shit eight years later.

3

The last two weeks have been a living nightmare. The number of hours I've slept can be counted on two hands. Every time I drop into oblivion, I dream of Xander. His suffering. His pain. Is he even still alive? Not that what they'll reduce him to can be called 'alive'. Maybe it's already done. Making a Revenant is almost instantaneous for the stronger Anima mystics. Why wouldn't it be the same? Though what Xander will become is worse than a Revenant.

So much worse.

My face in the mirror is gaunt-cheeked and hollow-eyed, my hair limp and lifeless. Olly fares no better. We've lost a family member. *Another* family member.

Our parents died in the mayhem that followed the Great Reveal five years ago. When everyone else discovered what had been living alongside them. The takeover was as effective as it was sudden, though it turned out they'd been planning it for decades. The evil majority had double the number of mystics to the Unbound, hence our cool moniker and them just being known as a big group of greedy arseholes. By me, anyway. The Guild held strategic positions across the world—government, army, police, financial institutions, schools. They were already in power. Establishing total rule was easy.

My parents worked in the Scottish government. Nomags like me, Olly, and Xander, and the rest of the population. The polite term for humans without soulkinetic magic. Xander tried to tell them about mystics, but they didn't believe him as readily as Olly and I. When the coup happened, they fiercely resisted, regretting that they were warned and didn't listen. That they hadn't trusted Xander. They convinced him to approach his family, despite the obvious reluctance on all sides, and became one of the first nomag leaders with connections to the dissenting mystics.

They stood up for what was right, despite their fear. Despite the danger.

And they were silenced. They weren't made Revenant, thankfully. Just your normal execution. Xander cried over their deaths as hard as me and Olly, blaming himself. Another reason to love him.

Because there's only one lot to blame, for all of this.

Sick of stewing in my grief, I force myself outside into a February day as cold and grey as my own depression. Greasy drizzle frizzes my hair and slicks my cheeks. I hunch my shoulders and guide my feet around the compound, my gaze on the scuffed toes of my boots.

The compound—named Compound 21—is the Dawson family homestead. Xander's parents opened their property to the Unbound, more welcoming to other mystics than they'd ever been to their number-two son. Though at least they let him stay in the house instead of banishing him to the cottage hidden in the trees like a dirty secret. Of course, as huge as their mansion is, it's not big enough to house thousands of people. It's an island in a hostile sea. We have to spread out, limit our numbers in groups. We hide to protect ourselves after the general populace were incited against us. The arsehole majority does what corrupt governments have done since the dawn of time to retain absolute power—lie, cheat, and threaten.

Thankfully, most Anima mystics aren't strong enough to rip a soul from a person and make a Revenant, quick and easy, or we'd all be meat puppets, even with the added protection of a soul anchor.

The rest of humanity lives a normal life like the proverbial goat, swallowing whatever is fed to them. As if the Anima mystics don't reap from their number to build their army of Revenants.

Sure, the bad guys blame it on us. But still.

And now they've taken Xander. He made the gruelling training bearable, the terrifying skirmishes bearable. I fought hard to keep him safe. What's the point if he's no longer here? We're already outnumbered and outmatched. Our defeat is inevitable. The one thing stopping me from putting a gun in my mouth is I couldn't do that to Olly. I'm his only family left. He has a boyfriend, but he's stuck in another compound and isn't exactly available for regular cuddles.

I'm sure the evil pricks will take him, eventually. Or Olly. And then *I'll* have nothing.

I sigh and kick a stone instead of falling to my knees and sobbing in the wet grass. It clangs off the perimeter fence, scattering droplets and shivering through the barbed wire wreathed in climbing plants. Shivering through the Essentia mystic who formed the vegetative barrier, too, no doubt. I stomp along the boundary, drizzle in my eyes and my teeth clamped on my lip to keep in the little mewling sounds I hate.

I'm an ugly crier—red face, swollen eyes, streaming nose.

Not like some of Xander's sex bunnies, with tears shimmering in their big, beautiful orbs, a lovely flush on their cheeks, and a delicate sob or two. I wail like a fox with its leg caught in a trap.

I walk faster, almost jogging, as if I can outrun grief and loneliness. Moisture curls in my lungs and chills my belly. I'm so intent on scowling at my shoes that it takes thirty seconds for the noises to penetrate. Excited voices. Shouting. The call of a name.

Now I'm running. *Sprinting.* The gate emerges from the mist, flanked by two watchtowers. A dirt track curves away between the trees. A lone figure limps closer. My heart spasms, already in pain, too wary to hope.

Xander was slender before, but with muscle definition that could turn me into a babbling idiot from one flash of a bare shoulder or the dip of a bicep. My mind quit altogether whenever he took off his top, which, unfortunately for my brain function, was regularly in summer.

His dark-green fatigues, the same ones he was wearing two weeks ago when they captured him, hang off his frame, the trousers riding low on his hips and ripped at the knees. His cheeks are concave beneath the scruff of a beard, every bone pronounced. There's not an inch of skin that isn't covered by filth, bruises, or scratches.

He stumbles and falls to one knee, head bent, his hair clumped in greasy spikes. One of the guards—Phoebe or something; I'm sure they had a fling for about a day—leaps from the tower and fumbles at the gate, the bolt and bars screeching as she unlocks them. One half of the barrier swings open. Her partner jumps down, nearly landing on his face.

"Wait! We need to check if he's—"

Phoebe holds a hand out to Xander. He raises his head. His hand reaches for her. My heart soars into my mouth.

Oh god, he did it. He escaped. He's not a—

His fingers clamp on Phoebe's throat and rip it out. Blood splatters his upturned face and beads in his eyelashes. A feral grin shows a flash of white teeth through the red mask. Phoebe crumples in a heap, too surprised to gurgle a protest. Xander shoves the bloody lump of tissue in his mouth, and chews, still grinning. My stomach pitches, and I swallow hard.

"He's Rabid!" the second guard yells, completely fucking redundantly in my opinion.

His rifle swings. Xander goes from crouched and chewing thoughtfully on his piece of Phoebe to instant attack, launching himself like a cheetah at a gazelle. He slaps the guard's gun to the side and a burst of bullets tears up the track. The guard lands on his back, Xander on top. Xander punches him in the face. Again. And again and again and again until there's nothing left but blood and a horrible, wet smacking sound. All while I gape, breath and limbs frozen, my fragile hope withered and gone.

Grunts gallop from the house behind me. My wide gaze zips between their readied guns and grim expressions to Xander, who's holding his hands up to the sky as if fascinated with his pretty, red gloves. He wiggles his fingers. The drizzle slithers pinkly down his slim and battered forearms. A crimson puddle haloes the second guard's head.

I throw myself at Xander. No time to think. No time to wonder if his fists will pound my face into oblivion. The grip of my Glock brands my palm. Xander's eyes lock on mine, still bright and lime green and intoxicating, but there's no hint of personality in his face, only rage and bloodlust. His hands tug at my shirt. I slam the butt of my Glock in the centre of his forehead and jump clear as his eyes roll. He slumps on top of the second guard, his cheek in a river of gore.

I struggle to pull in a complete breath. My lungs are locked, my skin bloodless. I manage tiny sips of air instead of passing out. My hand cramps on the Glock, but my muscles refuse to relax.

"Xan?" Olly chokes. "Oh, god, *Xander.*"

His distress knifes me in the stomach. He takes a tentative step beside me. His throat bobs, his face washed of colour. Freckles stand out like specks of dried blood. I imagine I look no better.

"We have to…" He swallows again, and it clicks. "We have to put him out of his misery."

"Oh, *now* you want to shoot him," I snarl.

Olly's expression crumples and the heat of my anger sputters under the relentless drizzle, solidifying to a lump of ice in my chest.

"I'm sorry," I mumble. "But you were right—if he's alive, there's hope."

The grunts shuffle around us, every weapon trained on the unconscious Xander and the grisly remains of the two guards. Fingers tighten on triggers. One twitch from Xander and his body will be shredded worse than his victims'.

I can't let that happen.

"No one comes back from being Rabid," Olly says dully.

"Has anyone ever tried?"

Olly yanks his gaze from his best friend. Hope flickers in his eyes.

"We need to secure him in his room before he wakes," I say in a rush.

3

"You can't take a Rabid into the compound," gasps one of the grunts.

I don't spare him a glance. Time is of the fucking essence here. There will be carnage if Xander wakes up. Or if someone tries to stop me.

"You get his head, I'll get his feet," I say. "We'll tie him with this."

I tug the canvas belt from around my hips, whipping myself in the leg. Without hesitation, Olly rolls Xander onto his back and slips his hands under his shoulders. He gags, but doesn't let go. I loop my belt around Xander's forearms and tighten the D-ring until it pinches his skin. Olly lifts Xander's torso from the mud and blood, Xander's head lolling on his chest. I grab his feet, my cold fingers curling around his ankles. I gulp down my own gag.

Xander smells like a wild thing—of earth and old blood and a body that hasn't seen a whiff of soap in a fortnight. The stench kicks me in the back of the throat.

I hoist his legs into the air. Olly shuffles rearwards. The grunts part around us, their expressions incredulous.

"I'm telling the Captain," the same one blurts.

He joined us a week ago after his compound was overrun, which is why I don't remember his name. Their Terra and Essentia mystics formed the usual protective barrier using the soul of the earth and plants to cloak the existence of the compound, unless another mystic breached it. Their mistake was trying to blend in without a fence. A bad guy literally walked across it, the magic alerting them to the presence of other mystics.

"Tell the Captain," I say to the incredulous grunt. "I'm sure he'll want him alive."

Olly and I trot across the lawn, Xander jiggling between us. Urgency claws at my stomach and quickens my steps. My breath puffs on each exhalation, splattering water from my lips.

Please don't wake up. *Please* don't. Not yet, not yet, not yet. Don't make me kill you.

I could have done it in the heat of battle when he begged me to, saving him from this exact awful fate. But not when I have him here, in my hands.

A red lump swells on Xander's forehead. Olly jumps up the front steps. My toe hooks the edge and I skid to my knees, my breath catching at the scalding pain. I scrabble to my feet without relaxing my grip on Xander, and hustle into the spacious hall, the parquet floor overlooked by a balcony and double staircase. My combats slip down my hips, no doubt baring my arse crack to anyone who dares to look. We hot-foot it up the steps, expecting to be stopped any second by a furious shout or by Xander bucking in our hands, his fingers extending like claws, his teeth clamping on flesh. The people we pass whisper and shrink away.

Our boots scuff mud on the carpet of the first-floor corridor. Xander's room is sandwiched between mine and Olly's. We dump his limp form on his bed and he bounces in our haste. Blood streaks the rumpled covers. The sheets still smell like him—the spicy-clove scent of hemp and bergamot, not the stink of abuse and neglect.

What the hell did they do to him?

I pant through my mouth, sweat and rain in my eyes, and toss my belt on the floor, the metal rings clinking. It's too rigid to secure Xander without the risk of cutting off his blood supply, so I tie one of his wrists to his metal bed frame with a resistance band he uses for exercise. His skin is gritty. *Sticky.* I stare at a mark on the dusky wall behind the headboard, probably from repeated slamming into the plaster with all the sex bunnies he humps.

I always wanted to be one of them. The only one.

Olly ties Xander's other wrist with a dressing-gown cord. I slip the knife from the holster at my ankle and slice a towel in two, using each half to bind his legs after tugging off his boots, choking on the wet, musky stench rising in an eye-burning cloud off the filthiest pair of socks I've ever seen.

Poor Xander. He loved long showers. The bathroom was always a steamy wonderland after he'd been in.

Olly joins me at the foot of the bed and we stare at our spreadeagled friend.

"Not it on giving him a sponge bath." I touch a finger to the tip of my nose a second faster than Olly.

"Dammit," Olly sighs.

4

What better way to demoralise your enemy than by stealing their loved ones and reducing them to a beast? Rabid in every way. We don't know how they do it. The soul is still there, so the soul anchor must be working. We can't exactly ask. Whatever the method, it's not pleasant. The Rabid's body tells the story of abuse when they can't. Some of them talk, though it's usually curse words and graphic descriptions of what they're going to do to you. Most seem to lose the power of speech alongside their humanity. They retain enough instinct or residual memory to return home on their release, where joy at their appearance quickly turns to a bloody nightmare of tangled bodies and screams.

Until we knew what to expect, of course, though being prepared doesn't make it any less harrowing.

Phoebe should have commanded him to stop and prove he was human and, when he failed, shot him in the head. She let her past dalliance cloud her judgement. I don't blame her. Had it been me on the gate, I would have rushed right out just the same.

Love is pain and foolishness. An unrequited shitstorm of longing. Or maybe I'm biased.

Olly sighs again. "Do I really have to bathe him? I thought

you'd fight me for it."

"Don't be inappropriate. Xander wouldn't want me to see him naked, and definitely not in this state."

"No, I suppose not."

My shoulders hunch at the words.

He couldn't have fibbed and said Xander would have loved to be naked in front of me? In my weaker moments, I asked Olly what Xander said about me when I wasn't there. It was always platonic, sometimes teasing, and never the declaration of love and wantonness I ached for. Though telling his best friend he really wanted to fuck his sister wasn't a conversation any sane person would have.

Still, a girl can dream.

Clattering from the corridor announces the arrival of Xander's latest sex bunny. She sashays through the doorway in a fug of some overly citrus perfume that stings my nostrils. Celeste can make drab combats and a shirt look sexy. I hate it. She's a carbon copy of the rest of them—short, curves for miles, big tits (excluding the guys, of course), and the ability to deep throat a garden hose. The exact opposite of me. Apart from the deep throating. I haven't tested my limits, except that one time with a banana out of curiosity. I gagged and drooled a lot, but maybe that's what men want.

Celeste places a booted foot on the polished wooden floor, and recoils, slapping her hand over her nose.

"What is that *smell?*" she gasps.

"That would be your beloved," I snap, and Olly elbows me in the ribs.

"Come in and talk to him," he says gently. "He should wake up soon. How hard did you hit him, Quinn?"

He slides a meaningful glance between me and the egg of

a lump on Xander's forehead. Xander's eyeliner is all gone, though his lashes fan thick and dark on his sharp cheekbones.

He's so thin. Has he been running wild for days trying to find his way back?

"I'm sure more brain damage won't hurt him." My harsh words disguise the wobble in my voice and the lump in my throat.

Olly winces. Celeste slides forward another step, her hand still clamped to her face.

"Is he okay?"

I curl my fingers instead of shaking her. I want to yell, *no he's* not *fucking okay!*

A bubble of pain lodges in my chest.

He might never be okay. I barely coped with losing him the first time. I can't think about his chances of recovery. About the odds of needing to put him down like the rabid animal he is.

"He's very ill," Olly says diplomatically while I swing between seething annoyance and bitter despair.

Celeste bends over the bed.

"Poor baby," she mumbles through her hand.

Xander goes from limp to rigid in less than a heartbeat. His eyes pop open. He lunges against the straps and bites at Celeste, his teeth snapping on air since she's not that close. She shrieks and reels backwards, her ample arse colliding with a chest of drawers and upsetting the neat line of books—MM romance, Xander's third love after football and camping.

The sex bunnies are way down the list. After me and Olly and coconut ice cream.

Celeste bursts into tears and flees the room. Xander's pale gaze switches to us, his eyes mostly pupil with a sliver of green.

He bares his teeth and growls a warning deep in his chest.

I cock my brow at Olly. "Someone's ready for his sponge bath."

* * *

Unlike Celeste, I don't go far when I leave Xander's bedroom. I lean against the wall beside the door, tip my head back, and shut my eyes. Weariness crushes my muscles and quivers my legs. I listen to the snip of scissors through cloth and the unmistakable sound of Olly retching.

"Jesus Christ, mate," Olly gasps. "My fucking eyes."

A slosh of water, and Xander starts howling. The noise weighs on my chest, not helping the crushing, claustrophobic feeling creeping over me.

How the hell are we going to fix him?

"You okay?" I manage to wheeze, my lids squeezed tight.

"Yeah," Olly calls over the thrashing of limbs and the gnashing of teeth. "The straps are holding, but he is not enjoying his bath."

Xander roars in agreement. Someone coming down the corridor does an abrupt U-turn and scuttles away. I thunk my head against the wall, needing to focus on some other pain than the slicing in my gut.

"Come on, Xan the Man," Olly says, his pleading tone soft and heart-wrenching. "You can fight this. I know it. I know *you.*"

Xander snarls like a jungle cat. It hurts my throat just to hear it. Olly cries quietly while he washes his best friend. Tears streak my cheeks and slither down my neck. My lungs hitch. I ache to break down and sob, but I need to be strong for Olly.

For Xander. Or none of us will make it.

Olly sniffles. "It's safe to come in."

I suck in a breath, square my shoulders, and march back into Xander's bedroom. I give myself a second by focusing on the rest of his furniture rather than the man himself. A bedside cabinet with a lamp and his iPod in a speaker stand.

He listens to nature sounds to lull himself to sleep. Otherwise, he likes grunge and garage that I hate, but tolerate because I love him.

Opposite the foot of his bed is the door to his en-suite. Olly tips a bucket of soiled water down the toilet. On the other side of the bed, a book rests on the cushioned window seat. The glass panes look out across the wide lawn to the gate. It's closed now, but people are still milling about.

My gaze drops to Xander without me having to think about it. My gaze always goes to him wherever he is in a room. He was either completely oblivious to my obsession or he ignored it because it made him uncomfortable.

I don't know which is worse.

The sky-blue sheet is pulled up to his armpits, baring his shoulders and arms where they're pinned to the headboard. Streaks of blood and mud mar where we dropped him. He may be cleaner, but he's not exactly fresh and the scent of animal lingers beneath his hemp and bergamot shower gel. I try not to look at where the sheet clings to his hips and thighs.

"Is he naked under there?" I say, achingly casual.

Olly drapes a pair of jeans and a t-shirt from the chair onto the bed and drags the chair over to me, gesturing for me to sit. He upends the mesh rubbish bin and perches on it.

"I couldn't exactly dress him in his current condition," he says. "Couldn't shave him, either, though he'd hate the beard.

His clothes also need to be incinerated. They're a health hazard."

I glance at the filthy pile on the floor. "So what do we do now?"

"Hell if I know. This was your idea."

"You're going to remind me of that every time it gets tough, aren't you?"

Olly smirks. "Damn right I am."

"We should probably feed him. He's so thin."

"I could count his ribs, Quinn. And he's covered in bruises." Olly swallows a couple of times. "Those fucking *bastards,*" he spits, his voice cracking on the last word.

"They'll pay," I hiss. "No matter what happens."

Xander watches us, his eyes flicking back and forth. A low growl continues to rumble in his chest. He tenses and relaxes his arms and legs, testing the bonds.

"We need better restraints," I continue in a less demented tone. "Handcuffs at least. And sedatives, so we can dress him and move him around without getting our faces chewed off. Or we could use that dog-catcher pole someone bought for capturing a Revenant, though it wasn't particularly successful as I recall."

Olly nods, exhaustion already carved into his face.

"Let's start with the food," he says.

5

The food turns out to be a battle of near-miss nips to my fingers. Breaded chicken—the blandest thing I could think of beyond watery soup, which just wasn't going to work.

Beast-Xander doesn't have the delicacy or patience for eating from a spoon.

I dangle a strip above his mouth, scattering breadcrumbs on his lips. His tongue sneaks out to swipe at them. I lower my hand and he lunges for my wrist as soon as it gets close. I jerk out of reach, showering crumbs on the sheet.

"Bad, Xander!" I scold. "No biting or you don't get fed."

"He's not a puppy, Quinn," Olly sighs.

"You say that, but what the hell are we going to do about toilet stuff? I suspect he's forgotten he's house trained."

Olly drops his face in his hands with a resigned, "Fuck."

I tip my head and shove the chicken strip in my mouth, forcing myself to chew and swallow. My stomach threatens to rebel, wound too tight for food. I make a show of licking my lips and rubbing my belly, like an idiot. Xander scowls and snaps his teeth.

"Are you going to behave?" I say, the next strip wiggling just out of reach of his straining mouth. "Good boys get chicken. Bad boys go hungry."

"For the love of Christ, Quinn," Olly blurts, his chest hitching, "don't talk to him in that baby voice. He's not a fucking child, either."

I flinch at the hot words, nearly losing my grip on the chicken.

Treating Xander like a puppy or a kid is the only way I'm getting through this. He's feral and needs to be trained. I can't think of him as the fiercely loyal thirty-one year old I've known since he was ten, who tangles my stomach in knots with a smile and who always included me in games with Olly, so I didn't feel left out.

Xander, shock-horror, has always had abandonment issues. I suspect it's why he dumps the sex bunnies first—so they can't leave him.

Not that any sane person would leave him.

"I know he's not a child," I say, striving for calm, but my voice is rough. "It's called a coping mechanism. Unless you want me to follow in Celeste's footsteps with the screaming and sobbing? Because I am a hair's-fucking-breadth away."

Olly scrubs his face hard enough to leave pink streaks. "I'm sorry. It's just... I hate seeing him like this."

"I know. I do, too. But I have to believe he'll get better. Otherwise, what the hell are we doing?"

"What if he doesn't?" Olly whispers.

"Then we keep trying. He'd do the same for us. He wouldn't give up."

Olly scrubs his face again, and I swear he rubs off a few freckles. He blows out a breath, sucks in another, and straightens on the mesh rubbish bin.

"You're right. Do what you want, talk to him however you want, and I'll shut my mouth."

"Wouldn't that be a nice change?" I grin.

He sticks out his tongue, proving that thirty-one-year-old men can still be overgrown children.

I turn back to Xander and point a finger at him. "No biting."

The chicken strip touches his lips. He tears it from my grasp and swallows it barely chewed. He opens his mouth and grunts. I feed him more chicken.

"He's doing it, Olly," I breathe. "He *listened*. That's progress, right? That's progress already."

"That's progress," Olly agrees in a wobbly voice.

I try to squash the flutter of hope. It's too soon, too fragile. I'm not sure I'll recover if it ends up being dashed.

Xander gulps the rest of the strips. I coax him to drink water through a metal straw. He resists at first, liquid dribbling into his beard scruff, then the cool water hits his tongue and he sucks hard, cheeks pinching. I take the straw away before he makes himself sick. He gives me a dissatisfied whine, and I have to stop myself from tousling his hair.

The greasy flop is a bit beyond a sponge bath and I'm sure Beast-Xander would chomp on my arm if I dared to touch him.

"I'll go get Celeste now he seems calmer." Olly slaps his hands on his knees, and rises.

Xander grumbles at Olly's sudden movement, every muscle tensed.

"And by calmer, I mean less bitey."

Olly disappears out the door. Xander stares at me, head cocked. His nostrils flare as if he's trying to catch my scent. His full belly forms a little mound beneath the covers.

"You look strange with a beard," I say to fill the silence. "Like a sixteenth-century rogue."

Xander offers no response. His chest rises and falls, air hissing between his teeth.

"Can you talk? If you talk, I'll give you a reward. There's still a tub of coconut ice cream in the freezer. We didn't finish it last time." My breath stutters. "Call me Q-tip and I'll buy you a fucking lorry load of the stuff."

I inch closer to the bed. Xander growls a warning.

"Speak to me, Xander. *Please*. I miss your voice. I miss *you*. I need—"

I hiccup, my fingertips swiping at tears. Olly's voice gets louder, cajoling Celeste up the corridor as if she's being led to a firing squad, not to pitch in and bring back the man we all love. She enters the room, hunched and wary. A ripple of disgust distorts her mouth before she smothers it. I curl my fingers instead of slapping her face and telling her to fuck off, the ungrateful, disloyal bitch.

"See, Celeste? He's calmed down. Just don't get too close this time." Olly guides her to my vacated seat. "Talk to him. Tell him who you are. Tell him who he is. We have to remind him."

She nods, rallying herself, her face pale and lovely. She sniffs at the air.

"At least he doesn't smell so bad," she says, and I clamp my teeth on my own growl.

Olly makes soothing gestures at me over Celeste's stupid head.

"Quinn and I will be next door," he says quickly. "Yell if you need us."

He tugs me from the room.

"That vacuous twat doesn't deserve him," I hiss outside Olly's bedroom door.

His mouth twitches. "You say that about all of them."

"So? It's true."

His smile softens. "You know I think you'd be the best person for him. He's the twat for not noticing."

My eyes sting and I turn away, a tickle creeping up my nostrils. I clear my throat, but no words come out.

Olly takes pity on me. "You want to wait in my room? Give them an hour?"

"I'm going to get some food." I sniff. "We can see if Xander wants to eat more after Celeste works her magic."

At Olly's snort, I head back down the corridor to my room, keeping my eyes fixed forward instead of peeking through Xander's door. Celeste's voice sounds whiny, but at least she's talking. In my en-suite, I splash water on my face, the cool liquid wonderful on my flushed skin. I meet my eyes in the mirror, and flinch.

I look haunted. Grief has hollowed out my own cheeks, not to mention the trauma of watching Xander return to us Rabid and slaughter a comrade and an ex-sex bunny. My freckles stand out like specks of mud on a white sheet, my hair a frizzy halo.

"Q-tip," I say, and bite back a sob.

I shove away from the mirror and stride past Xander's room without looking. Silence follows my footsteps, but Celeste is probably sulking at Xander's lack of proper attention beyond grunts and snarls. People try to engage me in conversation— all curious and fearful about Xander—but I brush them off. I'm surprised a certain Captain isn't one of them, enquiring what in the actual fuck we think we're doing. In the kitchen, I make myself a ham sandwich and eat it standing over the sink. The clock on the cooker says four thirty-seven.

5

It's getting dark and I didn't even notice.

I make sandwiches for Olly and Xander since we're unlikely to join everyone else for dinner, Xander especially. I slice an apple and pour a glass of orange juice, then carry everything up on a tray. Celeste stomps from Xander's room and dodges past me, her mouth pinched and her cheeks flushed.

"Wow, Celeste," I sneer at her retreating back, "twenty minutes. That's commitment."

"This isn't what I signed up for," she says, her nose in the air. "There's nothing of him left, anyway."

"Don't you fucking say that. He'll come back. He's a fighter. He doesn't let anyone treat him like shit."

"You're kidding yourself, Quinn," she says, and skips down the stairs, not a care in the world.

"You undeserving, weak-willed cow," I yell after her.

Olly pops his head out his bedroom door. "She quit already? That wasn't even half an hour."

"Lucky for him, he has us. He doesn't need anyone else."

"Preach, sister," Olly says.

He trails me into Xander's room. Xander greets us with a flash of teeth. The sheet has slipped down to his waist from his struggles or from Celeste ogling the slightly damaged merchandise. His chest is smooth and bare and bruised.

His brother always mocked him for his lack of chest hair, his own pecs smothered in a rug of blond. Yuck. I'll take Xander's perfect, hairless torso any day. I'll take Xander full stop.

Olly wasn't kidding about his ribs. I count each one to the dip of his abs, his muscles still defined even with the weight loss. His stomach tenses and falls with each breath. Despite his condition, my brain cells start to melt.

"Don't drool on the sandwiches," Olly says.

My cheeks flush. "Sorry."

I place the tray on the bedside table and tug the sheet up, ignoring Xander's growl. Olly munches on his sandwich, perched on his bin seat, while I feed Xander. He tries to bite me, but it's half-hearted. He inhales the sandwich, crunches the apple slices, and slurps the juice. Darkness falls. The sounds of everyone gathered for dinner drift up the stairs, though it's sombre. No laughing. Grumbles of discontent and unease. Olly and I talk to Xander—memories from our childhood and growing up together, stupid situations he got himself in, the sexy little troublemaker. His eyelids flutter, his belly sated. I trick myself into thinking the night will be an easy one.

But it's not.

6

First off, Xander hates the dog-catcher we use on him, thrashing and yowling as soon as it clamps around his throat.

I found it in a forgotten basement room, a rusted key protruding from the metal door. The space contained a dusty bed in one corner, a tiled shower in the other corner, and a toilet without any kind of privacy screen in between them.

Logically, the best place to contain a Rabid, but I want Xander in his own space, where he's comfortable. Where the familiarity, the scent, may trigger him back to himself.

Xander's parents used the cell to imprison rogue mystics before the Great Reveal—Anima ones, anyway, since they have a boner about power and status and sucking out the souls of people and animals. They gave them the chance to change their nefarious ways before delivering the final solution. I've wondered if that's why his parents never joined the dark side— shunned themselves for killing their own. They were duped as much as the nomags, believing they were essential enforcers protecting their secret society from extremists. Now *they're* the extremists, along with the rest of us rebels. From what I know of them, their philosophy and attitude seem way better suited to the Guild.

Bet it rankles not to be on the stronger side.

I pick at the knot of the resistance band around Xander's headboard, pulled tight from his constant struggles. He snaps at me, and I wince at the click of his teeth.

He's going to break his enamel.

"It'll take both of us on this pole to control him," Olly says uneasily, "and even then, we might fail. Can't we let him pee the bed?"

"And who do you think will have to strip the pee-soaked bed and give him another sponge bath?"

"Fuck," Olly sighs.

Xander grabs for me when the knot slips open. I leap backwards and he claws at the air, the resistance band whipping my thighs. My heart rate climbs, but I force myself to release his legs, dodging around Olly. Olly's knuckles whiten on the bar. Xander bucks and kicks, hampered by the sheet tangled around his hips.

"As soon as you release the last one, take hold of the pole," Olly says through his teeth. "I don't need to tell you how catastrophic it'll be if he gets free."

I nod once, my mouth dry. The cord loosens. Xander grabs the dog-catcher and jerks it side to side, taking Olly with it.

"Help!" Olly squeaks.

I lunge for the bar, wrapping my hands around the metal above Olly's desperate grip. With much grunting and swearing, we lever Xander off the bed and he leaps around like a demented toad, rattling my teeth together. I steadfastly fix my gaze on his blazing, furious eyes and not the flapping bodily bits I've never seen before. He throttles himself, tears running down his cheeks, clawed hands straining to reach us. We wrestle him into the bathroom and over to the toilet, though it takes a few attempts. He keeps kicking off the wall and shoving us back. I rap my head on the door frame. Olly slams his hip into the towel rail.

We're both panting for air in the cramped room, our faces dripping with sweat. My hair sticks to my cheeks and gets sucked into my mouth. Xander snarls on each exhale. His skin is slick and his exertions are not making him smell any better.

We finally get him over the toilet, too close to kick at the wall anymore. Xander refuses to turn around, alternating between grabbing for us and trying to rip the pole from our hands. His growls echo off the tiles. We heave, making him choke, and the backs of his legs hit the porcelain. He overbalances and sits hard on the toilet seat. Bottles and toothpaste scatter under his flailing arms.

"I swear to god, Xander, if you don't take a piss, I'm going to leave you to lie in it all night," Olly grunts, ducking as Xander lobs his toothbrush at him.

It's bright pink and cream. A joke gift I bought him a couple of years ago.

The toothbrush clatters into the bath. A round tub of shaving cream smacks me in the cheekbone. Xander makes confetti of the toilet paper, then appears to run out of energy. He scowls at us, his shoulders heaving. He takes hold of a certain appendage I'm definitely not looking at and aims a stream of pee at Olly. Olly yelps and barges into me while Xander gleefully hoses our trousers and boots. A pungent odour fills the bathroom, the liquid itself orange and turbid.

"Oh, I'm definitely rubbing this in your face when you're better, you arsehole," Olly says.

We yank Xander off the toilet. His bare feet scrabble on the floor, slipping in the puddles. My muscles are shaking when we get him on the bed, somewhat diagonally. Olly receives a kick in the mouth trying to get him to lie straight. I grab Xander's arm while Olly pushes the collar into his neck, pinning him against the mattress. Xander's nails rake my already throbbing cheek. I curse, and jerk his arm straight, tying his wrist to the headboard. Olly dives onto Xander's legs so I can secure them. Once it's done, we stand at the foot of the bed, all of us shuddering and breathing hard.

"We can't do this every time he has to take a leak," Olly says, his face red. Blood glistens on his lip.

"We need a better set-up. Maybe we can get him to use a bedpan." I huff, and bury my fingers in my hair. "I don't fucking know. But he needs an IV. He's obviously dehydrated."

"Great," Olly mutters. "More piss."

I spin on my heel. "I'll get the medic. You clean up the bathroom."

"We need to have a discussion on job delegation." Olly raises his voice as I march out of the room. "At least ask if the medic will put a catheter in!"

* * *

I have to beg the medic to put in an IV line and hang a bag of fluids. Xander shrieks and spits at her. She doesn't stay long enough to place a catheter. Her rapid footfalls fade down the corridor. I pick up a roll of bandage she dropped, and wrap it around Xander's forearm.

"Wimp," I say.

Olly yawns wide enough to crack his jaw. His lip splits and starts bleeding again. The scratches on my cheek sting where the medic gave me a perfunctory dab with hydrogen peroxide.

"Do you think we can leave him alone?" Olly says. "Or

should one of us sleep here?"

"We can take turns sleeping here. I'll go first since you cleaned up his piss."

"I'm still *wearing* his piss," Olly mutters.

Me, too. That's probably why the medic wrinkled her nose when I darkened her doorway.

Back in my blissfully quiet, deranged-beast-free room, I peel off my pee-splattered combats and boots and dress in cotton, watermelon-patterned pyjamas. The corridor is empty. No more incredulous stares or grumbles about how reckless we're being, everyone tucked up in bed. Xander hisses in greeting, his nudity covered by the duvet. I spread a couple of pillows on the floor, and poke his iPod. Birdsong and rain weave through the room. My heart gives an unhappy lurch at the reminder of just how fucked up everything is, helped by Xander's glare, his eyes dilated and dark and alien.

He's never looked at me with hatred. Exasperation, annoyance—sure. But never hatred.

I bow my head to hide my tears and paw through his manky combats abandoned on the floor. The stench makes my eyes water even more.

I don't know what I'm expecting to find. We don't carry phones or identification on most ops. Nothing for the Guild to track us with.

Most of Xander's pockets are filled with the same dirt and grime that smeared his body, except the last. A sob escapes at the clump of mushrooms sitting in my hand.

When did he collect this? It must have been before he was captured, when he saw them and thought of me. Afterwards, he would have had more pressing things to think about.

Honestly, you admit once that you like identifying mushrooms and suddenly you're the mushroom lady.

I slip the clod between the pages of his latest MM romance novel to examine later, then click off the light and shuffle under my blanket.

"Goodnight, Xander," I whisper.

For a glorious second, there's silence.

Then he lets out a roar.

7

No one sleeps well on our floor that night, and probably not on the second or third levels, either. Banging on the walls and shouts of, "Shut the fuck *up!*" incense Xander further. His spittle finds me in the dark, reminding me of the drizzle and my miserable trudge around the compound, the empty futility of the future dragging at every step. The loss of Xander an ache in my gut and chest.

He's here, he's alive, but the pain won't fade. I need him back. I don't care if he never looks at me as more than a sister, and shags a million sex bunnies before we're all turned into Revenants. I just want him to smirk, call me Q-tip, and tease me like he always does.

I sing to him, though my voice quavers on the edge of tears.

He loved to mock me for belting out tunes like Celine Dion. Apparently, I sound more like Kermit the Frog after he's been stepped on.

Whatever. It's all about confidence.

Xander pauses, then howls alongside. I talk to him in a soothing tone—what it was like for the two weeks I thought he was dead, what we'll do when he gets better, how Celeste is a big boobily waste of space. Sleep comes like drifts of snow, whipping me then lashing away on a lick of wind. The curtains lighten from black to grey. A gritty slush of tiredness fills my eyes and muscles and brain.

The bedroom door bangs into the wall, jerking me from a decent snooze and rocketing my heart rate to hummingbird parameters. I leap to my feet, trip on the sheets, and sprawl across Xander. His legs, thankfully. Losing half my cheek to his teeth at the arse crack of dawn would not improve my mood.

Xander's growl vibrates through me. A block of muscle fills the doorway, silhouetted against the brighter corridor. A palm slaps the switch on the wall, and I squint through the sudden blaze. Xander's growls increase. The light bathes the world-weary figure, though he's only two years older than the captive on the bed.

"Good morning, Captain," I say, blowing a flop of hair out of my face and heaving myself upright, Xander's knee jabbing me in the tits.

The Captain's jaw tics. His blue-eyed gaze sweeps from my watermelon pyjamas to Xander hog-tied to the bed.

"I'm waiting, McTierney," he says.

Xander yowls and thrashes hard, the metal bed frame creaking under the onslaught. The Captain ignores him. I knuckle sleep from my eyes and stifle a yawn, or seven.

"Waiting?" I say.

"Waiting for an explanation on why, without any authority, you brought a Rabid into my compound and endangered the lives of everyone here."

"I thought you'd want him alive."

It's a lie, of course. Just like I lied to the grunt at the gate.

"Why would you think that?" The Captain's voice is careful and clipped, like the rest of him.

"Because he's your brother."

The jaw tic migrates to his eye. Xavier glares at me.

"He hasn't been a Dawson for over a decade."

"True. He's an honorary McTierney. Which makes him *my* brother."

To give Xavier some credit as the Captain of Compound 21, he wasn't cruel to Xander. He's matured from the little shit who needed to be dunked in a puddle. He treated Xander like any other subordinate under his command—civil and distant and not like they shared a house for their formative years.

He hates to be reminded of the familial connection.

"I don't care what you call him, McTierney. What is he doing in my compound?"

"He lives here."

Massive fists ball at Xavier's sides. "He lost that right the second he became Rabid."

Xavier's parents still live in the house, too, though they stay on the top floor. The first and second floors are for the door-kickers and trigger-pullers. Us grunts. The term is a little American, but it's pretty accurate.

And one doesn't mix with one's inferiors, does one?

"You're letting your attachment cloud your judgement." Xavier's voice softens from diamond to marble. "That thing is no longer a person. It's an animal. And dangerous."

"Call him your brother," I spit. "Claim him just once, you fucking robot."

"Morning, Captain!" Olly bleats somewhere beyond Xavier's bulk.

When Xavier remains immobile in the doorway, Olly squeezes into the room through the tiny sliver left between Xavier and the frame. He pops out, hair mussed, wheezing slightly, dressed in a t-shirt and boxers. Xavier twitches one brow in acknowledgement, but his gaze stays on me. Xander continues to growl his displeasure, his lime-green eyes burning through hair and scruff like the stare of a jungle cat.

"Sorry, sir," Olly continues, smoothing a palm over his head. "We were planning to talk to you this morning about the, um, situation. The day got away from us yesterday."

Xavier releases me from his icy glare. "He slaughtered Johnson and Hogue before dinner."

"Right, and, ah, it took us a while after that to… subdue him."

"What exactly is your end game here, McTierney?"

"We want to—"

"We're going to cure him," I say over Olly.

Xavier's brow jumps higher. "There is no cure for Rabidity."

"Only because no one's ever tried."

"My compound is not your laboratory, McTierney. If you think the fate of Johnson and Hogue was bad, it's nothing compared to the aftermath of a full-on Rabid attack."

Xander spasms on the bed, the sheets tangled around his hips. The frame shrieks another protest.

"Imagine if they *can* be cured, though." I keep my voice calm and measured despite the anger and frustration bubbling in my gut. "It'd nullify the psychological warfare they've been using to demoralise us since they returned the first Rabid wearing the face of a loved one."

"It's too risky—"

"Not if it works."

"We don't have the facilities or the manpower—"

"Leave that to me and Olly. We'll take care of Xander."

"Stop interrupting me, McTierney," Xavier growls, sounding

like his brother.

"What my sister is trying to say is we'll take full responsibility for Xander, whatever happens, sir," Olly cuts in.

"Like we always have," I mutter.

Xavier's brows crash together. Xander wrenches against his straps in the silence. The bed jumps forward an inch. Xander does it again and again, the frame screeching across the floor. Xavier's frown gets deeper and deeper as the bed lurches towards him.

"Xander!" I slap my hand on his chest. "Quit it!"

His skin is scorching and damp beneath my palm, his heart a fleshy, frantic thud. He blinks at my hand, but stops his manic thrashing.

"He's still in there," I say softly. "His *soul* is still in there."

"That is simply his life essence. His personality has been obliterated." Xavier tilts his blocky head to the bright corridor behind him and barks, "Walker!"

Olly and I jump. Xander clacks his teeth. Xavier's second-in-command eases through the doorway.

William Walker, a name as white and bland as he is. Xavier and William played with souls together—the non-ripping-it-from-a-body kind of playing that involved scrying and building anchors and tugging on them just to be a dick. They also went to uni together and dated the same type of Essentia mystic sanctioned by their overbearing and proud parents.

Manipulating the souls of plants? Well, that's barely one step above a nomag. And it wouldn't do to have the arm candy more powerful than the men they're fawning over.

"Check his anchor," Xavier says. "I can sense his soul, though it's weak."

Disgust crumples William's face. "You want me to touch… a

Rabid?"

One blond brow arches upwards. William's throat bobs, but he minces deeper into the room. Xander tracks his progress through narrowed eyes, a warning growl vibrating in my palm still stuck to his chest. William folds the sheet away from the foot of the bed, his lip curling higher as more skin is exposed, and places one fingertip on Xander's bared ankle.

I hold my breath, though I'm not sure why.

William's eyelids flutter and spasm. He gasps and yanks his hand back, staggering away to dry heave next to Olly, who looks unenthused by the proximity.

"It's—th-that *thing*…" William flaps at Xander, another gag wracking his frame. "Pure chaos. An unspeakable deformation… I-I can't see beyond."

A fleeting emotion passes over Xavier's face, too brief to process. "He's suffering, McTierney. The longer we keep him here, the more we'll all suffer."

I open my mouth, but William interrupts, his pale cheeks paler, and sweat-slick.

"We could give him to other mystics," he says, wiping his lips with a shaking hand. "Another compound that's better equipped to study him. A cure would—"

"No," Xavier barks, his expression returned to its usual granite. "I will not have one of my men kept alive as a test subject. And moving him only increases the likelihood of catastrophe."

"Then keep him here." My voice drops to a whisper clogged by desperation and tears. "Let Olly and me try. *Please*, Xavier."

Olly blinks at me, no doubt gobsmacked by the lack of my usual disobedient tone whenever I have to talk to Xavier.

It's a surprise for me, too.

Xavier's face remains impassive, but something stirs in his blue eyes—empathy, uncertainty, an ocular parasite? Is anything human even in there?

"You have two weeks," he says quietly, "then I'm putting him down."

My weight slumps on my arm, and Xander releases a startled huff of breath.

Mothering Christ, he needs to brush his teeth.

"We're rewiring his brain, his behaviour—two weeks isn't enough," I splutter. "It could take months. *Years.*"

Olly pales, but nods his head. Xander strains forward to sniff at my hand, outwith biting distance.

"If he gets free and you're still alive in the aftermath, I will make you wish you were one of the slaughtered." Xavier pivots in the doorway.

Olly flaps his hand. "But, sir—"

"Two weeks," Xavier says, and strides away, William scuttling after.

8

The day, barely begun, does not improve after that. Xander takes to the bedpan as well as he did to being manhandled over the toilet bowl with a dog-catcher. He pisses everywhere except the curved metal container. The colour and turbidity are better, but it still stinks. I strip the sheets from under him and Olly sponges him down. He doesn't like that, either. He also doesn't like me tucking a plastic cover under his bare arse while holding my breath.

Silver lining—his current state makes it very easy to ignore his nakedness. He's feral and I'm not into bestiality.

He eats, he drinks, he poops—in the bedpan, thankfully, though that makes the experience no less harrowing for me and Olly. I could have gone my whole life without knowing what Xander's shit smelled like. Olly gags five times on his way to the bathroom, carrying the bedpan at arm's length. He gags three more times taking a wet wipe to his best friend's butt crack. I change Xander's fluid bag and attempt to erase the last five minutes from all living memory.

Maybe this will be enough to finally cure *me*. Hello faeces, goodbye unrequited love.

Heated stares follow me whenever I venture into the rest of the house for food or fluid or five minutes of not having to breathe the hot and fragrant air of Xander's bedroom. Discontented mumblings dog my footsteps, quickly smothered when I whirl and give them a glare of my own.

I'm not sure what everyone's so peeved about. I didn't get any sleep, either.

Celeste keeps herself scarce, darting away should we happen to enter the same room. They're not in a relationship, but you'd think that getting multiple orgasms would inspire some loyalty towards a man.

Xander dozes like an animal, snapping awake at the slightest sound or movement, a growl sawing from his chest. Olly and I rest when he does, though it's not for long and it's not restful. I smother my relief when I escape to my room for the evening, Olly on Xander's floor.

But the second night is much the same—growls and roars and pissed-off people hammering on the walls.

* * *

"It's not fair what you're doing."

The low voice accosts me in the kitchen while I'm chugging coffee after a second night of interrupted sleep listening to Xander re-enact *The Jungle Book* through the wall. Animal parts only. Olly cajoled and soothed, his words breaking and scratchy, but Xander was unmoved.

Having insomnia from grief for the past couple of weeks, and now this, is really not helping my constitution. Beast-Xander is no substitute for the real thing. I miss him so much.

My mug clatters on the granite counter top, flecks of quartz sparkling in the weak sunlight. The grunt from the gate, the one who was going to tattle to the mighty Captain, shoves his shoulder off the door frame and steps into the room.

"To him or to us," he continues.

"I'm not doing anything to you," I say in a tone that screams *be very fucking careful.*

A few survivors from his defunct compound filter into the kitchen, joined by more from ours until there's quite a group scowling at me over my morning coffee. They sit at the table or loiter at the counters. One pokes her head in the fridge and comes up empty. My fingers clench on the smooth edge of the bunker instead of lobbing my cup into their smug, fake-sympathising faces.

"You're prolonging his agony."

Several heads nod, and my knuckles whiten.

"We're helping him," I say.

The grunt gives me a pitying smile. "He's too far gone. The longer he's here, the more dangerous he gets."

"Well, thank god we have a Rabid expert in our midst. Or is it really because you'd rather murder Xander than suffer the minor inconvenience of a bad sleep?"

"That's not Xander," whispers a girl at the table.

Short, curvy, and pretty—he's definitely banged her.

She hunches at my frown.

"Not right now, it's not," I say. "But we'll get him back."

I grab my coffee to keep my hands busy, and take a scalding sip. Almond-caramel heat curls into my belly.

"Spare yourself the heartache." Another condescending smile from gate grunt. "If you can't do it, *I'll* put him out of his misery. It's what he'd want."

My mug cracks on the counter, oozing brown liquid from the base.

"You don't have a fucking clue what he'd want. And if you

go anywhere near him, *I'll* murder *you.*" I sweep my furious gaze over the shuffling crowd. "How can you give up on him so easily? You"—I point at a skinny guy with glasses—"never would have made it through basic training without him." My finger stabs at other faces. "Tutored at uni. Rescued from that ass-hat of an ex-boyfriend. And *you*"—this to another luscious specimen attempting to disappear at the back—"saving you from the Revenant horde is what got him captured in the first place, yet you stand there and fucking *nod* at the idea of killing him. What, he's good enough to screw, but god forbid he needs your tender loving care?"

Heads duck, eyes downcast, but I'm too angry and exhausted to be mollified. I push through the people at the door, knocking flesh against wood.

"I hope you all go Rabid," I snap. "I'll make sure Xander puts a bullet in your miserable faces, you selfish bunch of twats."

"It wasn't me he was trying to save," the luscious sex bunny mumbles, though he at least has the balls—literally this time— to meet my gaze. "I panicked and ran into him. It was you he was aiming for. I scrambled away and… the Guild caught him."

I pause in the corridor, my back to all the judgy faces. Grief punches me in the throat.

Of course it was me Xander was trying to rescue. Sure, the Revenants got a bit grabby, but I was mostly fine. A blade to the noggin and controlled bursts of bullets put them down.

"But had you been in trouble, he would've been the first person to help you," I rasp at the guy.

No one disagrees. I stomp upstairs, teeth gritted, every muscle bunched as tight as my fists. Olly glances up, perched on the edge of Xander's bed, a bowl cradled in his hand. Dark circles ring bloodshot eyes.

"Look, Quinn! I got him to eat from a spoon." He brandishes the utensil like it's Excalibur and he's just pulled it from a stone rather than Xander's gob. "He… Hey, what's wrong?"

I pace at the foot of the bed, pivoting sharply on each apex, my hair whirling in a strawberry cloud. Each breath blisters in and out.

"Those *cunts*. Things get a little hard and they bail. They want to 'put him out of his misery'." My fingers slice a pair of jagged air quotes. "It's like he means nothing to them. They're all as bad as fucking *Xavier*. The second Xander stops giving them what they want, they abandon him. They—"

"Quinn!" Olly yells, and I realise he's been calling my name for a while. "You're agitating Xander."

Xander flails on the bed, howling. The bowl is on the floor, cracked in half in a puddle of milk. I swallow the rage slicing my throat.

"Ssh, Xander, ssh. I'm sorry. That was my fault." I rub his chest in firm circles. I ache to touch his face, his forehead, but can't risk losing a finger. "You're okay. Everything's okay. I'm not going to let anyone hurt you."

A sob bubbles into the void left by the rage. I swallow that, too, though it hurts more.

Xander calms, limbs twitching, his eyes dilated and fixed on me. I keep my palm on his chest, soothed by the heat of his skin and the drum of his heart. He has a bran flake stuck in his beard.

I raise my gaze to Olly, struggling to keep my shit together. "We have to move him. Somewhere secure away from all these euthanasia-happy arseholes."

"What about his cottage in the trees? I know he hated it, but it's out of the way."

"There's no proper bed frame. Nowhere to chain him to. And the bathroom is way down the hall. Also, people still use it to get wasted. Us included."

Olly's grin flares briefly. I tug at my hair, my other hand still leaning on Xander. His chest rises and falls. He's quiet, as if he's listening.

"The basement," I sigh. "There's a creepy cell down there, where I found the dog-catcher. I didn't want to use it, but it was stupid of me to think we could do all this in his bedroom."

"There's a cell in the basement?"

"Have you seriously never explored this place? It has a metal door with a key and everything. A bed, toilet, and shower all lined up next to each other. Proper brick walls. No one will know he's there no matter how loud he roars. And we can lock the door."

"How do we move him without people noticing? Without endangering everyone and proving Xavier right?"

I glance at Xander, and pat his chest.

"Sedation," I say. "Lots and lots of sedation."

9

A tentative knock on the door interrupts us. Xander tenses beneath my palm. A growl, not yet audible, tickles along my skin.

"Is it safe to come in?" a voice calls through the wood. "Is *it* safe?"

I snort. "*He's* safe as long as you don't stick a body part in his face."

Olly makes chopping motions at his throat on the way to the door. It opens to reveal William.

His watery-blue gaze latches on Olly. "Captain Dawson wants to see you in his office. Right now."

Olly glances at me and raises a brow. I nod.

"I'll make preparations while you're gone. Give the Captain my regards."

Olly presses his lips together, his eyes laughing for him. William's nostrils quiver. I turn away to hide a smirk.

Xander taught me how to wind up the snobs and the prudes he hailed from. We had a points system based on their reactions. Nostrils quivering in indignation—ten big ones.

Xander snaps his teeth. William's entire face tries to wrinkle in on itself.

Dammit—fifty points. Even as a beast, he's still kicking my

arse.

My humour fizzles. The door clicks shut, Olly obediently trailing after William.

What the hell does Captain High-And-Mighty want? I doubt it's anything good. He better not renege on his two weeks, as pitiful as it is.

I look at Xander. He looks at me.

"Can you behave yourself if I leave you alone for twenty minutes?"

He grunts. I take it as assent, though I hesitate in the corridor, my hand unwilling to release the doorknob.

What if someone realises he's alone and creeps inside, gun cocked? What if I return to blood on the pillow and glazed, green eyes? No spark of life.

I slip back into the room and lean against the closed door, suddenly shaky. Xander tilts his head in polite inquiry while I shiver against the wood.

"I'll wait for Olly," I say. "It's everyone else who can't be trusted to behave. You don't know any better."

I sit on the chair next to the bed. Tap my fingers on my knees. Leap to my feet and apologise to a snarling Xander for the threatening move. I pack a bag with his clothes, toiletries, iPod, and books. Back on the seat, I prod at the stinging scratches on my cheek for something to do.

I bet Xander still has my skin under his fingernails. I guess it's no worse than the lump on his forehead.

Olly returns five minutes later, his freckles standing out like the cereal crumbs in the milk puddle I've not cleaned up yet.

"He's sending me away," he says, dazed.

"*What?*" I screech. "Away where? And for how long?"

"Back to the school where Xander was taken. For two weeks,

maybe more. He says it's empty. After our clusterfuck, a bunch of compounds got together to sweep them out. The cowards had already fled. Xavier thinks Rabids got made on the property somewhere. Thinks Xander got made there."

I splutter and hiss like a busted tap before my words spill out in a burning rush. "You know what he's doing, don't you? Captain Up-Himself is punishing us for starting this without his permission. That's why he gave us two lousy weeks and why he's getting rid of you on some holy-grail mission, so I have to care for Xander alone. He wants us to fail."

Olly slumps on the upturned waste bin, his hands buried in his hair.

"You can't manage Xander yourself. He's too strong, too unpredictable." A hint of green colours Olly's pale cheeks. "But if I don't go, he said he's not confident in us being able to cure Xander so he'd… so he'd put him down sooner than two weeks. For the safety of the compound."

"The weasel-fucking, manipulative bastard!" I spit. "He can't do that."

Tears and despair shimmer in Olly's eyes. "You saw it this morning—they all want to shoot Xander and be done with it. Bury his body and forget."

Olly drops his face in his hands. His shoulders tremble as he sobs quietly into his palms. Panic blooms in my stomach like a rotten flower, its petals tasting of bile and rust. Xander's gaze flicks between us. His fingers curl and uncurl. Curl and uncurl. I put my hand on the nape of Olly's neck, his skin hot with distress.

"I can manage," I say, then continue to lie through my teeth. "Xander's already listening to me. Responding to me. Fuck them. Fuck *all* of them. We'll fix Xander in two weeks, and they can choke on their goddamn chagrin."

Olly sniffs and raises a hopeful chin. "Are you sure? But how will you—"

I wave a hand. "Let me worry about that. Maybe this doesn't have to be a holy-grail mission. If we can discover how they make Rabids, maybe we can reverse it. And if we find where the bastards have slithered off to, we can make them pay for what they did to Xander. When do you leave?"

"An hour."

An hour? A freaking *hour?!*

I breathe through my nose instead of hyperventilating. One breath, two. Five. Olly frowns, and I force a smile.

"Just help me set him up in the basement," I say brightly. Too bright. My voice could shatter crystal. "No one will get near his body except me."

Olly cocks his head.

"Okay, that sounded weirder than I intended. I meant I'll fight for him, no matter what. I'll do whatever it takes to get him back to us. Like you will."

"You can't do this alone, Quinn. You can't."

"I can. And what choice do we have?" I mutter the last.

Olly blanches, but rallies quickly. "I'll find whatever's there and come home as soon as I can. I'll sneak away any chance I get just to give you a break."

"I know." I squeeze his shoulder. "Everything's going to be okay."

Nothing is fucking okay.

My stomach heaves. I cough to hide a gag, and swallow hard. Bloody shards of anxiety slide into my gut.

"Stay here and watch Xander," I say with nary a wobble. "I'll get everything ready."

I stalk through the door on brittle legs before Olly can reply. As soon as I'm in my room, I sink to my knees, stuff my fist in my mouth, and cry into the carpet.

I can't do this on my own. I can't. I *can't*. I'll fail, and Xander will die because of me. Or I'll lose control of him, and *everyone* will die because of me.

I force myself upright, time trickling faster than the sweat on my spine. A line of snot connects me to the carpet, and I swipe at my nose. I ignore the babbling in my skull and toss some things in a rucksack, scooping my sleeping bag from under the bed. I carry everything, including Xander's stuff, to the basement without being seen. Dust puffs from the bed sheets in sifts of grey. They smell a little mildewy, but it's not like Xander is a fresh bouquet of scents, either.

I find the on-duty medic in the modified clinical wing and rap a knuckle on the door frame. He glances up from his tablet, his blond hair flopping over his glasses, a scruff of beard covering his jaw.

"Can I get an IV sedative—something fast-acting that'll knock a person out completely?"

Brown eyes widen behind his lenses.

"For Xander," I say quickly, and keep the, "*Duh,*" to myself.

"I'll have to check with Captain—"

"Xavier gave us two weeks. Any means necessary." I squint at the medic. "You stay on our floor, right? Give me some intramuscular stuff, too, and maybe we'll all sleep tonight."

That gets him moving. Arsehole. He draws fluid into four syringes from two separate bottles and holds two out to me.

"Intravascular. Direct into his cannula." He brandishes the other two. "Intramuscular. Draw the needle back before you inject to make sure you're not in a blood vessel."

I slide each set of two into separate pockets. "How long will they last?"

"About twenty minutes. Thirty, tops. Takes the IM about the same to start working, the IV only a few minutes."

Christ, will he even be sedated before Olly gets dragged away for his maybe-bullshit, maybe-legit mission?

I mumble my thanks and yank the door open, surprising William with his fist raised to knock. He peers over my shoulder.

"Captain Dawson is ready to see you now."

The medic nods and rustles around, gathering items into a leather satchel.

I lean on the door handle, the picture of nonchalance. "Something wrong with our beloved Captain? The stress of his brother's illness getting to him?"

William treats me to a full-face wrinkle. "That's none of your concern, McTierney."

"I'm just worried about his health." I slice William a smirk. "Like his brother, he's practically family."

The medic dodges around me and both he and William start down the corridor, talking in low voices.

"Why is he sending Olly back to the school and not me?" I call to their retreating figures.

William deigns to stop while the medic continues on and out of sight.

Watery blue eyes scan me from top to toe. "While it's not your place to question his orders, the Captain thought you'd wish to remain by Xander's side after your impassioned plea. Regretting it already?"

Prick. And Xavier's right, of course. I can't trust anyone to save Xander, except me and Olly. Leaving him now would feel too much like abandonment.

"Why not someone else? Having only me caring for Xander increases the risk of him escaping and tearing a bloody hole through the entire compound. Isn't that our great Captain's biggest fear?"

William gives me a cold smile. "The Captain knows what he's doing, McTierney, even if you do not."

Fuck them both.

I wait for William to disappear, glance both ways, then duck back into the medical bay. A foldable wheelchair lies propped against the wall. I crack it open and pile the seat with a first-aid kit, more syringes, the sedative bottles, cotton balls, and a kidney dish. I wheel my goodies to Xander's room, scattering cotton in my wake.

"Where did you get all that?" Olly says.

"The medic was very helpful."

I waste no time injecting the IV sedative into Xander's drip line before disconnecting him from the fluid bag, leaving the cannula in place. He doesn't growl once. I take it as a positive sign.

"Get your stuff while we wait for this to work," I say to Olly. "How long have you got?"

He tilts his wrist. "Thirty minutes."

"Cutting it close."

I bustle around, the action distracting me from the imminent departure of my brother and the monumental task ahead. Panic flutters in the background on lazy butterfly wings.

Xander whines low in his throat. He blinks at me, his pale eyes dazed and ringed by forest green. I stroke the dip of his chest.

"Go to sleep, Xander," I whisper. "Just for a little while."

His lashes drift shut and fan above his cheekbones, almost reaching the dark stubble on his face. Tension leaks from his muscles, deepening the tired caverns of his eye sockets. His ribs rise and fall with slow and measured breaths. I poke him. Nothing. My knife slices his bonds, the knots stiff and tight from hours of struggling. His skin beneath is grooved and striped red, but not broken.

"Are you definitely, positively sure he's unconscious?" Olly peers over my shoulder, using me as a shield.

I step to the side. "Let's get him in the wheelchair and find out."

"Funny," Olly grumbles.

We slot Xander's floppy arms into a t-shirt. Olly drags a pair of boxers up his legs. For a brief, glorious moment, Beast-Xander's animal scent is smothered by the clean smell of fresh laundry and a hint of bergamot.

"I never thought I'd say this," I gasp, hauling Xander upright, "but I'm glad he's no longer naked."

"Yeah, I've seen way more of him than I ever wanted to."

Olly parks the wheelchair beside the bed, the stash stored in the side pouches, and we manhandle a limp Xander into the seat. His head flops forward, his chin on his chest. I use the remains of his bonds to tie his upper torso to the chair and stop him sliding onto the floor. I place his feet on the rests and fold his hands in his lap. His nails are crusted with filth and blood, the bandage covering his cannula bright white against the rest of him.

"Scope ahead," I say, my knees popping as I straighten. "We'll take him in the servants' elevator. Don't let anybody see us."

Two pillows under Xander's sheets craft a vaguely human shape. I wrap my fingers around the rubber grips of the wheelchair and shove him into the corridor at Olly's signal. The wheels whisper as we race him to the far end, his body rocking softly.

The servants' elevator is a cramped, hand-cranked box. Olly has to straddle Xander's legs to fit inside. His gaze zips to Xander's bowed head inches from his crotch.

"I *really* hope he doesn't wake up," Olly says.

I spin the handle. The lift jerks into a bone-rattling descent. Reluctant metal squeals a protest. The thump at the bottom clicks my teeth together. Xander slumps deeper and deeper in the chair. I tug him higher and check his breathing—calm and even. His pulse thuds slow and heavy on my fingertips. Olly winces at the screech of the door and sticks his head through the gap, twisting his body. He flaps his hand and we tumble into the basement. Olly's phone starts ringing before we reach Xander's new bedroom, and we both jump. Thankfully, Xander remains an inert lump of muscle.

Olly wrinkles his nose at the screen. "Shit. Xavier's waiting. And not patiently."

"Xavier can go fuck himself," I say.

I unlock the metal door and wheel Xander inside, pocketing the rusty key, my fingers brushing the smooth plastic of the two syringes.

Olly whistles. "Christ, you weren't joking about it being a cell."

His gaze sweeps from the bed to the toilet and open shower corner. His phone bleats again. He flinches, silencing it with an angry swipe of his finger. We cradle Xander between us and swing him onto the bed. Olly's phone rings five times, stops for a second, then starts again.

"Go," I sigh. "I can secure Xander. Don't give that bastard

an excuse to cut our time any shorter."

Olly grips my shoulders, his expression grim. "I'll phone you every day and be here every second I can. Just… be careful, okay?"

He folds me in a tight hug, and I pat his back. His ringing mobile drives us apart. He pauses at the door for a final look at his sedated friend sprawled on the bed, and me, standing forlorn.

"I love you, sis," he says.

I manage a smile. "Love you, too, bro."

Then he's gone.

10

"What the hell am I going to do with you?" I say to the unconscious Xander.

What am I going to do, what am I going to do? echoes on and on in my skull. How am I going to keep him clean if he won't use the toilet? How am I going to get him *to* the toilet? How am I going to care for him, feed him, *save* him?

I stare at his slim shoulders, slimmer hips, and the black, dirt-stained soles of his feet. Bruises stipple his bare legs, even his toes. He whimpers in his sleep, and I force myself to move, shaking off the tendrils of a panic attack.

Don't think, just do. Whatever it takes.

And pray Olly finds a miracle cure.

I lock the door, trapping us both inside should the worst happen. At least my fatal mistake won't condemn anyone else. Xander will survive a few weeks on my rotting carcass, and on water from the low tap beside the toilet. Olly can brick up the room and forget about us both.

I shiver, handcuffing Xander's wrists to the bed using the ones I'd glimpsed while searching for the dog-catcher. I'd thought they were fixed to the frame rather than detachable, otherwise I would have commandeered them, too. The bracelets at the foot of the bed have longer chains to secure his ankles, the key for all of them almost hidden in a giant dust ball beside the toilet. Bandages and cotton soften the edges of the metal. Water sloshes into the kidney dish—cold, but Xander shouldn't mind. I straddle him on my knees, and massage gel into the sharp bones of his jaw. Bristles rasp beneath my fingers. I inhale hemp and bergamot straight from the tub, though the familiar scent flares an ache in my chest. I steady my hand and shave the beard Xander would have hated were he himself enough to hate it. The water in the kidney dish turns brown and opaque. Pale, clean skin forms an invisible beard around Xander's mouth, the rest of him covered in grime.

He looks like himself. Like real Xander lay down to take a nap. He'll wake at any moment, cock a brow at my intimate position, and say, "About fucking time, Q-tip. Now lose the clothes and ride me like a cowgirl."

Or something more romantic.

I brush a greasy clump of hair off his forehead. My fingers continue on to stroke the lovely planes of his face. Warm breath tickles across my knuckles. I swipe an errant blob of gel from one nostril. His lashes flutter, and I snatch my hand away. A line appears between his brows. His body shifts under me. His lids crack to reveal green half-moons of sleepy awareness. I wait for something—a tiny flicker of Xander—but he blinks awake, and there's nothing except a foreign intelligence and wild alertness. His eyes narrow.

"No cause for alarm." I spread my hands and slowly swing my leg over him. "Don't mind me."

I slither lower. He tucks his chin to watch me. This may be one of many bad ideas I'll have, but I wrap my arms around his waist and bury my face in his hip. He jerks, metal rattling along the bed frame. Tension sings in his muscles and a garbled noise spills from his mouth.

"Talk to me, Xander," I beg. "I need to hear your voice."

He stills at the words, but says nothing. I squeeze him tighter, a clog in my throat. Pain and sadness stutter behind my ribs.

You'd think the way Xander was raised, he'd be cold and standoffish and loathe contact. But his hugs were the best—strong arms, warm, solid chest, the comforting smell of him. Maybe that's why he went overboard with the sexual activity—to compensate for the lack of tenderness and attention from his family. He was friendly to everyone, even his brother and that *really* pissed off Xavier. Despite his charmed upbringing, Xavier was the grumpy one. Xander could get hundreds of points in one interaction.

I admit, a little of his behaviour has rubbed off on me. I love pissing off Xavier.

I huff a few deep breaths to calm the imminent crying fit, choke, and say, "Jesus, Xander, you need a shower."

Maybe being clean will make him feel more human. I could get the plastic sheet and hose him down like an animal, but what if they did that after he was captured? What if it triggers him and makes him worse?

I slide out of bed and twist the shower on, hoping the water actually heats. Xander tests his new restraints. My fingers curl around the pole of the dog-catcher propped against the wall. The scrape and rattle of metal increase.

"I know you don't like it," I sigh, "but until you stop trying to claw my face off, we haven't got much choice."

Indecision and a lick of fear freeze me at the foot of the bed.

Olly and I struggled to control him *together*. How the hell will I manage alone? What if he wrenches free and literally claws my face off?

I lick my lips, and clamp the collar around his throat. Xander growls and bucks. I unlock his ankles, leaving the cuffs attached to the bed and staying wide of kicking range.

"If you're good, you get a reward," I say, my voice a little high. "You understand, Xander? Behave, and you get something nice."

He quits his thrashing and cocks his head. *Please*, let it mean he's listening. With a white-knuckled grip on the pole, I lean over and release his left arm. He doesn't immediately gouge out my eyeballs. My fingers hover over the final keyhole. I stare at Xander. He stares at me. He breathes. I don't.

"Are you going to behave?" I squeak.

He continues to watch me intently, but he doesn't bare his teeth or scowl. Am I getting through to him?

Am I about to be ripped apart by the only man I've ever loved?

The lock clicks. The handcuff clunks on the bed frame. My bandage and cotton padding scatters on the sheets. I clamp both hands on the dog-catcher, my palms slippery with sweat. I retreat a wobbly step, and another. Xander sits up. I don't yank on the pole, though I can't help a flinch. My heart thwaps against my ribs and swells into my throat. Xander curls one hand around the pole. The other follows just below it.

"Xander," I say, careful not to let the panic colour my voice, "what are you—"

He leaps from the bed. For a weightless, suspended moment, the collar throttles him. Then the pole skids through my clammy hands and rams me in the stomach, punching my air out and slamming me backwards into the wall. The shower mists my cheek as I whoop for breath, my hands on my knees.

Xander is a watery blur through my tears, charging at me.

"No, Xander!" I wheeze. *"Don't!"*

His legs tangle in the dog-catcher. I lunge for the door, my fumbling fingers grasping only syringes in my pocket. I pull at one, but it catches sideways in the lining.

Maybe I should stab my thigh through my trousers. At least I won't feel what Xander does to me. Or I will, but only for the first twenty minutes.

Gasping, I dive off the door. Xander bounces into the metal half a heartbeat later. He's spun the dog-catcher around, the pole sticking from his spine like a fin.

There's nowhere to run. Nowhere to hide. The bed sits flush against the wall in the corner. The shower hisses, steam purling upwards. My sobbing breaths are the loudest sound in the room.

Xander is silent.

I whirl to face him, trapped in the space between the corner and the foot of the bed, my hands raised as if I can defend myself against his animal fury. His body collides with mine, taking us both into the wall and punching my air out for the second time. His breath blasts hot against my throat, and an icy wash of terror prickles to my fingers. I scrunch my chin into my shoulder to protect my neck. I shove at him, but he captures my hands and pins them. He leans in, his hips against mine.

He only has a couple of inches on me, but he's stronger, even in his weakened state.

Frantic words tumble from my mouth, shaken by my heartbeat. "Xander, don't hurt me. You don't want to hurt me. Please, don't." Over and over and over.

The images of my fate are bright splashes of horror: Xander's teeth tearing into my skin, crushing pain, a burst of red to paint the wall.

I'm acting like prey—whimpering, shivering, frozen—but I can't stop.

Xander captures my wrists in one hand and grips my jaw with the other. I fight him, bruising myself on his fingers, but he tilts my head and I stare at the ceiling. He snuffles at my exposed throat. I bite my tongue to contain a scream. My pulse hammers against his lips, begging him to free it. I yank my arm. His grip tightens, crushing my bones together until I cry out. I keep yanking, my breath coming in bursts that don't seem to be oxygenating anything. I'm dizzy and sick and drenched in sweat.

My wrist pops free, leaving more flesh under Xander's fingernails. He buries his nose in my hair and seems unconcerned. I thrust my hand in my pocket. My thumb flips off a syringe cap as if I'm a seasoned medical professional.

"Xander!" I shriek, deafening myself.

Startled, he lifts his head and I jab the needle into the groove of his throat above the collar, depressing the plunger. He hisses and bats at my hand. The syringe flies from numb fingers and skitters under the bed. Xander spins me around, pressing my face to the wall. His fingers wrap around my neck from behind, squeezing until I can feel my pulse in my eyeballs. He fixes his teeth in my shoulder, not hard, not biting yet. A warning.

"Uck," he says, his breath scorching through my t-shirt.

"Wha—"

"*Fuck*," he growls.

A hysterical laugh bubbles out.

"Fuck," I pant in agreement.

I flex my fingers on the wall, preparing to push. Xander's weight disappears. He stumbles back, shaking his head. His knees buckle, but he catches himself, reeling another couple of steps. The wall holds me up since my knees also want to collapse. The heat of his body slowly leaches from my clothes. He blinks rapidly at me, then drops to his hands and knees, head bowed. The pole of the dog-catcher swings in an arc and rattles off the floor.

"Fuck," Xander says, and flops on his face.

11

My legs finally give out and I slide down the wall. I tuck my shaking hands into my armpits, but it sends the shivers deeper, across my shoulders, along my spine, all the way to my knees. My teeth chatter, worsening the headache zinging between my temples. My skull throbs from repeated contact with hard surfaces. My jaw aches from the imprint of Xander's fingers. There are red marks on my wrists developing into bruises and new gouges in my flesh that sting as soon as I notice them.

What an idiot I am. Clearly, it was too soon to get my hopes up. Uncuffing him was a terrible idea.

But at least he didn't actually eat me, or escape and eat everybody else. He *sniffed* me. And he *spoke*. Okay, it wasn't witty conversation, but I'll take, "Fuck," over howls and grunts any day. It means there's something going on in his head beyond animal cunning and bloodthirsty rage.

He's getting better. He's *going* to get better. I comfort myself with that rather than crawling from the room and huddling under my covers.

I crawl towards Xander instead. My lungs hitch, still unable to suck in a deep breath. Fear clenches my stomach, and I hate that.

I don't want to be afraid. Xander would never do anything

69

to hurt me, never give me cause to fear him. He'd fight anyone who dared.

But this isn't Xander.

His cheek is pillowed on the floor, his filthy hair falling across his forehead and hiding his eyes. I reach for him, hesitate, yank my hands away, and reach for him again.

"Now who's the fucking wimp?" I growl.

I unlatch the dog-catcher and roll Xander onto his back. His hand flops straight out. His pulse is a steady beat in the side of his neck, his breaths shallow, but even.

I should have asked the medic if repeated doses in one day is bad. Not that I had much choice.

Best not to dwell on what was to come after the sniffing.

I ignore the jumble of emotions whirling in my gut like a flock of startled pigeons, and heave myself upright using the bed frame. My knees quiver, my weakened legs nearly tumbling me on top of Xander when I crouch at his head. I jam my hands—still shaking—in his armpits and drag him towards the shower. Thankfully, the floor is smooth and the room is small. Water sizzles on my arse and lower back, my t-shirt rucked up. I yelp and drop Xander on my feet, twisting to adjust the temperature to a less scorching level. I lift his torso again and shuffle backwards, quickly drenched. My muscles strain to prop him in the corner. Water drums on us both, dripping from his hair, slicking his cheeks and plastering his t-shirt to his chest. My footsteps squelch to the bed and back. I cuff his wrist to the shower and his arm dangles, limp. I slump out of the splash zone, a puddle forming around my boots.

How much time do I have before he blinks awake and wants to wrestle—ten minutes? Five? Maybe two shots of sedative will leave him too sluggish to do more than glare and grumble in displeasure. I should cuff him straight to the bed, but I don't want him to stay dirty.

He got this way because of them, either from their abuse or from being tossed out to live like a wild thing. I want to fix him.

I squirt his hempy-smelling shampoo into my palms and scrub his hair, my fingers smoothing out the tangles. Bubbles gather on his closed eyelids and glide down the tip of his nose. He huffs a sigh that splatters droplets from his lips. I flinch and my boot slips, depositing me hard on my arse. My heart hammers, my headache fiercer. Xander's eyes stay closed. Cursing myself, I clean the rest of his face, scraping the bubbles from his eye sockets and getting right behind his ears. His arms and legs feel too thin beneath my hands. Dirty water swirls from his feet and splatters my thighs. I pick the crud from under his nails, most of it my skin. His fingers curl in mine and I back up so fast, a wave of water follows me.

I stand and shiver in the opposite corner, my hair heavy and wet on my shoulders. I swipe a palm over my face. Droplets plop onto the dusty floor.

Xander paddles his limbs like a dreaming puppy. His head tips back into the stream from the shower and he opens his mouth, lapping at it, the ball of his tongue piercing glinting in the light. Water-beaded lashes flutter open. Black spikes of hair frame his eyes and cheekbones.

He's beautiful, even when he's feral.

I straighten my spine instead of hunching like a cornered rabbit. "Remember what I said about behaving?"

A long, slow blink. Xander seems to be having some trouble focusing, his eyes half-lidded. His arm jerks, yanking on the handcuff and rattling it against the shower rod. He pulls on it, again and again. His gaze clears enough to swing to me.

"Fuck," he says.

"That's right. No nice things for you. You're going to stay in that shower and finish what I started." I mimic scrubbing under my arms. "You stink, Xander. Even an animal washes itself. Don't make me get a hose."

This is good—firm, sure voice. A gentle scold. I'm the alpha here, not him.

He stops tugging on the cuff. Trembling limbs lever him to his feet where he leans on the wall, his clothes moulded to his chest and hips. Fingers grip the hem of his t-shirt at his throat and tear it from his body with a wet ripping sound, leaving scraps of material circling his biceps. My eyes follow the path of water slicking his neck to his pecs and the cobbled plane of his stomach. A lucky drop slithers down the groove of his hip to the waistband of his boxers. I stop my eyeballs from examining that area too closely. I creep forward and scoop the shower gel from the floor.

"Hold out your hand," I say.

Xander's burning gaze performs its own assessment. He slides his boxers down his legs and kicks them at me. They splat on my boots. I stare into his eyes as if I'm trying to see the back of his skull.

My cheeks flush. "Hold out your hand."

"Fuck," he says.

My focus tries to slip south, but I rein it in somewhere around his ribs. His perfect, sexy ribs.

He is my best friend. My *brother's* best friend. There will be no ogling, especially when he's not himself. And naked and slippery and wet...

I rip my gaze from his belly button.

Shit, that was close.

"Fuck?" Xander inquires, head cocked.

"Hand," I counter.

He snorts, splattering droplets, but holds out his palm. I squirt gel in a shiny ribbon, then hug the bottle to my chest.

"Let's try a second word, though I commend your first choice." I flick a sopping clump of hair over my shoulder. "How about 'thanks for taking care of me, Q-tip. I've pined for you my entire life.'"

He circles a soapy hand across his chest, swiping under his armpits, awkward with one wrist chained. Bubbles glide down and down and—

"Fuck me," Xander says.

My eyes zip to his face. "What?"

His pupils are dilated, his lips half-parted.

"*Fuck me,*" he purrs.

There's no averting my gaze now. His hand falls to his erection, where the crown is flushed and swollen. Much like my entire body. He strokes himself—long, slow pumps that suck the air from the room. My clothes start to steam.

Speaking takes three attempts. "You had your chance. Bad boys don't get... *that.* You have to behave."

My pulse throbs in the roof of my mouth. In my tongue. My fingertips. Years of yearning flare together into one delicious ball of heat.

Xander thrusts into his fist, his hips flexing, giving more power to each stroke. My heart quivers as if it's sprouted tiny wings. They beat against my ribs and tickle the back of my throat. My cheeks blaze hot enough to dry the rest of me. I stare at the floor.

Xander gives a deep, growling, "Fuck me."

"Are you going to fight when I collar you and chain you to the bed?" I say to the polished stone. "You only get a reward if you behave."

But not that kind of reward, right? *Right?!*

Xander falls silent. I risk a peek. He's no longer touching himself, though it doesn't look like he finished. No, um, tell-tale splatter, and his erection still juts thick and proud from his hips.

I've never even touched a penis before, never mind his. My first and only time was thirty seconds of the boy jabbing his fingers between my thighs before he replaced them with his cock, neither particularly pleasant. He kept asking if I was okay and I kept saying I was fine, teeth gritted against the pain. Anything to get it over with.

So, sex ed, an awkward fumble, and a book I bought to avoid being a complete noob—the trifecta of my sexual experience. Not to mention the many and varied fantasies of Xander, none of which were anything like this.

I watch him watching me. I feel a little woozy given all my blood is in my face and between my legs.

"Turn off the shower," I say in a commanding tone.

He twists the dial. I dig out a towel for each of us and flap one at him.

"Dry yourself."

He rubs the material over every inch of his nakedness. I turn my back and squeeze the water from my hair, patting my clothes as best I can. My fingers wrap around the dog-catcher. Xander's lip curls, but he stays silent. I fasten the collar around his neck.

"If you behave, you get a reward," I remind him, sounding

more confident than I feel.

Nerves flutter in my belly. I unlock the cuff from the shower rod. Xander lets me walk him to the bed. He stretches out on his back.

I nod at the cuff dangling from his wrist. "Secure that to the frame."

The bracelet snicks shut around the metal. I breathe a little easier, though my heart has never beat this hard before. Xander frowns at the clean pair of boxers I hold out to him, but he pulls them on, one-handed. He watches me lock the rest of his cuffs without a single twitch.

"Fuck?" he says.

"Soon," I gulp. "And only if you behave."

I'm lying. Of course I am. Anything to keep him pliant. If he gets frustrated, I'll find something else to distract him. I can't have sex with him. That would be wrong on so many levels. For one—Xander in his right mind wouldn't want to. It doesn't matter what Beast-Xander wants. Beast-Xander is primal. He feeds on violence and blood and flesh.

And lust is simply another kind of hunger.

12

"What happened to your face?" Olly says.

My finger hesitates over my phone screen, tempted to hit the button and cancel the video call. I duck my chin and curl a little tighter against the wall of the basement corridor. I'm dressed in pink cotton pyjamas with limes on them.

"Xander and I had a slight disagreement about the shower," I say, my voice light.

"He got close enough to grab you?"

"He surprised me. It won't happen again."

I shift on the thick carpet. Sconces line the walls, the opulence of the mansion continuing into this corridor and stopping at the metal door beside me.

"Are you sure you can handle—"

"He's making real progress," I say brightly. "He didn't even try to rip out my jugular."

Olly frowns, his expression worried. The glow from his phone turns his face blue and reflects in his eyes. He's lying down, a pillow and mattress all that are visible in the background.

He chews on his lip. "So you got him in the shower?"

"I got him to wash himself. You should see him—he looks like Xander even if he doesn't act like it yet. I'll send you a photo tomorrow."

"Is he sleeping?"

"Yeah. He perked up for our shower altercation, but the sedative I gave him earlier must still be in his system."

Not to mention the second dose I stabbed him with. I'm not lying about him being sleepy, but he was still awake when I left the room. Still demanding I fuck him.

Not exactly what I want Olly to hear on our phone call.

Xander was very good for the rest of the day—eating everything he was offered without trying to bite my fingers, using the toilet while I pretended not to listen, no growling at me. The thought of why he was being good swoops through my stomach and clenches certain muscles that have no business clenching because it's not going to happen.

"What are you planning to do with him tomorrow?" Olly says.

"What?" I yelp.

How could Olly know? Did I mumble something without realising? Or is it written plain across my face?

"How are you going to keep the momentum going with his recovery?"

"Oh. Right." I clear my throat. "I might read to him for a bit. Talk about his background. Show him photos. He seems to respond well to reward-based training."

"What kind of rewards?"

"Oh, uh"—another throat clearing—"you know, ice cream, chocolate. Sometimes I pat his arm."

He wants me to do more than pat his fucking arm.

"So you're managing okay?"

"We're doing fine. It's going to be tough, and I really wish you were here, but it's all under control. No need to worry.

You're the one in dangerous territory, not me." Olly opens his mouth, but I rush on in a too-loud, too-bright voice. "And I forgot the best part! He spoke—he said a real human word."

Olly shoves up on one elbow, his eyes wide and hopeful. "He did? That's awesome! What did he say—your name? His name?"

"Well, it wasn't the best word in retrospect, but... he said 'fuck'."

"He said...?"

Olly blinks at me. His phone screen starts shaking, the image blurry. It sounds like he's choking. I open my mouth to ask if he's okay, and laughter bursts through the speaker.

"He said *fuck?*" Olly whoops. His phone stops jiggling long enough for me to see his watering eyes and scrunched-up face. "Christ, I can't breathe. Of course that's his first word. Classic Xan."

I join in Olly's laughter and we giggle for a few minutes, setting each other off when our snickers begin to taper. It's a welcome release after the shit of the last few weeks.

I hate not telling him the full truth, but I don't want him wracked with guilt, worrying about me every second. What if he's distracted at a crucial moment? I can't lose my brother, too. I need him to think all is rosy so he can get on with his job and back to me in one piece. Hopefully with answers because I have no fucking clue what I'm doing.

Olly swipes a finger under his eye. "God, I miss him."

"Me, too," I whisper.

Sadness dims the laughter, quickly smothered by a sudden, breath-stealing wave of loneliness.

"You should tell him how you feel when he's himself again," Olly says.

I manage a lacklustre, "Yeah… maybe."

"Life is precious. You never know when you're going to lose someone. Or when that someone might be turned into a raving lunatic who tries to rip off your face."

"True," I snort.

We talk for five more minutes, Olly telling me about his day. The school where Xander was taken, where we fought the Revenants, was empty as reported. They're going room by room searching for secret passages and hidden vaults. All very James Bond. Olly tries to sound chipper and optimistic, but I can tell he's disappointed with his lack of progress and the thought of how long the investigation could take.

Maybe longer than the time we have.

I hang up, feeling better and worse, and slip back into the room, locking the door behind me. My phone screen guides me to my sleeping bag spread on the floor beside the bed. Xander's eyes glitter in the shadows. Metal scrapes softly on metal.

"Fuck me?" he mumbles, drowsy.

"Go to sleep, Xander," I say. "We'll talk in the morning."

Talk. *Sure.*

Quiet settles over the room. My eyes drift shut. I'm sore and exhausted, but my mind is restless.

I didn't lie to Olly about my plans for Xander tomorrow. I *will* read to him and talk to him and show him pictures. I *won't* do the other thing, but…

But…

But…

What if it helps? Xander is a pretty sexual guy. What if having sex brings him back to himself? And, okay, he might wake up in the middle of it, utterly horrified that I'm straddling him without consent. At least he'll be awake.

Go to sleep, Quinn.

I huff and roll onto my other side, punching my pillow. I wriggle to get comfortable. Wriggle some more.

I need to rest. Xander is like a newborn—I have to sleep when he sleeps or I won't sleep at all.

But what if…?

What if?

Olly is off chasing his own 'what if?' even when it's tangled in Xavier's bullshit manipulation. Shouldn't I do the same? Didn't I promise to do whatever it took? No matter what.

I lie on my back, wide awake and blinking at the ceiling. My heart canters between my ribs, a pulse throbbing deep in my belly.

"Fuck," I whisper to the dark.

13

I catch a couple of hours of sleep in between calling myself vile names and agonising over what I'm going to do when Xander says those two words to me again. What if I refuse and he reverts to fury and aggression? What if I accept and he recovers?

But it's practically rape. Beast-Xander may be fine with it, but Xander won't be, and it's his body.

Christ—his body. I've wanted to touch it, taste it, *feel* it since I was fourteen. I've wanted him to look at me like I'm the only woman in the world. To hold me and kiss me and whisper he loves me. I've imagined many scenarios over the years—Xander showing up at my door in the pouring rain having run away from uni to see me, soaked and shivering and saying he can't wait a moment longer. Or our car breaks down in the middle of nowhere at night and we decide to huddle together in the back seat to stay warm, hands wandering in the dark, pleading whispers and increasing urgency… Or he saves me from a Revenant and pins me to a tree, mouth frantic on mine, panicked at the thought of losing me.

Shame when he tried to actually save me from Revenants, he ended up in enemy clutches, not kissing me silly in the woods.

Never have I imagined Xander would finally want to have

sex with me and it's not even bloody him. That's just cruel. Though the real cruelty will be if he does get better, and he hates me for it.

Whatever happens, it'll be worth it as long as he's himself again. I've been pining after him for years. That won't change if he hates me or doesn't remember a thing. As long as he's *here,* I can take it.

I can take it.

I kick off the sleeping bag, the glowing clock on my phone reading 06:58. The room is as dark as it was at noon and at midnight and at two am. I fumble to the dimmer switch beside the door and twist it to the lowest setting. The bare bulb glows orange and sears my tired eyeballs as if I'm staring at a nuclear explosion. Handcuffs jitter on metal.

"I know what you're going to say," I sigh, "but we're having breakfast first. And coffee. Lots of coffee. You'll get a reward if you behave yourself."

I slip out the door and lock it behind me without once looking at Xander. The kitchen is quiet, a held breath before the rush. I should be getting ready for exercises—sniper training, then a stint on the gate—but Xavier can *really* go fuck himself if he thinks I'm turning up as normal like I had to do while I was grieving Xander's death.

He's already stolen Olly, he's not stealing my two weeks. This is more important than any of it.

I fry a cooked breakfast for Xander, part of me hoping a full belly will satiate his other desires. The smell of grease sinks into my churning stomach. I fill a cafetière and a separate teapot, piling everything onto a tray. I pick up a banana, but put it back, my appetite replaced by anxiety and butterfly wings. On the way to the basement, I focus on the smell of coffee and the swirl of rainbow colours in puddles of oil.

Nothing else.

The metal door clangs behind me. A slop of tea hits the tray and steams gently. Still ignoring Xander, I place everything on the floor, turn up the light, and spend a minute decanting hot beverages. I raise my head and he's watching me, the intensity sending a tremor through my pulse. The sheet has slipped down to bare his chest. His hands flex.

"I'm going to unlock some of your cuffs so you can sit up to eat." I pause and project authority into my voice, though it wobbles. "What do you get if you behave?"

A dark light sparks in his eyes. Beast-Xander's smile is slow and wicked and sharp.

"Reward," he purrs.

Fuck. Oh, fuck.

My shaking fingers unlock his ankles and his right hand. He shoves himself into a sitting position against the headboard. The sheet glides down his hips and thighs. I hold out a mug, the liquid shivering on the surface. Xander reaches for it, staring at me, and curls his fingers around the ceramic, giving the contents a cautious sniff. I hold my breath as he takes a sip. His nose wrinkles, and he pushes the cup at me. I give him the second mug. Another sniff. Another sip. His forehead clears, and he takes a bigger mouthful. A tension in my chest eases.

Xander hates coffee and loves Assam tea. Seems Beast-Xander does, too.

I watch him eat his breakfast one-handed and cuffed to the bed. I drink the coffee. My lips tingle where his mouth touched my mug. The liquid does nothing to drown the flutters in my stomach. Neither does Xander's hot, demanding gaze.

"Do you need to pee?" I say into the charged silence.

He blinks at me. I desperately think of some other delaying tactic. Another shower? A fake phone call? Flee from the room?

I wouldn't be doing this if Olly were here. I wouldn't even be considering it. Olly would be mortified. Disgusted. It's a shameful secret I'll never share unless Xander wakes up and yells at me for it.

Please, *please* let him wake up.

I lick my lips. Clear my throat. Curl my hair around and around my finger.

"I'm going to cuff you again," I say.

He bares his teeth, but offers no resistance, even wriggling lower in the bed so I can fasten his ankles. The bulge in his boxers keeps drawing my eye. All my blood rushes to the surface.

I can't do this. I can't *not* do this. He's my best friend.

Whatever was done to him ramped up his base appetites. What if I can channel them all into lust—the one appetite that I might actually survive? Then if his lust is sated, maybe it'll put him in a tranquil state. Make him more receptive. Make him remember. A good dose of dopamine never hurt anyone.

Xander flexes his whole body, a wave of movement that ripples to his hips, skin sliding over taut muscle. My breath saws in and out like I've run a few laps around the compound in the frosty February air.

No one else needs to know. If it works, we can both go to therapy. If it doesn't… then it'll be our little secret.

God, that sounds perverted.

I place my hand on Xander's chest and stare into his eyes. Long, black lashes, too long and thick for a boy. The fresh green of spring leaves bordered by the darker green of the forest. A blush of hazel almost lost around his dilated pupil. His heart knocks against my palm.

"Are you sure?" I search his gaze. "Xander, are you sure you want to do this?"

Like it's really his choice.

A rumble of assent starts under my hand and falls from his mouth in a growled, "Fuck me."

Muscles clench—mine this time. There's too much swirling in my belly to decipher. I turn away to steady myself and when that doesn't work, I rummage in Xander's bag, finding the wallet I'd taken from his chest of drawers along with his phone.

His driver's licence photo is the best—dark hair framing dark eyes, a sexy, sulky mouth. Not even pixelated black and white can detract from his gorgeousness or disguise the twinkle of mischief in his eye. I used to tease him about the photo to hide my drooling adoration. Of course, he had better ammunition with my licence where I look like a surprised twiglet.

Xander taught me how to drive, though it wasn't technically legal with him being nineteen and only having his licence for two years. We all shared the same car—an ancient, blue-grey Peugeot 106 that shuddered up hills and did nought to sixty in 2.5 hours. Xander was so patient with me, especially when I kept stalling, nervous and overexcited to have him close in the car and all to myself. He'd put his hand over my shaking one and talk in calm tones despite the other drivers hooting and gesturing around us. Then I'd pull away smoothly as if I'd done it a hundred times, aching to impress him.

He made me a mixed tape of my favourite songs to celebrate passing my test. I still have it, though tapes were already obsolete when he gave it to me. I don't even own a cassette player.

Sadness gathers in my throat and burns the back of my eyeballs. I peel open the main slot of Xander's wallet where banknotes would go, expecting to find one condom, maybe two, for a grunt getting lucky on a regular basis and not leaving the compound except for missions. I laugh at the contents, though it's strangled by the lump in my throat—five condoms, all bunched together in their shiny foil.

"You're such a whore, Xander," I sniff. "A responsible whore."

I swipe the tear that escapes onto my cheekbone and take a couple of deep breaths, or ten. Metal rattles impatiently. I clasp a pink and silver square, and face him. Xander struggles against the cuffs, curling and uncurling his fingers. He even curls his toes.

"I realise it's been over two weeks, which is an inordinate amount of time for you, but some of us haven't gotten laid in thirteen years and are still perfectly fine," I say with an air of bravado. "Two more minutes won't kill you."

It might kill me. There's a pressure building in my gut, a mix of nerves, excitement, and fear. I'm about to cross a line, about to hurl myself over, and there'll be no coming back from it. I'll have to live with it for the rest of my life, no matter what happens.

Fantasising about Xander was safe—a way to release the tension and keep myself sane, though I developed a slight masturbatory obsession and a well-stocked toy drawer. Still, it was healthy. *Ish.* I could be his best friend and not trail around after him like one of his sex bunnies, desperate for attention. I got the best bits of him, or so I'd tell myself. I got a relationship that would last for decades, not just a few weeks in his bed before the next bunny hopped on in.

Maybe I should be more worried about how this will affect *me,* not Xander. It's still not too late. I could stop, leave, try something else. I could contact a psychiatrist to help him. An actual professional who'll heal him, not harm him, like my bumbling efforts might. Though it is a little tricky since it's dangerous to leave the compound.

But time is tick, tick, ticking, and Xavier is enough of an arsehole to euthanise his own brother as soon as the day dawns after his second week.

I shove my pyjama bottoms off my legs and kick them away. The tails of the button-down top tickle my thighs, covering my modesty. There's a lot going on at the core of me—heat, flutters, nervous bursts of hot panic. I ignore it all and climb on top of Xander, straddling his legs. His warm skin glides against my inner thighs, his legs pushing to spread mine wider. I have a second of anxiety, but I'm still covered by the hem of my lime-patterned pyjamas.

"Xander..." I croak. I clear my throat and swallow a couple of times, but my heart is in the way. "Xander, if you ever remember this, please don't hate me. You're my best—you're my best friend. I just want to help you. And you're a demanding fucker. So, really, it's *your* fault."

I wipe my eyes, the edge of the condom packet brushing my lashes. Xander jerks his legs wider and I overbalance, slapping my hands on the scorching flesh of his stomach. His muscles tremble beneath my palms.

"All right, you impatient slut," I say to bolster my courage. "Keep your pants on. Or don't."

I laugh, and it's definitely hysterical. I can't seem to take a full breath.

I tuck my fingers in the waistband of Xander's boxers, and close my eyes tight enough for sparkles of colour to dance across my lids. I slide the material down his thighs and stop above his knees. His breathing is harsh now, matching mine. I risk a peek.

"Jesus, Xander. Why does every part of you have to be perfect?"

He growls low in his throat. It rockets my already tortured pulse. Numb fingers tear open the condom packet while I try to remember what I learned in high school, practising on an awful thing that looked like a pink kitchen-roll holder, plus what I've read in my book. I'm very aware of stroking Xander's shaft as I tease the slick and reluctant condom down his erection. He twitches in my hands, the delicate skin scalding and silky. I need to pause once the condom is rolled to the base to catch my breath and tell myself to stop shaking.

I raise my eyes to meet his wild, dark gaze. "What's your name?"

He cocks his head. His pulse jumps in the hollow of his throat, his skin already dewed with sweat.

I position myself above him, thighs spread, both of us quivering like virgins.

"What's your name?" I say with more force.

"Xander," he grunts.

I swallow a sob and guide him inside me, and *sweet motherfucking Christ*. Even with all the conflicting emotions and without any foreplay, I'm wet.

Hell, I've been in a constant state of arousal ever since he was sixteen and looked at me with sad eyes and blood on his mouth.

His hips flex and I feel him, stretching me, grazing that

ache deep inside and spreading it outward. The sight of him beneath me, in me, after all my fantasies and longing, is almost unbearable. His eyes flutter shut, the cords in his neck taut. He strains against his bonds, hands curled into fists, using the leverage to thrust inside me. My head falls back, my hair swinging. I follow his lead, meeting each drive of his hips. The smack of flesh and the rattle of metal fill the room. Heat and pressure build where we're joined. My heart beats too hard, too fast. I can taste it, choking me. It's too much. My body is overloaded with the touch and scent and essence of Xander. A scream clogs my throat, trapped behind my heart and stuttered breath. Xander groans, pulsing inside me, slamming deep. I yelp, and come furiously in a rush of heat and tight, tingling muscles.

I bow my head, struggling to catch my breath, shudders wracking my frame, little aftershocks zinging around. Xander's ribs heave against my thighs.

I pray for a hesitant, "What in the actual fuck, Q-tip?" but he just pulls out of me, sighs deeply, and falls asleep.

And then I let myself cry.

14

In my fantasies, Xander was always an attentive lover. Each orgasm he coaxed from me was a point of pride, my pleasure more important than his. He'd make me come again and again until I begged him to stop and begged him to never stop. He'd cuddle me after, stroke my hair, and tell me I was beautiful, amazing, a wild cat and a sex goddess all in one. He'd kiss my happy tears and say he loved me.

And in reality, though there was no cuddling or affection, he's still the best sex I've ever had—this beast wearing Xander's body.

I dress and tip-toe out of the room. My sobs stack inside my chest and burst out as soon as I curl in a ball in my own shower, scalding water battering my shoulders and head.

I don't even know why I'm crying. I'm not hurt, bar a pleasant ache between my legs. The sex was great. My first penis-induced orgasm. So why does it feel like my heart is broken?

I scrub my skin until it glows pink, and my sobs peter into pathetic snivels. My face in the mirror is red, blotchy, and haunted. I blow a bucketful of snot into a tissue. Cold water calms the swelling, leaving my eyes bloodshot.

In the kitchen, coffee soothes my churning stomach, my

appetite still AWOL. A couple of people enter the room, clock me at the kettle, and haste an exit without a word.

I guess I did go all sanctimonious bitch on them, but still. Fucking wimps. If they had anything to do with it, Xander would be in the ground already.

Anxiety sharpens its claws on my ribs. I dump my half-finished coffee in the sink and hustle back to the basement.

I can't leave Xander alone for long. What if he goes berserk or someone finds him even though I locked the door? No one else can be trusted to help. I'm the only one left to care for him. Breaking down is a self-indulgent luxury I can't afford. I have to focus everything on Xander. So the sex didn't shock him into his right mind? At least I tried. Time to switch tactics.

I shove the door open. Xander snarls at my abrupt entrance, but settles to lazy alertness when I tell him to shush. He completes the palaver of going to the bathroom practically docile. I leave his ankles free as a reward, his skin broken and scabbed despite my dressings.

I need a better system of restraint. Something not so rigid that lets him move around rather than being confined to the bed. What about a long leash? Or some kind of pulley? It would need to reach to the shower so he could choose when to clean himself and go to the toilet, like an adult human male. Though it's probably too soon for all his limbs to be free.

He's still dangerous.

It can't be helping his mental state—to feel like a prisoner again. Who knows how long he was captive for the two weeks he was missing. Rabids are rare, so it must take effort or time or both to create them, otherwise they'd move in hordes, like Revenants. Maybe the sick fucks abused him the whole time.

One day, I'll make them regret it.

I let the restraint ideas mull in my subconscious while I sit on the closed toilet seat and read from where Xander bookmarked his last MM romance. It's pretty dark. Taboo. The main character is abused by his father. The dad meets a woman and is quickly married. Suddenly, the protagonist has a step brother his father dotes on and spoils, all while his abuse continues, the dad convincing the new family his son is disobedient, wilful, a troublemaker. Scorching hatred of the step brother becomes an attraction just as boiling, and extremely rough sex where—

I snap the book closed, my cheeks flushed. "Jesus, Xander, that's pornographic."

He peeks at me through his lashes, his head leaning against the wall, his arms spread between the cuffs. The calculating gleam in his eye swoops into my stomach. I dive for his phone, and perch on the corner of the bed at his side, close but not touching. His cuffed hand tangles in my hair, and tugs, stretching my neck back and exposing my jugular.

"No hair-pulling," I say through my teeth.

The grip eases. Xander strains across to sniff at my shoulder.

"No biting, either," I say quickly.

His huff of breath tickles my ear and flares goosebumps to the nape of my neck. I hold his phone in front of his face and the screen unlocks. His wallpaper is a swirl of leaves on water. I click on the gallery icon.

"Let's see what you've got in here that might provoke a memory. You better not have naked pictures of sex bunnies." I snort. "Who am I kidding? Of course you have."

I scroll through the photos, selecting one every now and then to show to Xander with a fond, "Remember when we…?" or, "When did you take that?" and, "I'd totally forgotten about this!" There are various images of all three of us, of Olly and Xander, me and Olly, me and Xander, and some of my parents. Scenery from our many camping trips. The requisite boobs and butts and dicks of a few sex bunnies, though their lack is glaring compared to the rest of the camera roll. Then there are pictures of me—caught mid-laugh and unawares, my hair blowing around my cheeks, my face aglow; me buried in the sand; me buried in the snow; me aiming a rifle at a target, my eyes dark and furious with concentration. My breath hitches at the next one.

"I didn't know you kept this," I say, cradling the phone in my hands.

It's an image of one of those strips you get from a photo booth, where couples stare longingly into each other's eyes, or kiss and fool around. We'd been out shopping for a birthday present for Olly about six years ago when Xander spotted one of his latest sex bunnies, who was not too happy being such a brief conquest. He dragged me into the booth to hide and I dared him to take a strip of photos—to cement our cover story, of course. We perched a buttock each on the tiny stool and giggled while we mugged for the camera. For the last picture, Xander pulled me into his lap and told me to make my best sexy face. It was my favourite photo of all of them— Xander smirking over my shoulder, his sultry, come-to-bed eyes bordered by black liner, and me, looking startled and mildly constipated. When Xander plucked the strip from the basket, he laughed so hard, he collapsed on the floor and smudged his liner by rubbing at his teary eyes.

"No wonder you never have a boyfriend," he wheezed, "if that's your sexy face."

Despite the humiliating photo and Xander's merciless teasing, I still love the memory. Xander's warm hands on my waist, his chin on my shoulder, muscled legs under mine and my arse in his lap. I thought I might explode.

"I kept mine, too," I say. "The original. In a scrapbook under my bed. Which you are definitely not allowed to look at."

I clear my throat, fighting the burn of emotion. No crying in front of Xander. Only positive and healing energy allowed.

Xander makes a noise. A little hum. I twist to look at him, his phone clenched in my hand.

"Xander?" I search his face, a flicker of hope in my chest. "Do you remember?"

He seems to be searching my face for something, too.

"What is it, Xander?" I say, shivery and eager. "What is it? Use your words."

He cocks his head. I hold my breath. He opens his mouth.

"Fuck me," he growls.

"This is very unorthodox, Ms McTierney. There's only so much I can accomplish over the phone. The patient should be present in person for me to formulate an accurate diagnosis and therapy plan."

The dulcet tones of Doctor Lucy Cavendish melt into my ear canal, and my body instinctively relaxes against the wall of the basement corridor. Weak daylight filters through a single, high window near the stairs. The carpet under me has an imprint of my arse from all the times I've sat out here making calls.

"I understand that, Doc, and I really appreciate—"

"It's Doctor Cavendish, please."

I clear my throat. "Right. Doctor Cavendish. Well, as I was saying—I appreciate you taking the time to phone me back and discuss the, uh, the patient. He's not in any condition to travel."

It's not exactly a lie. Christ, can you imagine? Me leading Xander on the dog-catcher pole, trying to stop him from eating people. Members of the public gawping, then screaming as he grabs them. Not to mention if we happened across a mystic. All mystics give off a magical aura that other mystics can feel, and even us nomags have a signature they can detect from being in close proximity to the Unbound. It's like living with a cat and walking about with hair stuck to your clothes. Everyone can see you have a cat.

"I can make house calls for special cases," Doc Cavendish says, "though it would, of course, incur a further fee."

Yeah, I'm already paying a chunk of my inheritance just for this phone conference. And it took two days to organise, mostly through dogged perseverance and harassment of the doc's secretary. Who knows how long a house call would take to schedule? It's not like she can come to the compound. Trusting her with the information I have already might be a mistake. If she's one of the Guild, or a nomag minion to the arsehole majority, she'll have seen right through my flimsy explanations. Xavier would be pissed to know I've reached out to an external party, but I'm using a burner phone and he didn't give me much choice with his bullshit ultimatum.

I'm desperate here.

"He's too volatile at the moment, Doc—Doctor Cavendish, but I would like you to see him as soon as he's able," I lie politely. "Until then, any help you can give me over the phone would be amazing. I just want him to get better."

My breath hitches on the last.

I kept as close to the truth as possible with Xander's history— I told the doc he was kidnapped and abused, returning to us in an animalistic state. That he got too distressed when we tried to take him to a hospital or when people came to assess him. That the police and relevant parties were involved, yada yada...

"If he's a threat to himself and others, you should submit him into psychiatric care. I'm surprised the recommendation has not already been made by the emergency services. These facilities are equipped to deal with violent and unstable patients. I can refer—"

"Your secretary mentioned that. On several occasions. I'm afraid time and resources are a bit of a factor here, Doc—uh, Cavendish."

The good doctor sighs. "This is *very* unorthodox, Ms McTierney. I'm simply concerned that he will not receive an adequate level of care in this critical period after his abuse."

"Noted." I pinch the bridge of my nose, a headache pounding behind my eyeballs. "All I can say is, I will do anything for him. Anything at all."

"The best thing you can do is submit him for hospitalisation." The tapping of keys fills the speaker. "I appreciate your reluctance, but I cannot stress the importance of this enough. In fact, I'm willing to detain him in my facility with a substantial discount for the private treatment. Consider it an extension of the unorthodoxy of this situation. I can send a team of trained medical professionals to collect him. The sooner the better."

Is she so desperate to get her hands on Xander because she suspects he's Rabid? Is she trying to get the location of our compound, too? Or is she simply doing her job?

"I can't, Doctor Cavendish," I mumble. "Won't he heal if I give him patience and stability? Show him he's safe and remind him who he is?"

"From what you've described, I consider it highly unlikely."

I gulp. "But he's become feral as a result of trauma, won't he—"

"I'm afraid you're making an inaccurate comparison to children who have reverted to an unsocialised state through abuse and social isolation, where key mental and psychological developmental stages are missed. There are few documented cases of adult patients, and they would not exhibit these behaviours after only two weeks."

Under normal, nomag circumstances, maybe, but what about with magic? What about the chaos and deformity that William detected when searching for Xander's soul anchor? Shame I can't ask the doc about that without giving myself away.

I press the heel of my hand into my forehead. "Is there anything I can do to fast-track his recovery?"

"I believe I've made myself clear in that respect, Ms McTierney. The patient must be admitted. He needs a team of experts responsible for his diagnosis and treatment."

Xander just has me and Olly. And under two weeks. Lucky him.

God, we're fucking screwed.

I shove to my feet to pace off my anxiety. A haze of white blankets my vision and dizziness rolls through my skull, threatening to pitch me on my face. I lean my arse on the wall and lower my head below my knees, my hair forming a curtain.

When did I last eat something? I left Xander feasting on a lunch of chicken sandwiches and crisps. Was it really that single piece of toast at breakfast? My belly is mostly filled with coffee and disquiet.

Lucy Cavendish keeps talking, and I focus on her voice.

"The patient sounds as though he is experiencing a psychotic frenzy," she says. "He needs immediate hospitalisation, blood screening to rule out a physiological cause, then likely anti-psychotic medication to restore his normal faculties."

I raise my head, the swell of my pulse not helping the ache behind my eyeballs, though the wooziness has eased.

15

"He's shown improvement already from me reminding him who he is and from, uh, sex," I say, interrupting the good doctor on how I'm only making things worse and can't possibly heal him alone.

There's a weighty pause.

"What do you mean?"

"Well the, um, patient demanded sex. So I gave him what he wanted."

"A sexual appetite could be unhealthy in this case. Was his abuse sexual in nature?"

I rub a bloom of pain beneath my breastbone. "I don't know."

"It's possible that sex is a negative response. He has obviously experienced something acute and intense enough to shatter his identity."

"So if… So would letting him have sex make him worse?"

"I'm wary of drawing links to typical behaviours born of long-term abuse when this patient is presenting as something very different," Doctor Cavendish says. "I'm less concerned about sex reinforcing his regression when he sounds psychotic and dissociative. On the other hand, a compulsive sexual appetite could be an unhealthy coping mechanism."

I close my eyes as my stomach heaves. A fist in my mouth stoppers a stinging rush of bile.

He's already fucked me twice today. I'm starting to get sore, and not in a fun way.

"So, no sex?" I croak.

The good doctor laughs prettily. "As wonderful as the act may be between consenting adults, the patient doesn't require sex, Ms McTierney. He needs stable serotonin levels."

Oh fuck, oh god. Have I messed Xander up permanently? I should never have surrendered to those two, demanding words. How can I love him and do something so depraved when he's in no state to protest?

I took advantage of him just to get what I've wanted after all these years. What an awful bitch I am.

Doctor Cavendish launches into another appeal for Xander's immediate committal, the urgency of an accurate diagnosis, and the likelihood he'll need lots and lots of drugs to recover any semblance of his previous self. Shame and guilt clog my ears, my throat, my chest. I choke on the acrid taste of them. All I can hear is the same phrase over and over again.

What have I done?

What have I done?

<h1 style="text-align:center">16</h1>

Xander and I have not had a good day. After my call with the doc, I stayed up all night tracking down and reading some of the journal articles and books she recommended, all of which prove that what I'm doing—keeping him in the compound, having sex with him—are only making him worse and, without proper treatment, he won't recover. The good doctor wouldn't let me off the call until I promised to bring Xander into her practice for a proper assessment as soon as possible, and at least within the next few days.

If Xavier hasn't shot him in the head by then, I will happily deliver Xander into the arms of the psychiatrist no matter how risky it is.

I refused his demand for afternoon sex. I explained why in a calm and adult manner while he growled, "Fuck me," in tones of increasing frustration. When he realised it wasn't happening, he had a howling, thrashing tantrum.

And he's been having one ever since.

He's reverted to how he was when we first tied him to his own bed—snarling at me, roaring and fighting against his bonds, his pale eyes bright with murder and rage. He pissed the bed out of spite. He wrestled against the dog-catcher and gave me another bruise in my solar plexus, though I managed to keep a grip on the pole this time. I pulled about ten muscles hosing him down, then forcing him back on the bed and getting his cuffs on.

Exhaustion has turned my eyes to spiky balls. They're so dry, my lids scrape when I blink. Fog fills my brain. I find myself staring at the wall, no recollection of what I was doing. Zoned out. My muscles are sluggish. Horizontal surfaces sing to me a siren's song of sleep.

So, yeah—Xander's not happy and *I'm* not fucking happy.

I wipe sweat from my brow and step back, the drill falling silent in my hand. Brick dust speckles the toilet seat. A long loop of metal runs from the corner above Xander's bed to the opposite corner where the shower is. I give it an experimental wiggle.

I found it in an outbuilding containing a hodgepodge of garden implements and defunct appliances. It might have been some kind of runner for a ceiling-mounted pulley to shift heavy loads from one side of a room to another. I heated the bends to stretch the loop out more, then screwed one side to the wall, leaving the second side open and unencumbered. A security rail.

"What do you think of this, Xander?" I say while he glowers at me. Sweat from his latest struggle against the cuffs sticks his hair to his forehead and tangles it across his eyes. "In a few seconds, you'll be able to get up out of that bed and walk to the toilet and the shower all by yourself. Hell, you can stand and do yoga if you want to."

I talk to him as if expecting a reply, though he hasn't said two words to me since he stopped telling me to fuck him.

I miss his voice. Even Beast-Xander's voice.

I put the drill back in its carry-case, and fix a picture knocked askew. Several glossy photos decorate the walls. Images from Xander's phone, and mine. I got them printed online and delivered to our PO Box, picked up by one of the select few who get to leave the compound for short errands. Probably Shaun. Xavier sent his guard dog, William, to question me on what I was getting in the mail, like it's any of his goddamn business. The pictures show us all smiling, laughing, hugging. The ones from my phone are mostly of Xander, lots of them candid—Xander reading a book, a secretive little smirk tugging at the corner of his mouth; Xander pouring water over his head on top of a hill; Xander grinning at the camera. The contrast between the playful Xander and the snapping, snarling beast forms an ache in my chest that it hurts to breathe past.

"Right, let's give this a shot," I say in my too-bright, too-loud, I'm-seconds-from-bawling voice.

Xander bares his teeth. Ignoring him, I unsnap the cuffs from his ankles, wincing at the broken and weeping skin.

"You've really made a mess of yourself," I scold. "We'll get you cleaned and bandaged in a minute."

I fasten the two handcuffs together and clip one end to the metal rail, forming a decent length of chain. Xander digs his heels into the mattress and shimmies into a sitting position, the rail skimming the top of his head. He ducks and growls at it.

"Okay, so now I'll undo your right wrist," I prattle cheerfully, "and switch the left one with—ow! Xander, *no!*"

His teeth sink into my forearm. Tears blur my eyes at the crushing pain.

"Stop!" I yelp. "Stop, and I'll do it."

He pauses, his jaw no longer clamping down, though his

teeth stay in my arm. Animal calculation gleams in his eyes. A growl vibrates against my throbbing flesh, his breath hot.

"I'll do what you want," I say tightly. "You can't get any fucking worse than this."

His tongue swipes the mound of skin pinched between his jaws. He opens his mouth, and I jerk my arm to my chest. A red and white imprint of his teeth forms a complete circle on my forearm. Blood beads where his canines sliced skin. Nausea swells in my stomach.

"Fuck me," Xander says.

My lungs want to hitch. My arm smarts and stings, the deepest divots turning purple.

My voice wobbles. "Just let me finish what I was doing."

He grunts. His gaze tracks my shaking fingers as they slide the handcuff on the rail past the top of his head. I bracelet the metal around his left wrist below the other cuff, then remove the shorter one, leaving him fastened to the loop screwed to the wall. I ease off the bed, cradling my injured arm. Xander tests the new restraint, straightening his arm to its full extent and still having some chain to spare. His head turns to me.

His pupils are dilated.

He lunges off the bed. I gasp and stumble backwards, tripping on my sleeping bag and falling on my arse. The impact jars my wound and clicks my teeth together, stunning me. Metal screeches on metal. Xander crouches and drags the sleeping bag towards himself, reeling me in where I sit on top of the slippery material, blinking and dazed. He reaches for me and I scrabble away, slamming my shoulder into the door in my haste. I clutch my arm and pant and shiver, refusing to look at him.

"*Now,*" he snarls.

16

The command quivers to my knees. Fear curdles the coffee in my gut.

It's all I've had today. It's all I could manage past the guilt and worry and bone-melting exhaustion.

This is my own fault. I should never have had sex with Xander. Beast-Xander. He's come to expect it. Taking it away from him must have seemed like a punishment. Another torture.

But I'm scared to let him touch me.

Blood dribbles from my arm and plops on the floor. I force my gaze to lift. Xander stands, the sleeping bag scrunched at his feet, the cuff shining on his left wrist. His bruises are yellowing, his flesh filling out to smooth the gauntness of his cheeks and the curve of his ribs. Stubble darkens his jaw since he's not let me shave him. *My* punishment for refusing sex. His chest rises and falls in sharp, shallow breaths. His erection strains the front of his boxer shorts.

I swallow hard. "Just don't hurt me. Okay?"

There's nothing familiar in his face. Nothing but hunger.

I take a quivering step. Another. My heart quails under the intensity of his gaze.

"Tell me your na—"

But I've gotten too close.

Xander grabs my uninjured arm and yanks me forward. He spins me towards the bed. Air stutters in my lungs. Panic clenches my stomach. His body crowds me from behind, scorching hot and musky.

I suck in a breath. "Xan—"

His hand clamps the nape of my neck, forcing me to bend and shoving my face into the mattress. Despite the scrubbing I gave it, the material still smells faintly of urine and much more strongly of sweaty, pissed-off male. I struggle to push myself up, my half-chewed arm flaring a protest, but Xander plants his palm between my shoulder blades to pin me in place. His cuffed hand drops to the waistband of my leggings, the chain tickling against my thigh.

Maybe giving him a longer reach wasn't the best idea.

He rips the leggings off me, exposing my arse to the cooler air of the room. Goosebumps prickle up my spine. His knees force my legs wider.

"Xand—"

He slams himself inside me, and the rest of his name becomes a whimper.

It fucking *burns*. Coercion and inhaling piss haven't exactly put me in a sexy frame of mind.

Xander has no such problem. His hips piston against my arse, grinding my face across the bed. He thrusts deep and hard, an ache blooming every time he batters my cervix. He grunts with effort, his breathing ragged. Fingers bruise my waist. I try to breathe, to relax, but the angle of my neck makes it difficult.

Just fucking come already, I want to yell.

Xander loops an arm around my throat and drags me upright. Before I can take a welcome breath, his fingers throttle me. He drives himself harder, faster. My pulse swells behind my eyeballs and beneath the clamp of his hand. Black sparkles dance across my vision. Xander groans deep and low. His rhythm falters.

"Xander…" I choke, close to fainting.

He pounds what little air I have left out with the force of his final thrusts. His body shudders against my back, his grip on my throat easing. Oxygen rushes into my straining lungs.

Blood smears the covers from my wounded arm. My abused muscles tremble.

It's over. Thank Christ it's over.

But Beast-Xander isn't finished teaching me a lesson. His teeth sink into my shoulder—more pinching, crushing pain—before he finally releases me to scuttle away like a wounded little rabbit.

A little rabbit who wishes she'd said, "Fuck off," to his first, fervent, "Fuck me."

17

Xander growls at the soft clang of knuckles on the door. My heart leaps, and I jump to my feet from the stool at the foot of the bed, just out of Xander's reach.

"Quit your grumbling," I say. "I told you Olly was coming."

Something falls from between the pages of Xander's raunchy romance and flops on my boot. The clump of mushrooms Xander picked for me before he was taken. The ones I found in his filthy combats. I slip them in my pocket and place the book on the stool. I unlock the door and pull it wide. A rush of love and warmth and relief floods me at the sight of my brother's face.

He gives me a lopsided, slightly abashed grin. "Hey, sis. Long time, no see."

I throw myself into his arms, burying my nose in his shoulder and inhaling the comforting scent of citrus and wood smoke.

He smells like Dad.

Olly hugs me tight. His hand squeezes my shoulder, and I can't help a wince. He pulls away, holding me at arm's length. "You okay?"

I avoid his probing gaze. "Yeah, sorry. Think I slept funny."

Olly would have a fit if he could see my back. Marking me in the throes of (his) passion seems to be Xander's favourite thing now, no matter how many times I say, "No biting." Bruises stipple my shoulders in a colourful tapestry of blue and purple.

Olly flicks the scrap of material at my throat. "What's with the scarf?"

Xander's fingers left marks.

"Oh, you know," I say breezily. "It gets a bit cold down here."

"Feels warm enough to me." Olly keeps a hold of my arm, examining me from top to toe. "Have you lost weight?"

I kept the lights dim for our nightly calls. No need to worry him. Everything is under control.

I ease out of his grip. "Don't think so. I might have missed a meal or two, what with Xander—"

"You look exhausted, Quinn," Olly says, his expression creasing with anxiety and guilt.

"I'm fine. You're the one who looks tired."

There are dark circles around his hazel eyes, and his strawberry-blond hair is wilder than usual, sticking up at all angles.

Every call, he's more dejected, having nothing to report. No evidence of where or how the evil majority make Rabids. The days whooshing past with the finality of a guillotine blade.

"I'm concerned about you. Alone down here with him."

"You were never concerned about me and Xander being alone before."

Olly smiles sadly. "That's not Xander, Quinn."

"I know that." I scrape paint from the door frame with my fingernail. "I've been telling him about his life. I've got to when we went on that school trip to Fort Augustus. My kayak rolled me into the loch and he jumped in to save me, not realising he didn't actually know how to swim because no one had ever taught him."

Olly chuckles. "I remember you dragging him onto the shore. He had a plant in his hair and was coughing and spluttering. He said you'd need to give him mouth to mouth. Your whole face turned pink, but he didn't notice because his latest—what do you call them?—sex bunny came shrieking onto the rocks, calling him a hero, and almost cemented his drowning by smothering him with kisses."

"Tatiyana," I say, my lip curling. "I hated her."

"You hate them all."

"Yeah, well, do they have to be so… so… sex bunnyish?"

Olly's face sobers. "How is he?"

I nudge the door wider with my hip. "Come in and see for yourself."

Olly takes a deep breath and steps across the threshold. I lock the door behind him. Xander's warning growl transforms into a single word.

"Mine."

"What did he say?"

"Uh, well, he's—"

"*Mine,*" Xander hisses.

He's at the full extent of his chain, his left arm pulled behind him as he strains against the cuff. He tugs, and metal screeches. He scowls between me and Olly. He's wearing boxer shorts since he won't tolerate trousers or socks, and I'm still trying to respect *some* boundaries. His black t-shirt is pinned at the shoulder where I sliced it to get it past his cuffed arm.

"Mine," he snarls.

I clear my throat. "He's got a little, ah, possessive what with me being the only person he sees."

Olly flinches, and I want to kick myself.

"I would've come sooner, but—"

"No," I say quickly. "That wasn't a dig at you. You're trying to save him another way. It's more efficient to split our resources."

"He looks good," Olly says quietly. "Clean and well-fed. Have *you* been eating?"

He turns his searching gaze to me instead of the territorial Xander.

"When I can. I don't like leaving him alone."

Olly takes a step closer. Xander slides his cuff along the rail, facing off, teeth bared.

"Mine," he says.

"You remember Olly, right, Xander? My *brother* and your best friend? You were going to tell him something. Just like we practised."

He cocks his head. For a second, I think he's not going to do it, then he opens his mouth and in a monotone says, "My name is Xander. I am thirty-one years old. Quinn is better than you at football."

Hearing my name on his lips still gives me a shiver even though the emotionless voice is nothing like Xander's. Xander always struggled to hide what he was feeling in his voice.

"Quinn, that's *amazing*," Olly breathes. He sniffs, and knuckles one eye. "Except for the football stuff, which is absolute bobbins."

I wish I could share his excitement, but it's the same thing I get Xander to repeat before he attempts to bash his way out my navel from behind. Apart from the football bit. He says it all by rote and not like he believes any of it, or even understands it.

I have to hope his memories are still there, just deeply buried. That every improvement, no matter how tiny, is a win. Even when it feels so fucking hollow.

I glance at Xander. He's staring at me in the calculated way that makes me uneasy. Something feral and hungry shifts across his face. I widen my gaze at him, frantically trying to communicate *don't you dare say, "Fuck me,"* with my eyeballs.

Olly inches closer and Xander's attention snaps to him, his hackles raised.

"Careful, Olly." I stop my brother with a hand on his arm. "He's not quite ready for physical contact."

Unless you're me, then he loves it rough, hard, and fast.

"I see you got a better system of restraint." Olly tips his chin at the metal rail.

"Makes things easier. No more wrestling him over the toilet bowl. He washes himself, too. And he gets to stretch his legs. Show him, Xander."

Xander paces between the shower and the bed, the cuff scraping along the rail.

Olly grins. "Seriously, Quinn—this is brilliant. If this is what he's like after a week, who knows how much better he'll be after another? Even if I can't find anything at the damn school, there's no way Xavier can…"

"Yeah," I say gruffly. "No way."

Olly tilts his wrist, his watch catching the light. "I have to head back in two hours."

"So soon?" I say, a catch in my throat.

"You're working miracles down here. I feel bad for not contributing. And bloody Xavier is running us ragged. He definitely wants to find out how to make Rabids for his own means, not because he wants to help Xander." Olly waves his hands at me. "Now, shoo. You have a couple of hours to rest and do what you want. Me and Xan the Man will talk guy stuff. You deserve a break."

"Are you sure you—"

"We'll be fine."

"Don't get too—"

"I'll sit on the stool."

"But…"

Olly ushers me towards the door despite my protests. I find myself blinking in the corridor, the metal shut behind me. I wait five minutes, but no screams reach my ear pressed to the keyhole. I stagger up to my bedroom.

I should go outside, get some fresh air. The last time was days ago on my search of the outbuildings for something better to use than the handcuffs slowly slicing through Xander's ankles and wrists. Or I could eat something. I might actually be hungry for the first time since Xander stumbled up to the gate and munched on Phoebe's throat. A bath would be *awesome*. The heat would soothe the ache in my weary muscles and my poor, friction-burned lady parts.

I sway on my feet. Mechanically undress. My fist closes around the mushrooms in my pocket. I sigh, fishing the loupe and fungi field guide from my desk drawer.

I could use an app on my phone, but I prefer the old-fashioned way of identifying growing things.

I raise the magnifying glass to my bleary eye and peer through the lens. The specimen is a bit squashed and dry, but not preserved too badly between the pages of Xander's book. Glossy gills and a ghostly cap, with a thin, purplish stem. I work through the key of my field guide, picking up the loupe occasionally to check the mushroom's characteristics. My finger taps the species name.

Tenebris antrum. Dark cave mushroom. Locally common in

Scotland. Typically grows in underground caverns that lack natural light.

I slump in my chair, half-naked, the rest of my clothes askew, one foot bare. My tired brain struggles to compute much beyond one question.

What the hell was Xander doing in a deep, dark cave?

18

Xander's two weeks are up tomorrow. He hasn't shown any progress since Olly visited. Trapped in a psychotic state just like the good Doctor Cavendish said he would be if I didn't bring him in for tests and drugs. The sex probably didn't help. Shame that damage was already done before I spoke to her.

Olly phones every night, excited to hear about what Xander has been up to since he's still found no clue at the school. I lie to keep that hopeful light in his face. I'm carrying this burden for both of us. He doesn't need to know the anxiety chews a new hole in my gut as each day passes.

I tried to tell Xavier about the cave mushrooms in Xander's pocket, but William kept me waiting with his usual guard-dog smugness and I couldn't leave Xander on his own for that lengthy battle of wills. Loath as I am to concede to that prick. Olly said there's no indication of a cave system on any map of the private school estate. No cliffs or crags, no sinkholes or springs. No secret entrance from the buildings. Our Terra mystics scried the landscape and couldn't detect the shape of caves in the soul of the ground.

Olly's coming home tomorrow. Another mission failed. No doubt Xavier will let the axe fall hours before that, just to be a dick.

I glance at Xander. He's breathing softly, asleep on his stomach, his face innocent and relaxed, his lashes fanned above his cheekbones. His bare back rises and falls, a sheen of sweat still drying.

I never imagined sex with Xander could get tedious. No. Sex with Xander could *never* get tedious, but sex with Beast-Xander has lost its allure. I'm pretty sure I'm getting a yeast infection. I am nothing but a warm sex toy. There's no kissing, no affection, no intimacy. Not even a cuddle. Xander humps himself to climax, always taking me from behind like the animal he is, then climbs off, leaving me slumped on the bed, his cum dribbling down my thigh. Sometimes he has a piss or turns the shower on. Sometimes he shoves me out of the way and falls asleep. Like today.

I've definitely lost weight. My cheekbones cast their own shadow. My bruises have bruises in the shape of Xander's teeth. The marks of his fingers stipple my arms, my waist, my arse.

But every day I read to him, talk to him, tell him about who he really is. Who he needs to get back to. I beg him to get better, then have to stop because I don't want to cry in front of him.

Positivity. All we need is fucking positivity.

I sigh, and slide deeper into my sleeping bag. It's just gone midnight.

Xander's two weeks are up *today*.

My stomach churns. I throw the sleeping bag off and pace, padding on my bare feet, the light turned low. My cheery yellow t-shirt swishes against my legs, a sun decal grinning out from the centre of it.

Maybe we can run. If I threaten him with no sex, he might

behave. I can deliver him to Doctor Cavendish like I should've done at the start. Get him proper psychiatric care, no matter the risks of leaving the compound.

It's not too late.

A key scrapes in the lock.

My breath freezes. I slam to a stop and stare at the key beside my pillow. The *only* key. Or so I thought.

I dive for my bag. Xander snarls and shoves into a crouch, muscles tense. The door swings open. I whirl to my feet, my hand behind my back. William enters first, his pistol drawn. Xavier marches in next, his bulk making the cramped room even tinier. Xander's snarls increase. Xavier's blue gaze sweeps over him and back to me, as frosty as an ice-rimed loch.

"How do you have a key?" I wheeze.

"This is my compound, McTierney. There's nowhere I can't access."

Xavier and William pause at the edge of my sleeping bag, now perpendicular to the foot of Xander's bed given his extra range of movement. No grabbing me in my sleep. Not that I've had much sleep.

"You gave us two weeks," I say, striving for calm.

"It's been two weeks."

"It's barely midnight. That's thirteen days and five minutes, not two weeks."

"I'm not here to talk semantics with you, McTierney. I'm here to dramatically improve the safety of my compound."

Xavier and William turn identical expressions of disgust on Xander. Growls shake Xander's body. His fingers claw the mattress, his eyes narrowed and framed by black hair. His bared teeth shine in the gloom.

He's never looked more wild and dangerous.

"He's changed," I gasp. "He's different. Tell them, Xander. Like how you told Olly."

His growls continue with only a short pause for breath. Xavier feints towards the bed and Xander leaps for him, howling. The handcuff rattles taut and pings him backwards, slamming him into the rail. He shakes his head, stunned.

"Oh, yes, very different," Xavier says drily.

"It's not his fault that, even as an animal, he remembers you're a fucking arsehole," I say.

William's nostrils quiver. His pasty skin flushes pink.

"How dare you speak to your Captain that way, you soul-blind little—"

Xavier snaps his fingers. "Give me the gun, Walker."

William spares me another glare, then places the pistol in Xavier's waiting palm. Xavier raises the weapon.

"Step aside, McTierney. It's time to let him go."

"But Xander's in there. He's talking. He trusts me and lets me get close to him. With proper psychiatric care, he could—"

"I am not letting a Rabid leave this compound to wreak more havoc. I should never have let him remain in the first place." Xavier attempts an empathetic expression. "I'll make sure he doesn't suffer. A quick bullet to the head. You can wait outside with Walker while I do it. Then we'll bury him together."

My gut heaves. The sting of bile coats my tongue.

"Please, Xavier," I whisper. "He might not look it, but I swear he's getting better. Please don't do this."

Xander resumes his snarling, stalking up and down the length of the rail, the screech of the metal drilling into my eardrums. Xavier tracks him with the barrel of his gun and I dance along between them, sweaty and sick and unable to breathe.

"Please, Xavier. He's your brother."

A muscle tics in Xavier's jaw. "Step aside, McTierney. This won't get any easier by delaying."

"And delaying will only make your punishment worse," William chimes in, quite gleefully I may fucking add.

"She won't be getting punished." A spark of pity warms Xavier's eyes for a millisecond. "This will be punishment enough."

My hand tightens behind my back. I raise my arm and aim the Glock at Xavier.

"What about now?" I say. "Will I get punished *now*, Captain?"

"What are you doing, McTierney?"

"Drop the pistol and the key and get the hell out," I bark.

William scoffs. "She's not going to—"

I aim at his kneecap, my eyes narrowed in concentration. William splutters and skitters sideways, hiding behind the sizeable shield of Xavier. I return my aim to the centre of Xavier's forehead and repeat my command.

"This will not end well for you, McTierney," he says.

"Keep fucking talking and this won't end well for *you*."

The pistol clatters to the floor, followed by the thunk of the key. Two, huge palms rise to shoulder level.

"Is this really the way you want to play it?"

I smile grimly. "You gave me no choice."

I flick the Glock towards the door. William and Xavier mince backwards. As soon as they're in the corridor, I slam the metal shut and lock it, twisting the key hard enough to hurt my fingers. My breath comes in gasps, my heart shuddering along with the rest of me.

Then I collapse to my knees and rest my forehead on the

cool surface.

19

"We can't stay here."

My words are shaky but firm. I climb to my feet with the aid of the door handle, the Glock still clenched in my fist. Xander is agitated, growling softly and quivering. I stop just out of reach and say his name until he focuses on me and not whatever wild thoughts are flitting across his face.

There's only one place we can go and it's not exactly a secret. But I need somewhere to regroup. To plan. To pray Olly gets home soon.

"If you follow me and don't hurt anyone, I'll do whatever you want."

Xander cocks his head. "Whatever I want?"

I shiver at his words. The inflection is wrong, an undertone of menace, but it's still Xander's voice.

"Whatever you want," I say, my mouth dry, "but you follow me and don't hurt anyone unless they try to hurt you. Okay?"

His eyes darken, all pupil. His feral grin is the same one he wore when he ripped out Phoebe's throat.

This is the worst of my bad ideas. Banking everyone's lives—*my life*—on a promise I already regret.

But what choice do I have?

I ignore him for a few blessed minutes, stuffing items into

our bags and pulling on a pair of trousers and my combat boots. The gun stays in my hand.

I can't believe I faced down Xavier and William in my sunny nightie. Guess it's slightly better than any of my fruit-themed pyjamas.

Swallowing my heartbeat, I unlock Xander's cuff. It swings and rattles against the brickwork. We stare at each other, my breath held with the enormity of Beast-Xander being free. A pulse thuds deep in my belly. I wait for him to pounce. To bite and rip and tear and rape. He blinks at me, poised with the patience of a predator.

"Okay." My air shudders out. "Okay, good."

Christ, I can taste my own fear—metal and sweat.

I hold out a black t-shirt with a red dragon in the centre, its claws gripping a bleeding skull. Xander's favourite. Very goth. He pulls it over his head without complaint, but bares his teeth at the proffered trousers and boots.

"Put the boots on or we're going nowhere," I command, my words unflinching while the rest of me twitches and trembles.

Xander yanks the boots on, the laces trailing to the floor. He still looks great in his t-shirt, boxers, and boots, all slim shoulders, narrow hips, and long, muscled legs. I press my lips together.

There's no time to waste. Xavier could be amassing a group to storm the room. Or he might be barricading the exits, expecting us to flee.

I wish Olly were here.

I shoulder my bag and force Xander to wear his. The metal door squeaks. No one greets me with a, "Surprise, mothafucker," and a barrage of bullets. I wave to Xander and creep to the foot of the stairs, taking each step and pausing to listen. A soft glow from deeper in the house leaves everything in shadow. Xander's eyes glitter in the dark. I avoid the front and back doors, slipping into the large dining room and skirting around the tables and chairs. Xander moves silently, his breath stirring my hair and chasing goosebumps down my spine. His hot, eager breaths.

Don't think about it.

A security light shines from an outbuilding, sparkling on damp grass. A short lawn stretches to bare trees clawing at the night sky. The wooden frame of the dining-room window squeals and lodges half-way. I crawl through, my boots crunching on a narrow strip of gravel. Xander slinks behind me, fluid and graceful. Cold air chills my exposed arms and tightens my face. Xander appears not to notice. My pants puff white while his breaths gently steam around his cheeks.

"This way," I say, desperate to hear something human, even if it's my own voice.

I jog across the lawn. Xander purrs low in his throat. It takes all my willpower not to bolt, but that would only excite him more.

A branch scratches my forehead and tangles in my hair. I tuck my chin and plough through. The air smells of mushrooms and dead leaves. Snaps and cracks chart our progress. I stumble on the cottage out of luck rather than design, my bearings confused by the dark and the silent threat of the beast behind me, the quiet, watchful trees.

The living-room walls are composed entirely of glass, smudged by dirt and algae. It's a nice place to sit and watch the sun set above the branches, the space heated by the rays through the window. Twigs, moss, and rotten vegetation obscure the peaked, tile roof. The door closes quietly after us. Darkness settles in the hall. Xander is a vague shape. My heart kicks at his unchained, uncontrolled proximity, the air heavy with promise.

I wrap my fingers around a syringe in my pocket for reassurance. I still have two if 'whatever he wants' turns out to be something I can't endure.

It's okay. It'll be okay.

I realise I'm whispering it, and clamp my mouth shut. I spin on my heel and fumble along the wall. A black doorway yawns to my left, lightening as the space opens into the living room and adjoined kitchen/dining area. In the gloom, bottles and cans lie scattered on the table and floor. I pull the door closed and keep moving past the bathroom to the single bedroom at the rear. Next to it, a small mudroom leads to the back door and a tiny garden with a bench and a water feature clogged with leaves.

Or it was the last time Olly, Xander, and I were here. We squeezed on the bench, drinking wine and talking shit, laughing at nothing and everything. We all had a few vapes of Xander's weed. The rest of the night was beautifully mellow. Just three best friends hanging out. Xander gets more touchy-feely after he's smoked weed. Olly had to slap his hand when he kept stroking his thigh. He stroked mine, too, but I didn't complain. I had to fight not to open my legs wider while my body screamed, "*Higher!* Dear fucking god, please go higher."

I seal us into the bedroom and grope for the lamp next to the bed, the curtains already closed.

The window faces away from the centre of the compound so no one should see unless they're tromping through the trees. The guards on the fence have no cause to do that. Not yet.

Light floods the space, muted and yellow but glaring after

our night-time romp in the woods. I squint against the brightness.

Jesus fuck, Xander's eyes are dark and intense. Wicked.

I avoid his gaze and scan the room. The only furniture apart from the lamp and bedside table is a double bed with a box base instead of a frame, the covers crumpled and stained. I wrinkle my nose.

Definitely jizz. The savages. There's an unspoken rule that you clean up after yourself since lots of us crash here when we've imbibed a little too much, happy to be out from under the watchful gaze of Xavier and William and all the other mystics.

I shrug off my bag and strip the soiled sheets, dumping them in the corner to wash tomorrow. The covers from the drawer in the box base smell like lavender.

If only that were enough to calm the roiling in my stomach.

"We'll stay here for a day, maybe two," I babble. "Olly gets home in a few hours. He can help sneak you off-compound to somewhere Xavier can't touch you. We'll work something out. Get you to a psychiatrist. Everything's going to be okay."

I smooth a palm across the sheets, and straighten up. My back hits firm muscle and heat. A gasp slips out. Fingers grip my biceps before I can scuttle onto the bed, and escape. A nose brushes my ear. Every hair on my body crackles to attention. Nerves swoop into my gut. I swallow, and my throat clicks. I can't gather enough spit to speak.

Xander paws at my combats, his arms around and clamping me to the front of his body. One button pops open, but the fly has a whole series of them. Xander's snarl of frustration shivers down my spine.

"Xander," I squeak. "Wait—"

"Whatever I want," he growls.

"Right, but at least let me—"

My combats rip between his fists. Buttons ping everywhere. A hand grinds my face into the mattress, my arse in the air since this bed is lower than the one in the basement. Xander jerks my ruined combats to my knees, nearly taking me with them. He shoves my nightie up. He's making anticipatory noises deep in his throat.

I tell myself to breathe. This is fine. More of the same. It's uncomfortable, but a few pumps between my legs and he'll zonk out for the rest of the night. It's nicer than the cell. I get to inhale lavender instead of dust and piss and sweat. He's alive and safe for now, despite Xavier's best intentions.

This is fine.

His erection prods me in the arse. I bite my lip on a yelp.

"Uh, Xander, that's the wrong—"

He takes me from behind in one hard thrust, going where no man or beast has gone before. If I thought unlubricated vaginal sex burned, then this is a heated poker rammed into my colon and swirled around to rearrange my insides. I shriek into the mattress and try to crawl away.

Fuck my promise. This *hurts*.

Xander tightens his grip on my waist, the crushing pain pretty much lost in the conflagration of my internal organs. His hips plunge against my arse, knocking me off balance. I gnaw my lip to keep from screaming. Metal floods my mouth. Whimpers creep up my throat, but I cage them behind my teeth in case they drive him into a frenzy.

He's frenzied enough, thank you very fucking much.

Christ's sake, I think I'm torn, bleeding, and not just from my mouth.

My hands scrabble uselessly at the covers. I choke on lavender and my own blood. Somehow, the agony increases, Xander happily pounding my intestines into oblivion. A howl builds in my chest—a wail of torment and shame that'll no doubt trigger Xander's killer instinct. He'll snap my neck while he fucks me. Maybe he'll fuck me again before my body cools.

He grunts and spasms against me, shaking a whimper free. It turns into a whine when he pulls out none too gently, taking half of my guts with him. He wanders out of the room, leaving me sprawled on the bed, my breathing ragged, my arse throbbing, a bitter taste on my tongue. The muffled splash of water comes from along the hall. I slide my combats up, though it takes me two tries because my hands are shaking so much. My whole body is shaking. Something thick and warm dribbles down my inner thigh.

Xander pads back into the room. I flinch away, dropping to my knees, but he just kicks off his boots and flops diagonally across the bed. His breathing deepens thirty seconds later.

I should feel something. Probably. But all I feel is numb.

I crawl from the room, too sore and unsteady to stand. I reach the bathroom on my hands and knees. My teeth are chattering. My fingers and feet and heart have turned to ice. I manage to switch the shower on without getting up. Water patters on the plastic base. Mould stipples the limp curtain. I crawl into the steam and warmth and curl on my side. Sobs wrench out of me. Even that hurts my arse. I choke out a laugh, but it dissolves into a pathetic crying fit.

I brought this on myself. Made my bed, so to speak. And now I'm fucking bawling in it.

20

Dawn finds me curled on the couch under a blanket, weary and heartsick. Everything hurts.

I stayed in the shower for almost two hours, fuzzy and in shock. The heat failed to thaw the icy ache in my core. I dozed fitfully when I made it to the sofa, snapping awake, shaking and sweating, afraid I would find Xander bending over me, ready for more. *Demanding* more.

I'm really starting to hate Beast-Xander. Sure, he can't be blamed for his behaviour. He's just an animal. Whatever. Fuck that guy. I want *my* Xander back. I want Xander.

My lip wobbles, and I force myself up before I start howling again. I shuffle into the kitchen, the blanket clutched around my shoulders.

Focus on one step at a time—coffee first, then call Olly. Figure out a plan. Watch for Xavier and his goons.

We're lucky no one else was in the cottage last night. It never crossed my mind in my panic. It's not used every night, but it's a popular place for a shag and a bender. Too risky to stay another night. We have to get Xander out of the compound today.

My toe nudges a can of cider and it rolls across the cracked tiles, clunking into the fridge. I fill the kettle, select a mug, spoon coffee into a small cafetière. Normal activities. Comforting activities.

Footsteps pad towards me. My fingers jerk and spray sugar across the worn counter top. I grip the edge, my other hand clenched in the blanket. My shoulders hunch. I stare at the coffee, as if it will save me.

"Mor-morning, Xander. You want tea? There's a box of Assam in the cupboard. I put it there last time."

Bright and cheerful, if you ignore the wobble.

I can do this.

Xander's silence crawls down my spine. A tremor shivers up my legs. My shoulders have reached my ears, I'm so fucking tense.

"I'm having coffee," I say, high enough to shatter the living-room windows, "then we can—"

My protective blanket is yanked from my body. I stumble backwards and collide with muscle and heat, just like last night. *Just like last night,* my mind screams.

"Xander," I plead, "I'm a little sore from—"

He spins me around and slams my spine into the floor-to-ceiling cupboard next to the fridge. My head hits wood with a dull thunk. My teeth-shaped bruises throb their protest.

Xander is still wearing his dragon t-shirt and boxers, his erection bobbing through the gap, the button undone. He bunches my nightie in his fist at the level of my navel. One tug removes my underwear. He hooks my leg over his hip and buries himself to the hilt inside me.

Part of me welcomes the slight burn because it's bearable. Unlike anal sex, which I will not be having again this millennium. At least I can stand and shut my eyes and wait for it to end. It's our first time in this position, but not even that can make it enjoyable. There's nothing familiar in his face, only hunger.

This isn't Xander. Xander is gone. Xavier was right, the dickhead.

Xander's fingers clench on my thigh around his hip, hard enough to bruise. Again.

"Ow," I mutter. "Xander—"

He braces his forearm against my throat, choking the rest of my words, and forces my chin higher. His hand crushes my thigh. I struggle to breathe past the press of his arm. Flesh smacks against flesh. An occasional grunt. The sounds of a rutting beast. A brutal pressure builds in my chest, my gut, behind my eyeballs. The ceiling wavers and blurs.

I can't. *I can't.*

Hot tears splash my cheeks and drip from my jaw. A sob rips from my throat. I'm vaguely aware of Xander pausing mid-thrust, head cocked, but I'm in full-on, wailing-fox mode. I shove at him until it's just me in my body, hollow and so fucking done.

"I can't do this," I sob, over and over.

I shoulder past Xander, blinded by tears and snot and swollen flesh. I stumble to the couch, find my boots, pull them on. My lungs struggle to suck in a full breath and it wobbles back out. Xander stays in the kitchen, his boxers around his ankles, his dick limp beneath his t-shirt.

"I've loved you since I was fourteen!" I yell at him, every second word punctuated by a hiccup. "And you know what's ironic? If you were yourself, you wouldn't touch me like this. You—you wouldn't touch me..."

I weep into my hands, running for the front door and barking my shins off every piece of furniture. I claw at the lock.

Xander halts on the threshold of the living room, silhouetted by the light, his face in shadow.

"I fucking hate you, Xander." My voice cracks. "And I love you. I want you back. *You.* Only you. Sorry, I need some air."

I tumble out of the door and slam it behind me. The woods welcome me with wet fronds and dripping lichen, the chill soothing my flushed cheeks. Brambles scour my bare legs, but I don't stop. I run until dizziness drops me to my knees, then I sit and hug them to my chest and pant at the sky. Clouds scud across the blue in the gap between the branches. My heart calms, my hitching cries petering to the occasional whine. The cold feels wonderful on my abused arse.

I'm not sure how long I sit there, composing myself. Long enough for the wonderful cold to turn to shivers, my skin pale and blue.

My clothes are back at the cottage, as is my phone. And Xander. I can't leave him alone, especially unchained. The risk of him running amok has never been higher. Olly should be arriving home any time now. I need to call him, get him to meet me here. We can bundle Xander out of the compound in the boot of a car. No more sex. If he complains about it, then tough. It'll be the psychiatrist's problem. How stupid to think I could care for him. Rescue him. He needs professional help. I'll do anything I can to assist. Just not that. Not anymore.

My heart can't take it.

I scrub my face and climb to my feet. My boots drag through the leaves, reluctant to return. Tiny shoots of green spear from the ground as winter limps towards spring. A cluster of rubbery jelly ear fungus sprouts from a dead elder bush.

What if he demands sex as soon as I step through the door?

Then I sedate his ass and truss him up so tight, he can't move.

What if he's not there?

Shit. What the fuck am I doing, dilly dallying like an imbecile?

I lope for the cottage. The door shuts hard behind me.

Deep breaths. No, my hands aren't shaking.

"Xander?" I call.

Nothing. No scurry of footsteps or eager little noises. No growls.

The living room is empty. And the bedroom. By the time I reach the bathroom, I'm sprinting, heart hammering, a hot spike of panic in my chest. There's no one in the shower. No one in the mudroom or the garden. No one.

Xander is gone.

21

Xander

I open my eyes in a bed smelling of sex. Nothing new there. Except it's not my bed. I prop myself on my elbows. I recognise the lamp and the bedside cabinet, the lack of other furniture.

Okay, so it *used* to be my bed.

Did I bring Celeste to my old cottage? That might explain why I'm in my lucky dragon t-shirt and nothing else.

So why can't I remember? I never get black-out drunk. It's too risky to lose *all* my inhibitions. A guy has to keep some secrets.

I swing my feet onto the threadbare carpet. Vertigo rolls through my skull. I cradle my head in my hands, my elbows on my knees.

What the fuck did I do last night? I feel… weird. Not quite with it. Weak, my throat a little scratchy. My joints ache, like they've been stretched too far. There's a scent on my skin. Something familiar. Sweet and exotic, like coconuts and honey. Who smells like that? Not me. Celeste douses herself in some awful citrus stuff that's only good for searing your nostrils. The answer teases me, dancing out of reach. I frown at my toes. Unease curls in my stomach and I'm not sure why.

Did I break up with Celeste and bring someone new here? Why would I do that? This place is for chilling with Olly and Quinn.

I focus on remembering, but a sharp pain shoots through my head.

Time to find them to explain this mystery before I freak out. They'll know what day it is, even if I don't.

My clothes are in my bag beside the bed. I halt in the act of pulling on boxers. My arms and legs are… not right. There are marks on my wrists and ankles. Healing scabs and red circles like I was…

My stomach heaves.

Something's wrong. Am I still high? Am I ill? Why does it look like I was tied—

Bile shoots into my mouth.

Okay. Time to stop thinking about that unless I want to throw up.

I yank on a pair of jeans and my boots, and feel a little better. Except the jeans are looser than I remember. There are more clothes in the bag. Way too much. I root around and find a couple of books, my iPod, some kind of first aid stash with clinking bottles and empty syringes, plus the entire contents of my bathroom. My mouth twitches at the pink and cream toothbrush.

A present from Quinn. The cheeky cow. She said it was as gay as I am.

But why would I pack so much? The longest I've stayed when I didn't have to is one night. Most of the time I don't even bring a bag.

A ball of crumpled sheets lies in the corner next to another bag. I step towards it. A burst of fear hits me from nowhere.

I don't want to look. I don't want to know whose stuff it is.

Why, why, *why?*

I spin on my heel and stride into the hall before I even realise I'm moving.

"Celeste?" I hesitate in the corridor, head cocked. "Quinn? Olly?"

No answer. The house is silent and still. A shiver ripples down my spine, though the air is warm. I peek into the living room. A pair of my boxers have been abandoned on the kitchen floor next to a scrap of women's underwear. The unicorn on the front causes another inexplicable lurch in my gut.

Was that me? I'm not usually a fan of the rough stuff. Now, if a lady asks me to rip off her knickers, well, I'm not going to argue. But surely I'd remember having tear-off-your-pants sex in the kitchen? Plus Celeste prefers silky thongs to cotton.

Whose knickers are these?

"Hello?" My voice sounds strange—husky and uncertain.

I don't like it here. I've never liked it here, especially when I was banished so as not to embarrass the family. It's lonely, dark, and dingy. Only Olly and Quinn make it bearable. And they don't seem to be around.

My breathing gets shallow and rapid. Or rapider. I've been breathing fast ever since I opened my eyes. The dim room gets dimmer. The walls—closer. Air wheezes in and out of my tight throat. Hot panic surges in my gut.

The front door slams against the wall in my haste to open it, leaving a divot. I stumble outside and huff fresh, glorious oxygen. No one is around to see me almost lose my shit.

The need to find a familiar face is an ache behind my

breastbone.

I hustle towards the main house on a path I've taken many times before, when I was allowed to enter and scavenge scraps off the table like a mangy dog. If I hadn't found a second, better family, I'd be quite bitter about it. But I am Xander McTierney. Not blood related, thank god, though that may have made things easier.

Or more fucked up.

Where are Quinn and Olly? The thought of finding them worsens and soothes the panic. Which doesn't add up.

My boots kick through leaves. Water drips from trailing lichen, yet the sky is bright and clear. Shoots of green peek through the damp ground.

Is that a fucking snowdrop? I only know of it because of Quinn's fascination with plants and mushrooms. When the hell did spring get here? It was frosty and February only yesterday.

Was that yesterday?

More stomach churning, more nausea, more feeling as if someone's gripping my throat in their fist and squeezing like a bastard.

Has someone drugged me? Christ, have I been date raped? How does that even work for a guy?

But no—I trust everyone here. Excluding my shitty original family. Most of the other mystics are nice people. Though we did have an influx from Compound 14. I don't know enough about them yet except we're all on the same side. The good guys.

A burst of relief quickens my pace at the sight of the main house and the well-tended lawn bordering the rear and disappearing around the front. I half-expected it to be a ruin or gone completely the way my day is going. Figures move beyond the glass of the dining room windows, one of the windows open. I aim towards it. There's a shriek, and the shatter of ceramic. The window thumps shut, rattling the pane against the frame.

My breath catches and I whirl around, but there's nothing behind me. You'd think there was a Revenant charging at the window, but it's just me out here, shivering and sweating on the grass.

What in the actual hell?

I jog to the front. The wide lawn extends to the gate, flanked by guard towers, a shape just visible in each. Everything seems calm and normal. I leap up the steps, my pulse quickening.

Bang!

A bullet cracks into the door frame near my head. Splinters prickle my cheek. I trip on my own feet and sprawl face-first on the polished floor. My gaze lifts to a line of three people—grunts, like me, two from the destroyed compound, one a guy I play football with. Shaun. He has a crush on Quinn. His game goes to shit whenever she joins us.

All three aim their rifles at my face.

"What the fuck are you doing?" I screech.

22

I scrabble another frantic circuit around the cottage, as if Xander might be hiding in a drawer somewhere and I've simply overlooked him, but the place is cramped—people are not easy to lose.

How could I have left him? For all my talk of being the only one he needs to look after him, of doing whatever it takes no matter what, I was pretty quick to bail when the going got rough. Or rougher. It's been pretty fucking rough, I'll be honest.

But that's not the point. I swore there would be no further self-indulgent breakdowns. That Xander was more important than my fragile psyche. Yet what do I do? I bugger off into the trees to have a crying fit, leaving him alone and unbound in the cottage. I could have just locked myself in the bathroom like a normal person. Composed myself. Then taken control of the situation and established boundaries.

Instead, I abandoned someone who has abandonment issues in a place that triggers unpleasant memories despite the happier times we've had there. Xander still has days where he gets depressed and withdrawn about it. Beast-Xander has no doubt gone berserk.

How many people have I killed? How long until someone

kills Xander?

Xavier was right again, dammit—I already wish I was one of the slaughtered.

I burst out of the cottage and sprint around it in case Xander is, you know, just chilling in the fucking garden.

Nothing.

My throat aches with the urge to scream his name, but I don't want to alert anyone in case he hasn't made a move yet. He's a predator stalking his prey. Patient. Deadly. I might catch him in time. I'm also *persona non grata* in Xavier's eyes, so no need to draw attention to myself and have one of his eager minions drag me inside to see him.

My boot crushes a patch of snowdrops. A gunshot cracks beyond the trees, the sound echoing above the canopy.

"Xander!" I shriek.

I crash headlong into the woods. Branches whip my cheeks. My nightie tangles in every clump of brambles. Raspberry thickets scratch my bare legs.

Oh god, I've killed him. This is all my fault. *I've killed him.*

I stagger onto the grass, sobbing, sweat-soaked, my heart racing. There's no one at the back of the house and the reflection in the glass obscures my view of the dining room, the window now shut. I gallop around to the front. The lawn is empty, the guards still in their watchtowers at the gate. A commotion spills from the front door.

He can't be dead. Not after everything we've been through. Everything *he's* been through. He was the best thing in my life bar Olly and my parents. I thought I loved him enough to save him.

But I've failed. I let my own weakness condemn him.

Why did I leave him alone, free and wild? *Why?* I'm glad he never loved me back. I didn't fucking deserve it.

Excited voices echo from the direction of the hall. Yelling. The cacophony of a crowd.

Are those bastards celebrating over his dead body?

I'll kill them all.

With dread and rage warring in my gut, I mount the steps into the house.

23

Xander

The rifles waver at my calm and manly voice that may or may not be two decibels higher than my usual range. At this distance, the gun barrels gape as wide as the mouths of the grunts staring at me. Boots thunder down stairs and screech on the parquet floor, but I dare not remove my gaze from the three lunatics. My palms are flat on the ground under my chest, my body tensed to spring up and away.

Shaun lowers his gun. "Xander?"

"Yes, it's fucking Xander!" I say—again quite calmly. "Who the hell do you think you're looking at?"

Shaun's, "Holy shit, she did it," dissolves in an explosion of voices. A scrum of people surrounds me and, for a second, I fear I'm about to be trampled. Multiple hands grab and yank me upright. Palms slap my shoulders, my back, my arms. Someone even ruffles my goddamn hair. There are exclamations of, "Welcome back, mate!" and, "Jesus, he's back!"

"What do you mean 'back'?" My voice cracks. "Where have I been?"

And why can't I remember? *Why can't I remember?*

Everyone's talking at once, yet no one answers me. It's deafening and confusing and I've had a pretty stressful morning already.

If I had actually been somewhere, everyone's excitement at seeing me would be kinda cool. It's nice to feel wanted.

"Xander!"

My head snaps up at Olly's voice and, I swear, my knees go weak at the sight of him on the top of the stairs. Strawberry-blond hair, freckles, and limitless generosity. Just like his sister.

"Olly! Thank Christ. Everyone's been abducted by pod people. Can you please explain—"

Olly pelts down the steps, streaks across the hall, and collides with me so hard, I stagger back. Arms wrap around me, his face buried in my shoulder. He's a couple of inches shorter, the same as Quinn. I'm enveloped in his burning-orange-tree scent, and it eases the knots in my stomach.

"Goddamn, I missed you, Xan the Man," he says roughly, his breath hot through my t-shirt.

"Uh, Olls?" I clear my throat. "You're freaking me out. What the hell is going on? Where have I been?"

Olly releases me, rubbing at his eyes. Before he can put me out of my misery, Celeste appears at the edge of the crowd and launches herself at me like a Xander-seeking missile.

"Snuggle muffin!" she squeals.

I've asked her numerous times not to call me that in public. It's fucking embarrassing. She wants me to give her a cutesy nickname, too, but I just… can't.

Her legs clamp around my waist, her arms around my neck. She plants a sloppy kiss on my mouth. My nose starts stinging from her perfume. Something flickers across Olly's face, but he spies someone behind me, and beckons.

"There's Quinn," he says. "I was wondering why she wasn't with you."

My heart seizes, then thrums along uncomfortably fast.

Quinn was with me? At the cottage? My internal thoughts get higher and faster and end in a shout of *oh, Christ, what did I do?!*

I spin around, my hands on Celeste's thighs to steady her. She smacks kisses on my forehead, my cheeks, my nose. I can't see past her head or move in the cage of her arms. Her touch sends a tremor down my spine.

I don't want her to touch me. I want her to stop touching me.

"Right, Celeste, let me breathe." I peel her gently away and plop her back on her feet.

I scan the doorway, but it's empty and there's no flash of strawberry-blonde hair in the crowd still churning around me.

"Where's Quinn?" I say.

Celeste pouts and wrinkles her nose.

Olly frowns at her. "She was there a second ago."

The uproar finally settles. The crowd watches me, hanging on every word and movement. They press in close, closer. The air is stifling and sticky and catches in my throat. Firm fingers wrap around my forearm.

"Come on," Olly says. "We need to talk."

He leads me through the crowd. Yells and palm-slapping become whispers and trailing fingers. Celeste skips along after us up the stairs. Olly jerks to a halt, stopping me with him, and glares at her.

"Not you," he barks. "*You* can wait."

Her face settles in mulish lines. She sniffs, spins on her heel, and stomps down the stairs, quickly swallowed in the crush of people.

"Have you two had a falling out I'm not aware of?" I try to laugh, make my voice light, but it comes out a croak.

"I'll explain everything in a minute," Olly says. "But privacy first."

We go to my room. The door seals us into a welcome bubble of silence. My gaze falls on the bed and the scraps of material tied to the posts. My gut gives an uncomfortable lurch and my hand rubs it absently.

"Have I developed a kink I don't know about?" Again, my light tone fails. I sound wrecked. Lost.

The chair has been moved to beside my bed along with the mesh rubbish bin, turned upside down. A metaphor for my life right now and I still don't know *why*.

"What the hell is going on?" I whisper.

"Sit down, mate," Olly says. "What's the last thing you remember?"

I perch on the mattress. An unpleasant odour rises from the covers—musky, fungal almost. It teases my already sensitive biliary response. I shut my eyes and squeeze them tight, as if that will banish all the weirdness and help me remember.

At first, nothing happens. I pinch the bridge of my nose. Then my eyes snap open.

"Our pre-mission ritual! We were in the cottage eating coconut ice cream and watching an episode of *Battlestar Galactica*. Quinn made that joke about me being a Cylon."

Olly places his hand on my shoulder. His sympathetic expression scares the crap out of me.

"That was a month ago," he says softly.

I'm aware of my mouth flapping, my eyes bugging out. My chest locks and refuses to expand. Olly presses between my shoulder blades and guides my head between my legs.

"Breathe, Xander. You're okay. I've got you."

He pats my back. I whoop in air.

"A *month?*" I gasp. "But how?"

And then he tells me the whole, torrid truth. Words and phrases like 'Rabid' and 'slaughtered Johnson and Hogue' and 'Xavier was a fucking dick' bounce around in my skull.

Voices pass beyond the closed door. Someone knocks on the wood and calls my name. I don't know about Olly, but I can't say a thing. My brain is spinning. Imploding. I might actually faint.

"Another fact you should know," Olly says after the voices fade. "Celeste refused to help after talking to you for twenty minutes. She hasn't been near you in the last two weeks. Said it wasn't what she signed up for."

I manage a weak smirk. "No loyalty these days."

"I should've done more, too." Olly stares at his feet, his freckles bright in his pale face. "I should've argued with Captain Up-Himself. He didn't need me at the school, not specifically. I shouldn't have left Quinn alone."

"Where is—"

The door bangs against the wall, and rebounds. A massive hand slaps it steady. Olly and I leap about a foot. Xavier looms in the doorway. He always looms. His hand grips a pistol at his side. William peeks over his shoulder.

"Well, good morning, brother-mine," I say, though my voice lacks its usual bite. "Nice of you to check up on me."

Xavier shakes his head—a stubborn lack of response to a familial reminder that usually scores me at least ten points.

"She did it," he says, almost to himself. "That stubborn psycho actually did it."

"She's not a—"

Xavier's stabbing finger cuts Olly off. He aims it at both of us.

"When the crazier McTierney inevitably joins you, tell her to go to my office. *Immediately.*"

And with that burst of brotherly affection, Xavier spins on his heel and strides away, William scuttling after him. Olly quietly closes the door.

I swallow hard. "Where *is* Quinn? Why isn't she here?"

"Don't know," Olly mumbles. "Let me call her."

Her phone rings and rings, then goes to voicemail. Her tinny, cheerful voice says, "Hey, this is Quinn. I'm probably around, but avoiding someone. Leave me a message and if I don't phone back, it's you."

"Call me, *please*," Olly says after the beep.

His mobile chirps a second later. He frowns at the screen, then holds it out to me. A text bubble reads 'Can't talk now, Q x.'

"What does that mean?" I rub my face. "Can't talk or *won't* talk?"

Olly paces between the door and the window seat. "Don't know, man. All I know is you were difficult to handle and she had to care for you alone. She said she read to you, talked about your life, showed you pictures. You need to try and remember. Whatever you went through was some serious shit. She lost weight. Had bruises."

My gut clenches. I struggle to speak.

"Did I hurt her? Is she avoiding… is she avoiding *me?*"

Olly shrugs one shoulder. "That's what you need to remember. I don't get it, though—she knows it wasn't you, whatever you did. She called the Rabid you 'Beast-Xander'."

A tortured chuckle slices out of me.

"Christ, this is a lot to process." I dig the heels of my hands into my eye sockets until sparks ripple across my closed lids. "What if it's bad? Whatever I remember?"

"You'll still be my best friend. My brother." Olly clasps my shoulder again. "That's not going to change."

I sure hope so. But bruises, weight loss?

What the hell have I done to Q-tip?

24

I peer around the door frame, braced to witness a group of feral soldiers beating Xander to death with rifle butts. What I see is worse.

My fingernails sink into wood and are the only things keeping me vertical. My legs wobble. My vision wobbles. My heart soars, seizes, and dies.

Xander has his back to me, but I'd recognise his figure anywhere. I've memorised the dark flop of his hair, the spread of his shoulders, the narrowness of his waist, and the delectable curve of his arse. And wrapped around him like a fucking spider monkey is none other than the big-titted waste of space, Celeste, who doesn't deserve to breathe the same air, never mind touch him.

She's doing more than touching him. She's snogging his face off as if she single-handedly nursed him back to health, risking life and limb and sanity. And he's *letting* her.

My breath hitches. My dead heart spasms and bursts into flames.

Xander is back. Hale and whole and *himself*. No way would Celeste be dry-humping him otherwise.

The crowd around the happy couple shifts. Olly spots me trembling in the doorway, his eyes bright and shiny with joy.

He waves me over, a big grin crinkling his cheeks. I shake my head and back away. My feet trip down the front steps. I catch myself and stumble towards the cottage.

I can't do it. I thought I could bear Xander going back to his sex bunnies as long as he was normal again, but I *can't.* It hurts too much. Does he remember anything? Do I want him to? I don't know what would burn me more—Xander remembering it all and choosing to shag his sex bunnies as if our shared trauma meant nothing, or Xander being oblivious and me losing the tiny piece of him I could claim, even if it was only his beast self. And never being able to tell anyone.

Who am I kidding? It's the fucking first one, hands down.

I need a break. A break from *him,* even though part of me wants to spin around, rush inside the house, and throw myself at him, sobbing with relief. My arms ache to hold him, the real Xander, hear his voice, inhale his scent. Tell him I love him. Still.

I'm sure that would go down well.

I need time to process and heal. A chance to bury this period of my life so, when I do finally see him, I can treat him like I always have—like my best friend and a second brother, not the monster I came to hate.

I jog into the cottage and aim straight for the bedroom. My heart clenches at Xander's bag, the contents spilling out.

How panicked and confused he must have been, coming back to himself all alone. Was it my tears that triggered it? I wish I'd bloody cried the first time he was rough, and saved myself a lot of pain. Though it was probably a combination of everything, and cumulative.

I rip off my nightie and leave it in a pile on the floor. No way am I wearing it again. I dress quickly in jeans and a purple hoodie, tucking my mobile in my pocket and hoisting my bag over my shoulder. I leave the cottage without looking back.

Avoiding the front of the house, I creep in the rear entrance and up the servants' stairs. My phone vibrates. I flinch and bang my head on the door frame leading to the third floor. My thumb hesitates over the screen.

Olly. No doubt wondering where the hell I am. Wondering why I'm not fused to Xander's hip, crying and celebrating and gloating.

God, I want to be. But I can't face him. Beast-Xander twisted me up inside. He took everything and I have nothing left to give. Not right now.

I watch my phone screen until my voicemail kicks in, then type a quick message.

That'll hold him for about five minutes. He must be worried. Worried about what happened between me and Xander to drive me away. Guilty at not being there to help.

I can't think about that yet. I want to escape so badly, it tingles in my teeth.

I tuck the phone in my pocket and step into the third-floor corridor. Most of the rooms are offices and bedrooms for Xavier and his mystics, including his parents. The space is richly appointed, thickly carpeted, and reeks of entitlement. I stride towards the door at the end and raise my fist to knock.

Not that *he* ever bloody knocks.

"At least you follow some orders, McTierney," Xavier says behind me.

I whirl around and frown at him. "What?"

"Do I have to remove your firearm or are you going to behave like a rational human being this time?"

He looks me up and down. William glares from behind the

bulk of Xavier's bicep, Xavier's frame filling the corridor.

I smile sweetly. "Only if you get William to do it."

William's face attempts to wrinkle in on itself. I hide a smirk. So easy.

"You appear to have forgotten how much trouble you're in, McTierney. Threatening a captain of the Unbound is a serious offence. Not to mention wilful disobedience and endangering the entire compound."

"Did you see him?" I mean for it to be loud and smug, but the words come out timid.

"I saw him," Xavier says.

I nod once and turn to the door, shoving it open. "In that case, Captain, I'm ready for my punishment."

25

Xander

A wave of exhaustion hits, and I slump on the bed. Olly watches me with concern.

"You should get some rest, man. Let your subconscious mull it over in your sleep. I'll search for Quinn."

I nod, my head suddenly too heavy for my neck. My eyes sting, my nose stings, my throat stings. Sleep would be good.

Olly pauses, his hand on the door knob. He clears his throat.

"I'd change the sheets first if I were you," he says, and shuts the door behind him.

No shit. They smell like an animal has been rolling around in my bed.

Christ. Was *I* the animal?

Shuddering, I strip the covers. The mattress reeks of piss, and I swallow a gag.

Maybe I don't want to remember.

I wrestle the mattress over. The other side smells a lot nicer, but I'll still need to get a new one. I'll pester Xavier about that tomorrow. Should be fun. If he refuses, I'll threaten to piss on *his* mattress.

I spread fresh covers over the bed. The bonds around the posts refuse to loosen, even the resistance band. Gut twitching, I hack at the material with nail scissors until they fall apart, then toss them in the mesh bin after turning it the right way up and placing it in the corner where it belongs. I lie on my back and stare at the ceiling, hands crossed over my stomach.

I miss my iPod. Left it back at the cottage with the rest of my stuff. Bird song and wave sounds would be comforting right about now.

I killed *Phoebe.* We slept together a couple of times, but there was no chemistry. For me, anyway. And Hogue. He was a solemn, unassuming guy. A bit geeky. Pretty eyes. Got flustered when I flirted. I slaughtered them with my bare hands.

No. Not me. *Beast-Xander.*

It doesn't make me feel any better.

I sigh and turn on my side, tucking my hand under my cheek. My lids slip shut.

When I open my eyes what must only be two minutes later, Olly is perched on the chair by the bed, his fingers reaching for me. I jump high enough to bounce a little on the mattress.

"Jesus fuck, Olls."

My throat is worse than before—scratchy and sore. My muscles are stiff. Hell, my *bones* are stiff. A headache thumps at the front of my skull, politely requesting attention.

Olly sags in the chair. "Sorry. You've been asleep for two bloody days. I had to keep checking you were still alive. I worried you might wake up Rabid again. How are you feeling?"

"Need water," I croak.

He fills a glass in the bathroom and slops some on my arm in his haste. The cool liquid burns then soothes, gushing into my belly. I gulp a breath, slamming the empty glass on the bedside cabinet.

"How did you sleep?" Olly says.

"Feels like I didn't. Did you find Quinn?"

A head shake. "She hasn't been to her room. Won't answer my calls. Her last message said 'I'll call you when I can. Stop bugging me.'"

I manage a weak smile. "Sounds like her."

"She's never avoided my calls before."

"She's never avoided *me* before," I say, "except for maybe an hour after I did something to piss her off. Like when I tried to set her up with that guy at the gym."

"Oh, yeah. I've never seen her turn so pink."

We share a chuckle, but quickly sober. The absence of Quinn is an empty space in the room. In my chest.

"So, do you... remember?" Olly ventures.

I start to say no, but frown instead.

Did I dream? Maybe that's why I'm so tired. But what did I dream?

Unease climbs into my throat. A sensation like something rushing at me, barrelling towards me, sends fear prickling across my scalp. My consciousness scurries away from the phantom shape like a mouse in the dark, but the thing flaps and looms and spreads its wings, then launches itself directly into my brain.

My eyes pop wide. "Oh, fuck."

I scrabble for the bathroom and barely make it in time. The water is not half as pleasant in reverse. Bile nips my throat and nose and brings tears to my eyes. I heave over the toilet, hunched on my knees. I spit into the bowl, then sit hard on my arse, muscles aching. Olly hands me another glass of water.

My stomach lurches, but I keep it down.

"You remembered something," he says grimly.

"Oh, fuck; oh, god, Olls—it's bad. It's really fucking bad."

I roll the cold glass on my sweating forehead. I shut my eyes, but the images won't stop. In fact, they're more colourful, more graphic, on the black of my lids.

"You remember all of it?" Olly says.

"Nothing until… a room I don't recognise? A shower in the corner. I was handcuffed to the bed." My stomach flips, and I fight a gag. "I don't remember you. Only Quinn. Oh, Christ, *Quinn*."

My voice cracks. I wedge myself in the gap between the toilet and the wall. My bare heels squeak on the tiles, scrabbling to push me deeper into the space even though my spine is flush against the plaster.

Olly flops onto the edge of the bath. "Tell me."

"You don't want to hear it," I gasp. "I can't believe… Why would she… Oh, god… Oh, fuck."

Olly shouts my name. My head snaps up. He's crouched in front of me—when did that happen? He rubs my hands between his palms.

"Your skin is freezing." He lifts his gaze, his face pale. "You're scaring me, mate."

"You're going to hate me." A tear slides down to my jaw. My voice is broken. Bleak. "I've tried so goddamn hard not to be that guy."

"What guy?"

Olly's eyes are the only colour in his face. Even his freckles have paled.

"The guy who fucked your sister," I say.

He cocks his head instead of punching me. "You and Quinn

had sex?"

"Not sex," I wheeze. "She let me, but it was basically rape. I fucking *raped* her, Olls."

I stuff my fist in my mouth and cut myself on my teeth, tasting metal. I'm shaking, rattling my shoulders between the wall and the toilet seat. The sharp scent of vomit wafts from the bowl.

"You didn't rape her," Olly says firmly, still holding the hand not pressed to my mouth. "You said she let you. You're both adults. And you weren't even *you*."

"You don't get it. This was brutal. *I* was brutal. I'm talking anal without any lube or prep."

Olly blanches. "Okay… maybe I don't need all the details."

"She tried to crawl away." My voice doesn't sound like mine—high and strained and hitching. "I wouldn't let her."

I hide my face in my palm and sob into my knees. A tentative hand cups the back of my head.

"Xander," he says, gentle somehow even though he should despise me. It's been the thing I've always feared—that Olly would grow to loathe and abandon me like my own family. All because of Quinn.

I tried so hard.

"Xander," he continues, "this reaction is why you can't blame yourself for anything you did while you were Rabid. You would never hurt Quinn in your right mind. She knows that. She may have forgotten, but you've both been through something traumatic. She'll forgive you. Now blow your nose—you've got snot all over me."

He flutters a strip of toilet roll in my direction and tugs his hand from mine, his skin bleached from the press of my fingers. My laugh is watery, but I do as instructed, honking delicately into the tissue.

I sniff, dry my face, and finally have enough courage to meet Olly's eye. "I need to talk to her."

"Yeah, you both need to have a good, long talk," he says. And then he mutters something that sounds like, "You oblivious fucking idiots."

26

Xander

I'd love to talk to Quinn, if I could actually *find* her. Olly and I search the compound—every room in the main house (and there are many), the outbuildings, the garage, the woods, even the guard towers by the gate. The other bag has disappeared from the cottage. Quinn's bag. No wonder my subconscious shied away from looking at the contents for a clue.

It knew what I'd done.

But I still don't remember how my boxers and Quinn's ripped underwear got to be in the kitchen. I'm very happy not remembering. I have enough to torture myself with.

Olly scolds me whenever I start the blame and self-loathing cycle. Which is often. He says Quinn wouldn't have done anything she couldn't handle. But he wasn't there. He didn't see the pain on her face. And if she could handle it, why is she hiding?

Because she *couldn't* handle it. I broke her.

Maybe Olly is in denial about me calling it rape, but there's no doubt in my mind. It was brutal and not what she wanted, despite her initial consent.

158

She's vanished from the compound. No one we ask has seen her. A few of them are still wary in my presence. The rest are eager to question me on what happened, what Quinn did. How she healed me. Olly gives them a vague answer because I can't. We pretend I don't remember.

Celeste attempts to insert herself back at my side and I tell her in no uncertain terms to get lost. She abandoned me. People only get to do that once.

Quinn continues to leave Olly's calls unanswered. Her voicemail is full of his worried messages. She texts him. Things like 'Leave me alone, I'm fine' and 'I'll phone, I promise, just give me some time' and the one that breaks my heart: 'Does Xander remember anything?' I beg him to lie. He feels guilty, but he does, replying that I remember none of it, that I'm doing okay. Concerned for her.

The latter is true, at least.

After two days of fruitless searching, covering the same ground as if she might be keeping ahead of us like a crafty fox, I suck it up and go to Xavier's office. The door opens into a narrow reception area with a desk barring the way to the inner sanctum and a chair shoved in the corner.

It always reminds me of school, waiting for the headmistress to dole out punishment for whatever trouble I'd gotten myself into.

It happened a lot.

William glances up from behind the desk. His upper lip wrinkles before his good breeding kicks in and his expression smooths to haughty indifference.

"Good morning, White Walker," I say cheerfully.

He looks like one—frosty and pale, his blue eyes devoid of anything resembling a personality. A threat to anyone who dares steal Xavier's attention from him. I swear, if they haven't fucked yet, I will lose a lot of money to Quinn.

My humour evaporates. It resurfaces for a brief second at William's quivering nostrils.

"I'd like to speak to my brother," I say in a mild voice.

William's nasal passages flare wider than the Clyde Tunnel. He slaps his pen on the desk, and steeples his fingers.

"Captain Dawson is extremely busy."

"That's okay. I'll wait."

I make a show of settling in the chair. William rewards me with a facial spasm.

No doubt he's desperate to throw me out on my arse, but while that used to be acceptable behaviour for the rest of the Dawson family, we're now the good guys. Good guys don't toss other good guys out on their ear, even if the aforementioned good guys are massive dicks.

Of course, Xavier makes me wait an hour. I suspect it would've been two, but, on the sixty-minute mark, I stare at William's jugular as if I want to know what it looks like on the outside.

"What are you gawking at?" William hisses through his teeth, his eyes a little wide. His fingers flutter over his throat.

I jerk as if startled. "Hmm? Sorry, zoned out there. I've suddenly got an urge for raw steak. Nice and bloody."

No doubt William's regretting the soul anchor he placed in me years ago. Even he can't yank my soul out to save himself unless he removes his anchor, and that takes time and concentration.

He jabs at the intercom on his desk and Xavier magically finishes his busywork, appearing at the door and ushering me into his lair. I wink at William on the way past.

He made my lonely life hell after he paired up with my brother when we moved to Melrose. He deserves everything he gets.

Xavier's office is much larger than the reception area, the floor-to-ceiling window offering a view of the sloping lawn and front gate. A better, bigger view than the one from my room. Two leather chairs face his solid oak desk. He sits in the swivel seat behind it, and it squeals. I choose to stand.

"What can I do for you, Xander?" he says, copying the finger-steepling manoeuvre William favours.

He addresses everyone else by their surnames, except me. He can't bear to call me Dawson.

"Where's Quinn?" I say.

"You mean she's not glued to your side after ensuring your miraculous recovery?"

"Don't get cute. You know everything that happens in this compound, as you remind us daily."

Xavier leans back in his chair, his fingers tapping the arm rests. "What did the indomitable McTierney do to cure your Rabidity?"

I force myself to meet his cold, blue gaze. "She reminded me who I am."

"How exactly?"

"Read to me. Talked about my life. Showed me photos." I shrug one shoulder. "I'm still piecing it together."

"What do you recall of the process itself—being made Rabid? Is it a power we all have? By which, of course, I don't mean *you*."

"Good mystics don't turn people into monsters," I say mildly, "or are you thinking of joining the dark side?"

"Now who's being cute?"

"*Where is Quinn?*" I growl.

Xavier stands and faces the window, hands crossed behind his back. "Isn't it funny that the McTierney who was so desperate to save you, desperate enough to threaten her own captain with a gun, is nowhere to be found now you're restored?"

"She threatened you with a gun?"

"Apparently, I gave her no choice."

My hands ball into fists. "What have you done to her?"

"I believe the real question here is what have *you* done to her?"

I flinch. "I don't know what you mean."

Xavier turns back to his desk, resting his hand on top of his chair and mirroring my posture, though I'm tense and he's a smug bastard.

"Tell me, Xander—what's the last place you would ever want to go? Where would that place be?"

My face pales. My fingers are freezing again. A tremor courses up my legs.

"You sent her there?" I rasp.

Xavier grins. "On the contrary—she *asked* to go. Begged me, in fact. Now, why would one of your closest friends be eager to go somewhere so traumatic for you? Somewhere you're guaranteed to avoid?"

"Send me there," I spit, my voice wobbling.

How they made me Rabid is still a mystery, but my entire body rebels at the thought of the place. Sweat pools in the small of my back, though my hand on the seat is white and blueish. Anxiety grinds in my chest.

Xavier laughs. "I think not. You've just recovered from a debilitating condition. Returning to the scene of the crime, so to speak, would be horribly triggering for you. And until I'm assured your Rabidity is not simply suppressed rather than vanquished, you are consigned to the compound."

"You're grounding me?"

"I'm protecting you, Xander," he says, his patient tone ruined by the smirk on his face. "And I'm protecting McTierney."

* * *

I don't remember leaving Xavier's office. I must have looked a state—pale, sweating, shaking. Xavier and William will have lapped that right up.

The bastards.

I stumble into Olly in the corridor. He takes one look at my face and steers me to my bedroom. His expression is grim after I explain what happened. Why we couldn't find Quinn.

God, it hurts to know she ran to that place to get away from me. Clever bloody woman. Not that it's her fault. It's mine. All mine.

I don't want to go back there. But I will. For her.

She's obviously forgotten how fucking stubborn I am.

Unfortunately, my stubbornness only lasts until I'm curled in the space for the spare wheel in one of our 4x4s. The clunk of the boot and the knowledge of where I'm headed erupt in a panic attack. Olly and Shaun drag me into the dim light of the garage, my legs floppy and useless. A scream lodges in my throat, but I can't breathe to let it out. I can't breathe.

I can't breathe.

A paper bag is shoved against my lips. Olly, fuzzy and distant, holds my hand and tells me to copy him. Copy his breathing. In and out. The crinkle of paper slows to a rate less manic.

Dizziness washes through my skull. My heart has never beat so hard. I focus on breathing while Olly and Shaun talk in low voices. Shaun disappears into the shiny Range Rover and drives away in a puff of exhaust.

Just as well. I'm too weak and exhausted to try again today even if I wanted to. And I do. I need to get to Quinn. Talk to her. Tell her how goddamn sorry I am.

I'll have another chance in forty-eight hours. Shaun leaves the compound every couple of days to run errands. Thankfully, Xavier isn't inspecting all the vehicles that exit the gate with the intensity of a drug-sniffing hound. He's watching me and Olly. Or having us watched, but his minions are easy to lose. It gives us a few minutes to get me in my hidey hole, then for Olly to stay behind and run interference. Xavier will magically have 'just missed me' every time he comes searching.

Or that was the plan.

The second attempt goes much the same as the first. By the third—four long, excruciating days—I'm trembling before I leave my fucking bedroom. Olly's hand on my arm interrupts my furious and somewhat high-pitched cursing.

"Have you still got that first aid kit Quinn left in your bag?" he says.

I jerk my chin at my bed and he scrabbles under it, pulling the holdall out and rummaging around. Glass clinks.

"What are you looking for?"

Christ, my teeth are chattering.

He brandishes a clear bottle and an empty syringe.

"Medicinal help," he says.

Mist eases from the sodden ground and creeps around the tree trunks, tendrils exploring like ghostly fingers. Fitting, since I'm searching for evil.

Or the place where evil was committed.

I fist my hand in my pocket. The clump of dark cave mushrooms is in tattered bits. I let the pieces drift from my palm to the carpet of moss and loam.

Xander must have found them after he was captured. If he'd found them before the mission, he would have given them to me. On the awful day itself, he had no time to go spelunking. So he kept them as a clue to the location of the Rabid-making, knowing he wouldn't be in any state to say where he'd been.

He wanted the bastards found. Until I can steel my heart and face him again, it's all I have to cling to. Finding where Beast-Xander was born, ideally how it was done, and hunting down the vile pricks responsible.

Maybe by then, I'll have forgiven myself.

I hunch my shoulders and hustle through the misty woods, my eyes scanning the landscape, looking for something—*anything*—that could indicate the presence of a cave system.

It has to be here. If they took Xander away from the school, it could be bloody anywhere. But the tyre tracks of the van they shoved him into seemed to aim towards the forest, though they were soon lost beneath the churned mud left by hundreds of Revenants.

Olly said they searched as much of the estate as they could, but focused on the main house and outbuildings. If the Terra mystics couldn't find any indication of something underground, then it must not be there.

But I like to do things the manual way. The grunt way. Magic can easily get cloaked or confused. My stomping boots do not.

Maybe Xander remembers now. Maybe I should answer one of Olly's many calls and find out.

Maybe tomorrow.

I kick a stone and it cracks off the trunk of a pine canted over a slope. Water droplets patter on the exposed roots. The disturbed soil smells of mulch and damp. I pause on the edge, looking down into a grassy bowl. Another pine tree leans precariously on the opposite bank. Mist slithers and purls towards the bottom. My boots slide into a descent.

It's probably just a sunken clearing. Not a sinkhole.

I reach the base and take a cautious step on solid, unforgiving ground. Another step. Two. The grass gets a little spongier, but I'm sure it's no—

The roots of the grasses ping and snap beneath my feet. Mud hisses, taking the stability with it. A waterfall of soil and stone drops me into a black cavity, and I land on my arse in a bushel of cave mushrooms.

* * *

The screech of stone vibrates into my molars and drills an ache through my skull. Cracks zig-zag across the ceiling. I slap a hand to the top of my hard hat, squashing it more securely on my head and sending a cloud of dust puffing into the beams of the portable floodlights. My warm breath moistens the skin enclosed by my face mask. Condensation fogs my safety glasses. Two Terra mystics stand in front of me, similarly kitted out, their pale figures covered in pulverised stone and sweat. One has her palms aloft, manipulating the soul of the rock to hold up the ceiling. The other carefully extracts boulders from the blocked tunnel we've been digging through for the last six days. A rock crusher chugs and crunches in the background, muffled by my ear protection.

The Guild cowards collapsed the cave system before they fled the school. An impenetrable wall of scree and stone greeted me when I fell through the sinkhole into a small cavern, my buttocks smarting after my hard landing. The poor cave mushrooms were unsalvageable.

Maybe the cave-in confused our Terra mystics' magic, or the Guild cloaked its presence another way.

A rock groans. Dust poofs everywhere. Pebbles skitter.

"There's a space ahead," the male mystic shouts. "I think we've broken through!"

"Thank fuck," I mutter.

"What?"

"I said, 'Top work!'" I yell.

I skirt past the woman concentrating on keeping us from being buried alive. The man—Gerald? Ronald?—finishes rolling a boulder clear, his tall and skinny frame at odds with the power of his magical ability. A smooth corridor bends out of sight, blissfully free of rocks and obstructions bar a smattering of grit on the polished floor.

"The soul of the ground is more stable here," he says as I pass him. "I'll help Clarissa secure the roof."

"Excellent idea. I'll scout ahead, but I won't go far."

The dust and noise lessen around the corner. Lights glow from the ceiling, illuminating the tunnel to another blockage of stone about thirty metres away.

"Goddammit," I growl.

Two depressions in the rock wall reveal metal doors side by side. Opposite them, chunks of debris obscure three other potential doorways or corridors, a fan of gravel dirtying the floor. The handle of the closest door clunks under my palm. The entrance swings into a smooth and shiny room. A table sits in the centre, bolted to the floor. Plastic straps bristle from each corner. My heart kicks.

Is this the cell where Xander was turned?

A shiver shudders down my spine. I leave the door open and push through the second one. A semi-circle of black and flickering monitors fills the back wall above a crescent-shaped desk. One screen shows the corridor I came from; another, the cell. A maroon office chair lies on its side in front of the desk. I nudge it out the way and tap the keyboard. The central screen bleeps to life, showing a black background and glowing green letters, as if I've stumbled onto a spaceship in a sci-fi movie. The creepy text lists four dates. I use the roller ball embedded in the desk and select the earliest. Another screen flickers, revealing a cell.

But this one isn't empty.

A woman is bound to the table. Blood oozes beneath the plastic straps. A cloaked figure enters, and my heart shrivels at the shadows contained by the hood. Two hulking men follow behind. My stomach rolls as the footage continues. Tiny screams filter from the headset abandoned on the desk.

I fast-forward the video, but it makes it no easier to watch.

I skip to the next. A man. Pleading. Pain.

Oh, Christ…

Is this what they did to Xander? Is that his video right at the end? The date matches the time of his capture.

I force myself to view the whole of the second video. Bile squirts into my throat. The screen fades to black, reflecting my pale and panting face. Footsteps clomp along the corridor. I lean my palms on the cold desk and tell myself to breathe.

"Well look at this lot." Ronald whistles. "Found anything interesting?"

I clear the sharp taste of bile from my mouth.

"Evil," I say.

28

"This is all you found?" Xavier clicks his mouse, his slab of a head squared down to fit the small screen of my laptop balanced on the kitchen island. "What about Xander's video? Where's the file with that?"

I stroke the USB stick on a cord around my neck, hidden under my pea-green shirt. "They didn't have it—only those three—but we just broke through this morning. There are a hell of a lot of tunnels and caverns buried behind the rockfall. Maybe they use different servers."

My camera feed in the bottom-right corner shows my dull eyes and tired face, my skin made paler by a patina of rock dust. Clods of hair have escaped from my already messy ponytail.

"How is it that you stumbled on the underground cavern when several teams of mystics and nomags, including your brother, came up empty?" Xavier says, arching a brow.

I smile coldly. "I tried to tell you about the mushrooms, but your guard dog kept me away. And some of us don't need fancy powers to do a good job."

"Watch that mouth, McTierney," he says, though it lacks heat. He keeps tapping away at his mouse, muttering, "Goddamn bloody mushrooms."

I stop touching the USB before the lump under my shirt

draws his all-seeing eye. The kitchen is top of the range, the counters pink-veined marble and huge to accommodate all the staff and students. Everything has been left as if the bad little mystics will filter in at any minute, looking for a sandwich before they go avail themselves of someone's soul. They had time to cover their tracks, though, and buried their secrets beneath a shit-tonne of rock.

I clench my fingers in my lap to stop from rubbing the USB.

"What are your thoughts on the videos?" Xavier says, finally holding my gaze through the screen. "I assume you've watched them."

I shift on the padded stool. "As much as I could stomach. Is the sexual assault and rape tied into the ritual? I've never heard of soulkinetics using sexual magic."

Xavier grunts. "Neither have I. The routine of it with each victim—male or female—suggests as such, but I think it's to humiliate and break them down. It seems to me that although it takes only a few days to create a Rabid—"

"Longer if the victim is strong," I interject mildly.

"—it uses an excessive amount of energy," Xavier continues, a muscle twitching in his jaw.

"That would explain why we have so few videos," I say. "One roughly every twelve months. That's a long time to replenish, so it's probably all they can do. You saw the guy—that kind of evil takes a toll on the body."

Xavier rubs his face, stubble rasping under his fingers. "Yes, he was not a healthy individual. We should be thankful this ability is rare, otherwise we'd be overrun with Revenants *and* Rabids."

I wait until Xavier catches my gaze. "I want to be on the team that hunts him down. Him and his two sadistic cronies."

"I'll take that under advisement, McTierney," he says. "Get back to me if you find anything else."

The call ends and I shut the lid of my laptop, sliding painfully from the stool and leaving patterns of rock dust on the cushion. My muscles ache from hours of lifting heavy stones and feeding them into the crusher to give us space to move in the tunnels. More dust purls in my wake as I exit through the kitchen door and walk to the separate garage, my focus on my boots.

I've seen the lawn and the trees and the tyre tracks every day since I got here, but it doesn't soften the lurch in my gut. I made the mistake of inspecting closer and discovered the heel marks Xander left in the dirt.

The garage is a huge space of marble and glass, the no-doubt-expensive cars replaced with a dirty hodgepodge of 4x4s and SUVs . They flank the poor rock crusher that coughed and died this morning. I prop open the engine panel and root around inside, checking the spark plugs and following the oil line.

Olly texts me every day. He's finally stopped calling. I miss his voice, but I'm not ready to face him yet. Too ashamed of myself. Olly says Xander's struggling to accept what he did when he was Rabid—the parts that Olly knows about, anyway. Xander still doesn't remember anything.

I ask that every day.

A pinch of guilt tightens my ribs. I lean deeper into the engine compartment as if I can crawl away from it.

I should be there, supporting him. Even when we only slept a wall apart, we'd message or call at least once a day. I'd keep him abridged of my points for pissing off Xavier and the nostril-quivering William. He'd send me photos of interesting fungi he found in the woods and call me mushroom lady.

No wonder he hasn't contacted me. As far as he's aware, I left without saying goodbye right when he needed his friends. I'm sure Celeste is being pretty fucking comforting now he's back to his old self, the bitch. He's damn inflexible when it comes to abandonment. No one gets a second chance.

Not even me.

A tiny fearful, hopeful part of me thought he might turn up here, too stubborn to be kept away by nightmares and trauma. But his silence says it all.

He hates me. And I deserve it.

I swipe a tear from my cheek, huffing diesel and oil. Loneliness carves a hollow in my stomach.

What a fool I am. I've isolated myself in this fucking place because I'm a coward. The hard part was over. If I'd stayed in the hall, Xander would have spotted me, dropped Celeste on her arse, and hugged me instead. No question. All I've done is hurt him, maybe even hindered his recovery.

I should have phoned him. Acted normal. God, I'd give anything to hear him say that stupid nickname. It's all I wanted when he was Beast-Xander. It's all I want now. Then I'll know he forgives me.

So when a timid voice behind me mumbles, "Hey, Q-tip," you'd think I'd be prepared.

But I'm not.

29

The top of my skull clangs on the hatch of the engine compartment and my bleat of, "Fucking hell!" echoes in the garage. I spin around so fast, my ponytail thwaps me in the cheek.

I'm not ready. For all my pining and angst and homesickness, I'm not bloody ready. I haven't showered since yesterday. I'm covered in rock dust and engine grease. My mouth tastes like the bottom of a cave.

But there's Xander, wearing a black jacket that hugs his shoulders and emphasises the cut of his waist, the material dappled with water. The hood is up, perfectly matching his hair and framing the brilliant green of his eyes.

Eyes that are as uncertain and anxious as those two, whispered words.

Hey, Q-tip.

"Olly lied!" I gasp, a palm flying to my chest to calm the wild thud of my heart.

"Don't blame him," Xander says. "I asked him to."

"How much do you remember?"

His gaze drops to the floor. My stomach drops, too.

"Almost all of it," he says.

My calming hand fails to restrain my heart, which catapults free and flaps for the door. Humiliation prickles through my veins.

No wonder he can't look at me.

My legs spur me in the direction of my vacated organ. Cold sweat pops on my hairline.

"I have to go," I yelp, putting a whole Volvo between me and Xander instead of brushing past him.

"Quinn, wait." His voice catches.

Oh, fuck, I'm going to lose it.

I only realise I'm clutching a wrench in my fist when I'm sprinting across the lawn instead of following the driveway to skirt round it like I usually do. Rain pelts my face and beads in my eyelashes. Xander calls my name again, but I don't stop. Can't. Blind panic has seized my body and all I want to do is *get away.* I shoulder-barge the two-leaf door beneath the imposing central portico and slam it behind me, stumbling through a security vestibule into an opulent, oval hall under a domed ceiling with stained glass signs of the zodiac.

"Quinn, is that Xander?" a voice calls from one of the offices on my right.

"Uh-huh," I pant.

Crap. Of course he's chasing me. Am I going to have to do something really embarrassing like lock myself in a bathroom?

"Is he not coming in? He's just standing in the rain."

I halt my lunge for the stairs, my wet boots squeaking on the floor. My heart rate continues to rival a hummingbird's, but I turn on trembling legs and peek through the narrow windows flanking the door.

Xander is a black shape in the middle of the lawn. Grey clouds loom above him, pelting rain, his face obscured in the gloom of his hood. He sways.

Then he falls to his knees.

My boots hit the grass. Running again. No memory of opening the front door. Water blinds my eyes and sticks my shirt to my torso. Two steps from Xander, I slide on my knees and collide with his body, wrapping my arms around his shoulders and burying my face in his neck, tearing his hood down.

Hemp and bergamot and Xander—heaven.

His fingers clench in the back of my shirt. Dampness seeps into my shins. Xander's breath is ragged in my ear. As shaky as the rest of him.

"I'm sorry," I say. "I'm sorry."

What a bitch I am. Forcing him to come here because I was too cowardly to stay and talk. The stubborn arse. I should've known he wouldn't let fear and traumatic repercussions stop him. Not for long.

The USB stick digs into my skin since we're mashed together.

"You ran away," he says, his voice nearly lost in the patter of rain on his jacket.

I shake my head, as if denying the truth. "I couldn't watch you with Celeste. Not so soon after… And I was ashamed."

He tries to pull free, but I tighten my arms, burrowing closer into the warmth and pulse of his throat. Water drums on my head and slicks my hair to my skull. He relaxes, fingers unclenching. One hand cups my shoulder blade. The other settles on the small of my back, his nose behind my ear. Our thighs are pressed together. Our chests.

Fuck, I've missed his hugs.

"I'm not with Celeste anymore," he says.

"Oh." I sniff. "*Good.* That useless pair of tits refused to help."

His chuckle sends a little tremor down my spine that he can

definitely feel since we're fused into one body. Maybe he'll think I'm cold. Which I am. I'd struggle to get any wetter unless I rolled around in a puddle.

But I'm not letting go.

"Olly told me." The humour fades from Xander's voice. "I'm so goddamn sorry, Q-tip."

"You don't have anything to be sorry about."

Again, he tries to ease from my grip. I hide my face and cling worse than his sex bunnies.

"I hurt you." His shoulders heave under my arms. "Why… why would you let me treat you like that?"

I shake my head a second time. "It wasn't you. I forgot that for a bit. Olly doesn't know."

"He does now."

My cheeks attempt a blush, but all my blood has fled into my core with the chill. Except for a pleasant tingle in my gut at the feel of Xander in my arms. His hard, perfect body and glorious scent. Usually, he's warm, but we're both shivering.

"Why, Quinn?" he continues. "You still haven't told me *why*."

Doesn't he remember the kitchen? Me yelling that I love him? Have I been spared one humiliation?

"I wanted you back." My breath hitches. "I would've done anything."

The tears finally come. I cry into his neck, releasing all the pain and terror and relief. Washing myself clean. Washing us both clean. Xander has a couple of sniffles himself, and cuddles me tighter until we're only quivering from cold, not emotion.

"If you two are going to shag on the lawn, we're allowed to watch," someone shouts from the direction of the school building.

It forces us apart and we help each other stand. My joints are frozen, my clothes drenched. Xander isn't much better, though his jacket has protected his top half at least. We stare at each other, suddenly awkward. Spikes of black hair frame his cheeks, his skin slick with water.

I want to lick him, and welcome the urge. It's so normal. I was worried I might have actually fallen out of love after everything. And that would be sad. Easier, but sad.

"You saved my life, Q-tip," he says quietly. "I'll never forget that."

"You would've done the same."

His mouth twitches. "Maybe not quite the same."

I manage a blush. The gentle wind seems to slice through my sodden shirt, and my muscles spasm.

"Can you come inside?"

He glances over my shoulder. His pupils dilate, and a shudder rustles through his jacket. I hold out my hand. He takes it, squeezing my fingers, and lets me lead him towards the building.

"Do you remember what they did?" I say softly.

"Not consciously. But subconsciously? Yes. Olly had to sedate me to get me here."

My gaze sweeps the dripping grounds. "Where is Olly?"

"He stayed at the compound to run interference. My loving big brother forbade me from coming anywhere near you."

A smile tugs at my mouth. "Xavier will be furious."

Xander hesitates on the step, pulling against my arm. His focus bounces from our joined hands to the double door to the lawn and the tree line. He sucks in a breath and blows it back out, scattering droplets from his lips. At his nod, I guide him into the hall and up to the room I've claimed in the attic, ignoring everyone else. Rain taps on the skylight.

It's a small space with a sloping roof, but it's cosy and private, with an en-suite that's almost as large as the whole bedroom. Must have housed one of the teachers. The bath cinched it for me.

We take turns showering and change into dry clothes, Xander borrowing a pair of black combats that, of course, suit him perfectly. He steps out of the steamy bathroom after a very short shower by his standards. I flip the USB through my fingers, then hold it out to him. He plucks it from my hand after a pause. His skin brushes mine.

"What's this?"

"If you ever want to know what they did, it's on there." I raise my gaze to his. "It's the only copy. Xavier was looking for it, but I deleted the rest."

His throat bobs as he swallows. "Did you watch it?"

"Only long enough to see it was you, then… I couldn't."

His fist closes around the stick. "Will you watch it with me?"

My turn to swallow, though it clicks. "If you want me to."

I jog down to the kitchen to retrieve my laptop, apprehension jiggling in my stomach. I dodge the questions everyone throws at me about Xander's appearance, and bound back upstairs, breathless, my heart slapping against my ribs.

I know what happened in the other videos. It still sickens me. Do I really want to see that done to Xander?

But when can I ever say no to him?

He paces between the couch and the bed while I set the laptop on the wooden coffee table. We sit on the floor, our backs to the sofa, not touching. I hover the arrow over the play button.

"Are you sure?" I lick my dry lips. "It's going to be tough to watch."

Tough—fucking understatement. I might scream, throw up, faint. Probably all three.

Xander's face is pale, his pulse fluttering in the hollow of his throat, but he nods.

"I have to know."

"Okay, well, be prepared for me to lose my shit."

"You and me both," he says.

He grips my hand in his, and I hit play.

The video shows the cell carved from bedrock, the walls somehow shiny and smooth. Xander is strapped to the table in the centre. His biceps flex as he fights the bonds, the hard edge of plastic digging into his wrists. The cloaked figure stands at his feet with their back to the camera, tall and painfully thin, hood drawn. Two men flank Xander's head, both thickly muscled with shaven hair. One has an eyebrow piercing. The other has the tattoo of a skull on the side of his neck.

I recognise all of them from the other videos. The hooded figure is the Rabid maker. He likes to watch before it's his turn.

"You're crushing my hand, Q-tip," Xander says next to me, and I jump.

"Sorry."

Nothing has happened yet, but there's already a sick swirl in my gut. My heart is beating so hard, I can taste it.

I know what's coming.

Eyebrow-piercing fumbles at the cord securing his jogging bottoms and shoves them down his hips. No underwear. His dick bobs free, partially erect. Xander's fingers tighten on mine this time. I clamp my lips together. Eyebrow-piercing strokes himself and there's a considerable length to cover, his crown huge and purple.

On the table, Xander sneers. "You think this'll be the first time some guy has come on my face? Prepare to be disappointed, arsehole."

It pulls a laugh from me despite the atrocious situation. Beside me, Xander manages a weak smile before his gaze is yanked to the screen. The light reflects in his eyes, playing his abuse in miniature.

On the video, Xander's face is calm, his expression controlled, though his voice wobbled when he spoke. He's breathing fast, his hands clenched into fists. He knows what their plan is, knows these are the last few moments of his life. He might survive for a while as a Rabid before someone shoots him. But he'll never be himself again.

And he's fucking terrified.

My throat closes at the sight of him struggling to be brave and defiant. Beside me, Xander clicks his tongue piercing on his teeth, though he seems unaware he's doing it, his focus fixed on the laptop.

Neck-tattoo exposes himself and joins his companion in the synchronised dick-stroking. He's not got as much to wave around as Eyebrow-piercing. Both of them get aroused no matter the gender of their victim. The Rabid maker observes their work in silence. The only sounds are the slap of flesh and an occasional grunt. Xander stares at the ceiling of the cavern, grim and pale. Both men climax, then all three exit the room, leaving a spitting and furious Xander with ropes of cum across his cheeks and forehead.

The video jumps to the three mystics back in the cavern. The time and date in the bottom corner of the screen show it's the next day. White streaks have dried on Xander's skin.

Like the other videos, it's been edited to cut the footage of their victims when they're alone.

Neck-tattoo fiddles with the table between Xander's feet. A metal rod pops out, connecting the straps between Xander's ankles. Eyebrow-piercing performs the same action at Xander's head and his arms pop free, the straps at his wrists joined by another rod. Xander throws his legs over the table and totters onto his feet, hopping a couple of steps. Eyebrow-piercing grabs for him and Xander swings the pole between his wrists, aiming for a temple shot. Eyebrow-piercing ducks and Xander spins around, tripping over the bar between his feet and sprawling in a clatter of metal. Eyebrow-piercing hauls him upright and slams his stomach into the edge of the table, bending him over, pinning him with his larger body. A hand drops to the waistband of Xander's combats.

"Ah, shit," the Xander beside me whispers.

"Don't you fucking dare," the Xander on the screen growls.

I bite my lip, tasting metal.

Eyebrow-piercing tugs Xander's trousers down, exposing one smooth flank to the camera. Xander bucks, wrenching himself backwards and knocking Eyebrow-piercing on his arse. Neck-tattoo hammers a fist into Xander's skull. Xander slumps across the table, limp and blinking, eyelashes fluttering. Neck-tattoo leans his weight on Xander, lying diagonally across his back. Xander tries to kick, but can't get any height or power from his hobbled ankles. Eyebrow-piercing approaches dick-first. He slams it into Xander. Xander's cry morphs to a snarl of, *"Motherfucker,"* over and over again, a little more ragged each time. I wince with remembered pain.

"I'm sorry I did that to you, Q-tip." His voice is rough, but he releases my throbbing hand and slings his arm around my shoulders, tucking me into his side.

"It wasn't the same," I croak.

Swallowing hard, I force my gaze to the screen. Neck-tattoo takes his turn. The Rabid maker watches in silence.

They rape him the next day, too. And the next. The edited clip starts early enough to show Xander flinching as soon as the door clangs open, admitting his abusers. But he doesn't plead or beg them to stop. He curses at them even when his voice breaks.

They move on to beating him with rods and thin wooden switches. That explains the cuts and bruises. Xander screams, unable to escape the onslaught. Each scream slices into my chest, my gut, my brain. On the third day of the beatings, Eyebrow-piercing and Neck-tattoo pause, thick chests heaving, sweat beading their shaved skulls. Blood drips from the switch in Neck-tattoo's fist.

"Is he ready yet?" he says.

The hooded figure swoops to the head of the table. His crooked back hides whatever he does, but Xander whimpers low in his throat.

The figure straightens. "Continue."

He strides to his place at Xander's feet, his face nothing but a glimpse of concave cheeks and dark sockets beneath the shadow of his hood. A switch whistles through the air. *Thwack*. Xander screams.

My muscles are rigid, my hands clenched in my lap. I twitch at each fractured scream, a shriek building in my throat. Tears drip from my jaw, knocked loose by my chattering teeth. I stab the spacebar and freeze the video, capturing Xander mid-agony, his back bowed, mouth wide, eyes squeezed shut.

"Don't," I croak, rocking slightly. "Don't make me listen to you scream anymore."

He calls my name a few times before it registers.

"Hey, Q-tip, hey—you're okay. Come here."

He pulls me into his lap, caging me in the comforting warmth of his body, my spine to his chest. His arms wrap around me and I hug his forearms tighter, his legs pressed to mine from thigh to ankle. He rests his forehead on the back of my neck, his breaths scorching down my spine.

"I'm sorry," he whispers. "I'm sorry for making you watch this, but I... I can't do it alone."

His arms quiver beneath my fingertips. He's the one witnessing his own torture yet *I'm* the one who needs comforting. I take a deep, steadying breath. Another. I manage to nod after a minute.

"Can we at least mute it?"

Air huffs to my nape, and I shiver.

"Maybe we should've done that before I started screaming," he says.

He loosens his hold enough for me to bend forward and cancel the audio. My shaking finger taps the spacebar. The on-screen beating resumes in silence bar the rasp of our breathing, a click as we swallow, and Xander's heart thudding against my spine. The absence of sound is somehow better and worse. The only focus is Xander writhing in pain, his mouth stretched in a mute howl, the flash of his bared teeth.

They beat him for another three days. The change in him is traumatising to witness. His cheeks are gaunt, his eyes feverbright with fear and pain. His clothes are sweat-soaked, blooddappled, and soiled since he doesn't appear to be released to use the bathroom.

"He's ready," the Rabid maker says.

The figure stoops over him at the head of the table and throws the hood back, revealing a face more haggard than Xander's. The man's skin is sallow and tight to a skull covered in wisps of light hair. He places his bony fingers on Xander's temples. His deep-set and bloodshot eyes roll in their sockets, his lids fluttering as if he's having a stroke. Xander's pupils dilate, his face washed of all colour. Then his life, his personality, disappears from his eyes, leaving an empty shell, his muscles slack.

Dead.

His body convulses on the table. Awareness rushes into his face. And horror.

"That's how he does it," Xander breathes in my ear, awe-struck and appalled. "He yanks the soul, then puts it back in instead of leaving it out for a Revenant."

"But what about the soul anchor?"

Xander shrugs one shoulder. "He's powerful. Maybe he can bypass it. Or destroy it?"

I couldn't see it on the other videos—the manipulation of the souls. The Rabid maker hunched closer to those victims, hiding their faces. Their terrified and occasionally soulless eyes. It all happened too fast. Xavier thought the Rabid maker was implanting some monstrous magical parasite—maybe even a piece of his own twisted soul—and that's why William could only detect chaos and deformity when he tried to check Xander's anchor when we first subdued him.

The Rabid maker sucks out Xander's soul and shoves it back in, over and over again. A clump of his wispy hair drifts onto Xander's cheek. Each time Xander's soul returns, he's more frantic, more lost, his eyes wild and haunted. I don't need sound to read the words on his lips.

No. Please. *Don't.*

He thrashes like a mad thing, a piece of his sanity gone in every cycle of soul/no soul, until there's nothing left but bloodlust and rage.

Goodbye, Xander. Hello, Beast-Xander.

He bucks on the table, gnashing his teeth, his chest expanding on each silent roar. For a second, he looks at the camera, his eyes alien and ferocious, the animal intelligence still able to spear anxiety deep into my gut. The video stops. Neither of us speaks for five minutes. His heart slows to a steady drum against my vertebrae.

"That's what I was like?" he says. "My memories of how I acted don't quite do it justice. The urges and emotions were… overwhelming."

"I'm going to kill them all," I say.

He shudders. "Christ, I knew it was going to be bad, but that… that was fucking awful. Yet why torture me first? Why not go straight to the soul thing?"

"Maybe he needs you in a fragile mental state. Maybe that's how he gets past the soul anchor." I huff, enjoying the restrictive hug of Xander's arms around my torso. "I can't… I can't even imagine…"

He cocks his head, his chin hooked over my shoulder. Kind of like that time in the photo booth—me sitting in his lap, slowly melting into a puddle of goo as explosive as old dynamite. If I turn my head, will my lips graze his cheekbone or his mouth?

Get a grip, Quinn. He's just watched a nightmare video of his own rape. Don't be a sick bitch.

"Say that again," he says.

I frown, distracted. Did I say the sick bitch part out loud?

"What?"

"You said 'I can't." His muscles tense around me. "You… you yelled that at me. In the kitchen. My old cottage."

"Um, we've dwelt on the past enough for one afternoon. Let's do something else."

I try to wriggle free, but his grip tightens. He props his feet over my ankles, pinning my legs.

Shit. Now my heart is beating hard. Can he feel it?

His mouth brushes the delicate curve of my ear. "Q-tip?"

I swallow. Crap, where has all my saliva gone?

"Uh-huh?" I say.

"Is there something you want to tell me?"

"Not at this particular moment," I squeak. "Don't you want to lie down? Process what you watched?"

"I don't want to think about it ever again. I'd rather stay here."

He shifts his hips. My breath catches before I can clamp my lips together.

What is he *doing?*

"Maybe *I* need to lie down," I mutter.

"Maybe you should admit what you said in the kitchen."

"Maybe you should let me go before I claw out your kneecaps," I growl.

He chuckles, and it shivers right into my ear and down my spine.

"I don't know why, but seconds after I've watched two guys gang rape me, all I want to do is tease you. How is that, Q-tip?"

"How the fuck should I know?"

He sits quietly. His arms rise and fall with my rapid breaths. His exhalations tickle through my hair and drop into my belly to form a big ball of tingles.

"What if I tell you something?" he says softly.

"What?"

"Something I should've told you years ago."

"What?"

He hesitates, then, "I love you, too," he says.

My heart flutters, but I smother the movement, like slapping a palm on a butterfly before it can gaily fly off and get ahead of itself, dancing all over the place.

"Like a sister, right?" I say drily.

His fingers stroke up my ribs. The tiny touch sends a surge of heat between my legs.

"No, Q-tip," he whispers, "not like a sister."

31

Xander's arms are around me, crossed under my breasts. His fingers continue their light, tickling stroke up and down. Up and down. My muscles clench so hard, it's practically an orgasm.

What the hell is he doing? Is he so desperate to forget the video, he'll shag the first woman he gets his hands on? That sounds like him. Or are there remnants of Beast-Xander that have his hormones all confused?

"Don't be ridiculous," I splutter. "You've never looked at me that way."

"I've looked at you that way for *years*."

"But… what about the sex bunnies?"

He laughs and I feel it everywhere our bodies touch. I get a little woozy.

"Sex bunnies?" he says.

I can't see his face with him hugging me so tight, but he's definitely smirking.

I scowl. "Oh, I'm sorry—all your fascinating and witty gentlemen and lady friends."

"Defence mechanism," he says. "I was hoping it would fade."

"What the hell are you talking about, Xander?"

"I had a crush on Olly, but got over that pretty quickly. And shagging *sex bunnies* won't make your brother hate me, but sleeping with his sister definitely will." Xander sighs and rests his forehead on the back of my neck. "Shit, I was doing so well. Olly is going to kill me."

My head is spinning, the wooziness now twirling around in my gut and chest and tangoing with my heart. I'm glad Xander can't see my expression because my eyes are bugging out and my mouth is flapping.

He fancied *Olly?* He says he loves *me?* Hearing those words has been in every fantasy since I was fourteen. My reaction was usually to snog his face off and bedazzle him with my sexual prowess, not sit dumb and blinking.

I pinch myself. Nope, not dreaming.

Xander huffs, stirring the small hairs on the back of my neck and sending a fleet of goosebumps racing across my shoulders. "Did you just pinch yourself, Q-tip?"

"Olly already knows how I feel about you," I blurt before I can tell myself to shut up. "He says you're a twat for not noticing."

Xander releases me, and I nearly puddle into his lap. His fingers squeeze my ribs, attempting to hoist me upright.

"Turn around," he rasps.

He tries to help, but I've become a splay of long legs and gangly arms. I end up collapsing in his lap, eliciting a grunt. I straddle his thighs, my hands on his shoulders, his chin tilted up to meet my gaze. I'm so close, I can see the blush of hazel around his pupils, the dark green bordering his iris. His eyeliner has smudged from the rain. He looks beautiful and wild and dazed.

"Olly knows you're in love with me?" he says, still raspy. "He *wanted* me to notice?"

All my blood has pulsed south. I'm sitting in his lap. I'm sitting in *Xander Dawson's* lap. His sexy, pouting mouth is inches from mine. I can taste his breaths. His spicy-clove scent is subtle yet fucking overwhelming.

"God, Q-tip, don't look at me like that," he groans. "I've not got a leash on my control right now."

He buries his face in my throat and his lips find the hollow between my collarbones where my pulse is going berserk. His fingers knead my lower back. My spine dissolves. It arches me closer to the cradle of his hips. The throbbing place between my legs finds the hard and throbbing place between his. I make a noise like a choking pigeon.

"Fuck," Xander says. *"Fuck."*

He blows a wobbling breath, which does nothing to alleviate the muscle spasms and tingles crackling all over my body. His mouth glides up the column of my throat, not kissing. Just soft and wicked lips trailing across my skin. He forces my chin higher, nuzzling my jaw. Gentle pressure in the small of my back slides me snug against him. My tattered moan joins his, but he keeps his hips still—no grinding, no thrusting. Only the maddening stroke of his lips on my throat.

I'm hot, flushed, dizzy. There's an ache between my legs desperate for friction. I tremble with the urge to rub myself on the ridge of his erection, a knot of tension flaring at the base of my spine. Everything between my knees and navel is tight, yet swollen.

There's no risk of confusing Xander with Beast-Xander. His touch is intimate, a glorious torment. No roughness or demand for immediate pleasure. Xander is nothing like him.

Real Xander. *My* Xander.

The laptop is still on the coffee table behind us, the video asking if we want to play it again.

Hell to-the-goddamn *no*.

"Christ, I really want to kiss you right now," Xander purrs into the sensitive spot beneath my ear.

My garbled noise says I would be amenable. I'm reeling, untethered, yet safe in his hands.

How have I been so blind to his true feelings? And vice-bloody-versa?

Xander shifts his mouth to the opposite side of my throat and traces his lips to the curve where neck meets shoulder. More goosebumps erupt.

"Is the unflappable Quinn McTierney actually speechless?" he murmurs on my skin.

All my blood is in my crotch so, yes, my speech centre is a little parched right now. There's nothing in my brain except the feel of Xander's firm body, the press of his hands, the brand of his mouth.

He leans away. I whine at the loss of contact. My eyes are closed, but I don't remember closing them. My heart is as swollen as the rest of me, and lodged in my throat. It's difficult to breathe past.

Does everyone feel like this when they finally get the person they want? How do they stand it? How can they find the will to stop?

Quivering fingers cup my face and slide into my hair. My lips part, aching to be claimed.

"Say something, Q-tip," Xander whispers.

A warbling, "Hmm?" is all I manage.

I wrangle my eyelids open. Xander's tender smile is something I always dreamed of, but never thought would be directed at me.

"You're so goddamn beautiful," he says, and I swoon.

I'd be embarrassed about it, but he growls and his hips flex, grinding his erection against yearning flesh with a delicious burst of friction. A thrum of need sings down my nerves. I make a strangled sound that might be his name, and writhe in his lap. The noise he makes leaves me tighter and wetter and utterly intoxicated.

"Fuck, Christ, sorry," he pants. "That was my fault. But we have to stop."

He grips my hips and eases me down his thighs, breathing hard, his head bowed. He must catch my pout out of the corner of his eye because he flashes me a grin.

"For now," he clarifies. "Don't let the erection fool you—this place gives me the creeps. And I need to talk to Olly. Make sure he's all right with this."

I gape at Xander. "You're going to ask his *permission?!*"

"Since I plan on making love to his sister until I pass out," he says, grin widening, "it'd be rude not to."

32

Xander holds my hand all the way back to the compound. Shaun came to pick us up since he was only half an hour away, running errands. He glances at where we're sitting in the back seat, a small frown between his brows. Xander's thumb skims my knuckles back and forth, like when his fingers stroked up and down my ribs, and I forget about Shaun.

My skin is still tingling from Xander's lips on my throat. His version of making love may give me a heart attack, but Beast-Xander left a lot to be desired.

I'm going to have sex with *Xander*. Not animal sex, but proper meaningful and intimate sex with the guy I've loved for fifteen years. I need to keep pinching myself.

I'm not worried about Olly's reaction. He'll be ecstatic to hear the news. Though Xander's fingers start tapping his knee the closer we get to the compound. We pull up to the gate, and Xander gives the guard peering at us through the window a cheery wave.

It's the condescending prick from Compound 14, the one who got all sniffy at letting a Rabid in, then offered to put Xander out of his misery because 'it's what he would have wanted.'

If any of them had had their way, Xander would be rotting

in a grave right now, not sitting beside me. I never would have known he loves me.

The stupid fuckers.

The guard's face wrinkles at the sight of Xander. He's one of Xavier's minions, always so eager to feed him information in the hope of special treatment and attention. From his expression, he had no idea Xander had sneaked off the compound.

On his watch, too. That's got to sting.

I wiggle my fingers at him—or one finger in particular—as Shaun motors through the gate and up the long, sloping driveway bisecting the lawn. Shadows from the setting sun creep across the grass. Shaun pulls smoothly into the garage and the automatic shutters lower behind us. The Range Rover has barely parked when Xander tugs me out the car with a quick, "Thanks, mate!" I hurry to match his stride, my heart stumbling along at his eagerness to get me in the compound.

The sooner he talks to Olly, the sooner he can finish what he started.

Oh, man. I'm definitely going to faint. What if he notices how inexperienced I am? What if I'm not very good? What if I turn into a blushing, stuttering fool?

"You still with me, Q-tip?"

Xander glances over his shoulder, taking the stairs to the first floor two at a time. I nod, managing not to trip over my feet, which feel about four times their normal size. His hand squeezes mine, and I'm grateful for the reassurance. He pauses to take a deep breath outside Olly's bedroom door.

Maybe I'm not the only one who needs a little reassurance.

I knock on the wood and push the door open at Olly's shout of, "Come in." He's sprawled on his bed on his front, heels kicking, staring at his phone. He shoves himself up on one hand.

"Hey, babe, let me ring you back," he says at the screen in his palm. "Quinn just got home."

"Bye, Andy!" I call as Olly's thumb taps the phone, ending the video call with his boyfriend from Compound 2.

He swings his legs over the edge of the mattress. "I didn't expect you both so soon. Weren't you there another week, Quinn?"

"Uh, yeah, I guess I was supposed to be... whoops."

"Also, thanks for answering my calls, *sis*. Not that I was worried or anything or that Xander had to be tranquillised to come out and see you."

Olly's gaze falls to our linked hands. Xander drops me as if I've burned him, but it's hard to be mad when his rush to get me in the house changes to hesitation and fidgeting.

He's nervous. That's so fucking cute.

"Xander has something he'd like to tell you," I say helpfully. "Or maybe ask you is more accurate."

Xander slides me a brief look of panic. I press my lips together to hold in a laugh and give him an encouraging head tilt instead. He stares at his boots, then raises his eyes to Olly.

"So, um, Olls..." He clears his throat. "Quinn said you know how she feels about me."

Olly's gaze flicks to me. He cocks a brow, and I give him a secret smile. He folds his lips on what would no doubt be a grin, turning back to Xander.

"And?" he drawls.

I cough to hide a snort. Xander wrings his hands.

God, I want to rip off all his clothes. How can he be so confident and sure with everyone else yet still be anxious about where he stands with us? The adorable idiot.

"And that you wanted me to notice?" Xander's voice rises.

"What's your point here, mate?" Olly says, giving him nothing.

I stare out the window, my shoulders shaking with the strain of not laughing. I focus on Xander after a few seconds since I can never keep my eyes off him for long.

"So… you wouldn't mind if I noticed and, um"—he shuffles his feet—"reciprocated?"

My facade cracks, and I hoot a laugh. "Have mercy on the poor guy, Olly."

Olly's grin bursts free. He rolls off the bed and pulls Xander into a back-slapping hug. Xander blinks at me, somewhat stunned.

"I'm just winding you up, man," Olly chuckles. "Have you finally come to your senses and noticed Quinn has been pining after you for years?"

"Excuse me, hardly pining," I say. At Olly's look, it's my turn to shuffle my feet. "Okay—pining."

"You don't hate me for wanting to be with your sister?" Xander says slowly, as if he can't believe it. "But what if we have a fight or break up? What if you have to pick sides?"

Olly eases Xander away, his hands on his biceps. "I've told you already—you'll always be my best friend. No matter what. But, since it's also my sworn duty as a big brother, if you ever hurt her, I'll have to kick your arse."

Xander smirks, yanking Olly into a headlock and ruffling his hair. "Sure you will, shorty."

Olly wriggles out of his hold and bounces onto the edge of his bed, aiming his grin at both of us.

"So you had a good talk, then? Honestly, you pair are the

worst. I told Quinn she should tell you how she feels. And you"—he stabs a finger at Xander—"you could have talked to me."

Now we both shuffle our feet.

"Do you love her?" Olly says.

Xander aims that smile at me again—the one that makes me go all wobbly.

"Of course I love her. Do you know how fucking hard it's been not to show it?"

Olly leaps up and gathers us into a group hug. Xander wraps an arm around me, his lips warm and curved into a smile on my cheekbone.

"You idiots," Olly says affectionately. "I'm so happy for you."

"Since we're all sharing truths," I say, giving my brother a squeeze, "Xander had a crush on you, too."

Olly's head pops up, and Xander flushes.

Bless his bisexual little heart.

"It was only for a short while," he says. "Then you met Andy and I got over it pretty quickly."

"Were you just hedging your bets on which McTierney would fall for you?" I snort.

Xander squirms. "No. It was a teeny-tiny infatuation. Nothing serious. Nothing like…"

"Well, I can't fault your taste," Olly says, poking him in the ribs.

We break apart. Xander keeps his arm around me, sliding it lower until his hand curls around my waist. I run my nails up the back of his neck to his nape and scrape gently through his hair, earning a shiver. His fingers tighten on my hip bone.

"We have to go," he says in a rush.

Olly rolls his eyes. "Christ, at least do it in Quinn's room so

I don't have to listen."

"That's the plan. My mattress should be condemned."

I cock an eyebrow at Xander. "Plan?"

"I've planned this for a long time," Xander says, his voice husky.

Olly flaps his hand at us, and we tumble out of his room. I don't remember taking ten steps down the corridor, too aware of Xander pressed to my side, his fingers circling my hip bone.

The door shuts and, finally, we're all alone in my bedroom.

33

Xander's eyes are dilated and dark, but they're all him—hungry yet gentle. Fierce yet reverent. Deep and drowning. He circles behind me while I stand a little awe-struck. I lean into his solid chest, and his lips find my hair. His arms hug my waist, his fingers slipping under my shirt to splay his warm hands on my belly. Skin to skin. Need clenches in my gut and punches my breath out.

Fuck, I'm shaking already. We've not even kissed yet. Hell, I might swoon when we do.

"Full disclosure," I say, my voice high. "I've only done this with one other guy. We had sex once. It wasn't fun. No, um, other stuff, either. Also, Beast-Xander doesn't count."

Am I babbling? Feels like I'm babbling.

Xander's nose grazes my ear. "Are you telling me that you're a foreplay virgin? That no one else has slid their fingers inside this perfect body or put their mouth between your legs and"—he sucks on my ear lobe—"tasted you? Is that what you're saying, Q-tip?"

My knees buckle. His arms tighten, pressing me against him, against the hard pulse of his erection. He shudders at my strangled noise, his breathing already ragged.

"Fuck, you're going to wreck me."

I gulp a sob. "I think I need to lie down."

He turns me carefully in his arms to face him until I'm pressed to every glorious inch. One arm around the small of my back holds me upright, firm and safe. He strokes my cheek with his other hand, tracing to my jaw and catching my bottom lip.

"You can't be nervous," he says, his gaze on my mouth, "not after what we've already done."

"That wasn't you. I've never had sex with *you*."

He lifts his eyes, and a bolt of heat flares everywhere we touch.

"But I have a lot to make up for."

"You don't—"

He lowers his head, and my words dry up. He's so close, I can taste him—breath, heat, need. One tiny tilt, one strong heartbeat, and he'll be kissing me. I've imagined it so many times. Of course, he'll be amazing. I, on the other hand, may be a disappointment. I'll just follow his lead and hope he doesn't notice.

"A *lot* to make up for," Xander whispers, and slants his lips across mine.

Flutters, tingles, throbbing. Hell, they were bad enough at the mere fantasy of his touch. The reality is stunning—a firework in my brain that sparks in a fizzy cascade. An eager noise ripples up my throat, and Xander shudders, though his kiss stays gentle and lazy. A glide that traces my lips. A teasing nibble. I bury my fingers in his hair, desperate for an anchor since my knees are quivering.

Every part of me is quivering.

He tilts my chin, not deepening the kiss, but giving himself a better angle to explore with only his mouth, his hands doing nothing but holding me steady. The tender pressure is maddening. Excruciating. No tongue, no hip movement, no friction to soothe the ache between my legs. I flush beneath the onslaught, frantic for more, my fingers tugging at him, pleading. I'd be embarrassed by the sounds I'm making if I wasn't too busy licking at the seam of his lips like a crazy person. He groans and opens his mouth. My tongue swoops in, meeting his with an electrifying buzz. God, the slickness, the heat. And a hard, smooth little ball stroking across me.

I forgot about his piercing.

Goodbye muscle control. My brain seizes. My knees give out, forcing Xander to hook an arm under my arse and jiggle me higher, my feet a couple of inches off the ground, my body moulded to his. My legs dangle, too weak to even wrap around his waist, though they really fucking want to. The kiss doesn't stop—a starving battle of tongues and teeth and broken moans. He snogs me dizzy. Breathless. He tastes like oranges and walnuts.

Perfectly delicious.

He walks me backwards, my feet still not touching the ground, and guides me onto the bed. His weight settles between my thighs, and I gasp at the sensation of him on top of me. A surge of heat clenches every muscle. Xander shoves up on his hands, panting. His lips are swollen, a flush pinking his cheeks. His eyes are hooded and dazed, as if he's drunk.

Christ, he's so fucking beautiful.

"You weren't using your legs at all there, Q-tip," he says, his voice husky.

It helps my dignity to watch his control fray when mine shattered into a million pieces the second he kissed me. I've spent so long hiding how I feel, but now I'm exposed. Now, all my secrets are out and I can finally show what he does to me.

I lick my lips. "I… just, um… I…"

Okay, that wasn't the response I had in mind. Something more witty and intelligent, less drooling bedazzlement.

Delight shines in his eyes and stretches his mouth into a grin, which really doesn't help my wit or intelligence. Kneeling between my splayed and useless legs, he places his palm over my thudding heart, then captures my hand and puts my fingers on his chest. A fleshy fist knocks hard and fast against his breastbone.

His grin softens to a tender smile. "My legs weren't far behind."

He lowers himself onto me, trapping our hands between us, and feathers kisses across my lips until our hearts pound harder, faster. I open my mouth. His tongue finds mine and the gentle kiss becomes a wild and plunging tangle.

That piercing will be the death of me.

He rests his forehead on mine, eyes shut, breath trembling out. I blink and he's bouncing off the bed, his heat and weight suddenly gone, trailing my startled whine. He smirks over his shoulder, wedging my wooden chair under the door handle.

"I'm not going anywhere. But no doubt my pissed-off big brother will be stomping this way soon. And I'm not getting interrupted." Xander leaps on top of me, nuzzling my throat with a mumbled, "Now, where were we?"

He trails slow and searing kisses to the dip between my collarbones and licks my throbbing pulse. I arch my neck in invitation. Hell, I arch my whole body. Deft fingers pop the buttons on my shirt and spread the material wide. My bra is red silk, the straps thin and criss-crossing over my breasts and around my shoulders. Xander purrs in appreciation. His fingers splay on my ribs as his mouth scorches every inch of uncovered skin. His tongue tastes my cleavage, my belly button. I squirm at his intense yet patient exploration, sweet frustration a hot ball in my gut. His fingers flex in my waistband, and a rush of anticipation curls to my toes, but he just hoists himself to recapture my lips. His mouth curves on mine at my needy whimper.

I'm pretty sure Olly heard it two rooms away.

"Something on your mind, Q-tip?" Xander says.

"I've had thirteen fucking years of waiting. If you don't touch me properly, I'm going to explode."

He chuckles between sultry kisses, drawing a winded and whiny, "*Xander,*" from me.

"Don't worry." He dazzles me with a wicked smile. "I'm about to make you explode several times, and I plan on savouring the hell out of it since some of us need a rest after one."

I manage to cock a brow. "How much of a rest?"

"Not that long, you cheeky cow."

My laugh turns to a choked groan when he punishes me with a roll of his hips. My eyes flutter shut, my muscles spasming, questing for more. His laughter chases goosebumps across my flesh as he dots kisses down my torso to my quivering stomach.

I love that he's still playful and teasing even when he's driving me exquisitely insane.

He unbuttons my combats. My pulse throbs deep in my belly and awakens a scatter of nerves. I lift my hips and he tugs my trousers off, then seems to get lost somewhere, staring at my crotch.

I clear my throat. "Um, so I don't really do sexy underwear. I like colours. And patterns."

I shut my mouth. What an idiot. How old am I—twelve? I couldn't have bought a couple of thongs or even something lacy in case of emergency?

My hands sneak down to cover the sprinkling of hearts on white cotton. At least the red matches the bra.

Xander captures my fingers. He raises his gaze, and my pulse stutters into a canter.

"Fucking hell, Quinn," he growls. "I don't do rough, but I really, *really* want to rip off these adorable little panties. With my teeth."

My breath wobbles out, then in, then out again. Xander bites his lip and walks his shaking fingers across the love hearts on my underwear from hip bone to hip bone. I jackknife into a sitting position. He sits hard on his heels, blinking at me.

"That's it," I gasp, scrabbling at his t-shirt, utterly demented. "You're getting naked. I can't take it anymore."

He grins as I wrestle with his clothes. He tries to help, but I bat his hands away. His t-shirt flutters off the side of the bed. Although I've seen him half-naked lots of times—and fully naked as Beast-Xander—the sight of his toned and sleek muscles still short-circuits my nervous system. I grab his waist, and squeeze.

"Up," I say, aiming for confident command and hitting screeching weasel.

He rises onto his knees. The position stretches his stomach taut, his combats low on his hips. My gaze travels past the fascinating ridges and planes to his face. At this angle, he's all cheekbones and glittering eyes. He swallows hard, and now I want to taste the column of his throat and feast on the rest of him.

I can see how he got distracted. How he's in no rush for this to end.

Keeping my eyes on his, I unfasten his trousers and tug them to his knees, taking his boxers with them. His tongue wets his bottom lip. Bent over as I am, my breath must be brushing a certain quivering piece of anatomy filling my peripheral vision. He shivers, seeming to have trouble focusing on me. My turn to grin, all filthy and wicked.

"What do *you* taste like, Xander?" I whisper.

His groan catches in his throat. The sound echoes in the pit of my stomach and flares between my legs. His lashes flutter shut, his hands flexing at his sides.

"I'm supposed to be making it up to you," he says, his voice tattered.

"You will. You are."

My fingers wrap around hot, velvety skin. I slide my mouth over the head of his cock. Warm and salty-sweet. He gives an agonised, *"Fuck,"* and it's the sexiest noise I've ever heard.

My orgasms can wait. What other glorious sounds can I wring from him before he retakes control and returns me to a gibbering puddle?

I tongue the underside of his shaft, sucking him deep, then trace the ridge of his crown. He's so solid, so smooth. His pulse batters against my fist. His fingers curl in my hair, though his grip stays gentle.

"I thought you'd never done this before," he grinds out.

I roll my gaze up his trembling figure. His head is flung back, his eyes squeezed shut, dark lashes fanned above flushed cheeks.

"I read a book," I mumble around him.

"Of course you did." His ribs heave. "Fuck, Quinn, what are you doing to me?"

I swirl my tongue along the length of him, encouraged by the urgency in his tone. The frantic surprise.

The book said it was all about confidence. And saliva. If I think I can give a great blowjob, then I probably can. Also, not to be afraid. I may feel stupid bobbing up and down, but, with his dick in my mouth, he no doubt thinks I look fabulous. There was also a part about rubbing his tummy.

I pet Xander's belly. His hips twitch. A guttural moan rips from his mouth and I can't help a moan in response, muffled around him. His hands grip my arms. I find myself propelled onto my back, his very hard and very naked body on top, grinding against my not-so-naked places. His feverish lips devour mine until I'm making those eager little noises again. My unexpected mastery of him dissolves to need and want and a terrible, wonderful ache where his cock, damp from my mouth, surges against my already wet panties.

Frenzied hands remove my bra, my underwear. Xander pauses on all fours, his bowed head level with my navel. He sucks in a breath. Another. Effort shudders across his shoulders. He lifts his gaze, and the jagged force of his need arches my spine.

"My turn for a taste," he purrs. "Then you're getting thoroughly fucked til neither of us can walk."

My heart explodes into a shimmering sparkle of confetti. Xander places a light kiss between my legs, and I yelp. He smirks at me, his firm hands spreading my thighs. He curls his tongue and the ball of his piercing catches on his front teeth.

My, "Oh, god," is shaky and untethered.

Grinning, Xander bends and delivers a big, slow lick,

dragging his tongue piercing through my slit.

"Holy fuck!" I yell, writhing on the bed in a full-on spasm.

Never mind tingles—this is goddamn ecstasy.

"Mmm," he hums against me, his hands splaying me open, "I knew you'd taste good."

He continues his long, slow licks, stroking that wonderful ball of metal over my slick and throbbing places. Pleasure skates down my thighs and rolls in my belly, flushing my skin with heat. His soft lips nuzzle my clit and he lavishes it with strong flicks of his tongue.

My words are a garbled mess. I'm not even sure what I'm trying to say.

"Fuck, Xander. Oh, *god*—Xander. Please."

Maybe that was it.

I flail on the bed. His hands pin my thighs. My hair is across my face. I inhale it and puff it out with every gasping breath. He raises his gaze to mine, though I can barely focus and I definitely can't stay still. Meeting his eyes while his face is buried between my legs, his jaw working, pulses through every muscle. Then he slides a finger inside me, and I'm done. I'm gone. I wail his name really fucking loud.

Just when I think I may stop flopping around like a headless eel, he darts his piercing across my swollen clit and crooks the finger still inside me. This time I sob his name, faint and delirious, and attempt to form a human pretzel. The thrum of pleasure finally fades to limpness and panting, my heartbeat the only thing I can hear.

The mattress bobs. My lashes flutter, but it's as close as I can come to opening my eyes.

"That was fucking hot, Q-tip," Xander whispers in my ear. "But I really need to be inside you now."

His mouth swallows my moan. He breaks away to fumble for his combats and hooks out his wallet of five million condoms.

"Shit, did we use protection?" he says, a foil square caught in his fingers.

It takes a ridiculous amount of effort to speak, my body still in shock.

"At first," I croak. "But we don't need it."

"You sure? I mean, I'm clean—I get tested. Xavier ordered them to take blood and swabs in case I had a disease after being Rabid."

"I got an IUD ages ago. You know—for all the sex I hoped we'd be having."

He grins, and frisbees the unopened condom off the side of the bed. "Better late than never."

He kisses me before I can gather my senses. His fingers tangle in mine and only then do I feel his slight tremor. Still, he holds himself off me, searching my face. His name catches in my throat. He gives me a gentle, tender smile, and finally claims what has been his for years.

34

The sensation of Xander Dawson inside me is beyond description. Beyond tingles or fireworks or ecstasy. My fantasies pale to the reality of him—his silky skin, that sexy hint of hemp and bergamot, his weight between my thighs. He slides deep on a long exhale and we pause in the moment, neither of us daring to move, as if unable to believe we're finally here, finally doing this after years of turmoil and unsatisfied yearning. Sex with Beast-Xander was animal rutting—emotionless and mechanical. Nothing compared to this.

"Bloody Christ," Xander groans in my ear.

I laugh, and his fingers tighten in mine. He raises his head from where it dropped to my shoulder, his eyes bright and dazed.

"If you keep chuckling, Q-tip, I'm going to lose it in two fucking seconds."

I fold my lips to contain the joy bubbling in my chest, though it fizzes through my veins.

"Thought your control would be perfect by now."

He kisses the smirking corner of my mouth. "Not with you. Never with you."

He flexes his hips, curling himself somehow deeper, the stroke of him an ache. A branding flare of heat. He swallows my hitch of breath and doesn't stop kissing me as he glides into a lazy, eager rhythm—shallow pumps of his hips spreading the ache to my gut and thighs. Then he buries himself to the hilt, slowly withdrawing so I can feel the full length of him touching every part of me. Another plunging stroke and I rise to meet him, grinding hip to hip, my stomach taut, my pulse pounding full and heavy.

"God, Quinn," he rasps, "you feel so fucking good."

A whimper catches in my throat, and his tongue swirls into my mouth as if trying to taste it. His piercing strokes me to the same beat as his body between my legs, strong and sure. Tension swells in my centre, gathering from the press of his hot, greedy mouth and the glorious thrust of his hips. I grip him hard—hands, thighs—and take every inch.

"You're shaking," I murmur.

And he is, though his rhythm doesn't falter. He destroys me with his shallow strokes and slow, deep thrusts, my skin tingling and aflame. Nerves sparking. Heels digging into the mattress. Hands clutching his.

"I know," he says, his voice husky.

I sob his name. Our kiss grows frantic. My hips buck, the building pleasure arching my spine and rushing towards the peak. It's huge. Overwhelming. I can't keep still.

"Xander," I gasp, "you're going to make me come—so fucking hard."

"Oh, shit," he groans.

The sweet panic in his voice, the loss of control, spills me over the edge and his cries join mine a second later. He pulses inside me, my muscles clenched around him as I writhe. His hips rock, milking the orgasm to its last flutter and sizzle until we collapse together, panting and slick, our heartbeats drumming on bone and flesh. He buries his face in my neck, his hands still gripping mine, his scorching breath flaring goosebumps along my nape.

"I love you, Quinn McTierney," he mumbles.

Tears burn the back of my eyes and clog my throat. I swallow a couple of times.

"I love you, too, Xander Dawson."

Great, now *I'm* husky.

He gathers me into his arms with gentle kisses and flops us onto our sides, my back to his front, my body wrapped in the warmth and scent of him.

"Is this the aforementioned rest period?" I say.

He nips at my ear, and I yelp a giggle.

"Oh, I'm not done yet. I just want to hold you for a minute."

He cuddles closer. His hands wander, mapping the contours of my skin by touch alone—thighs, waist, ribs, the flat of my stomach. He brushes the underside of my breasts, tickles along my pubic bone, but goes no further.

"You get all wriggly when you're horny," he purrs.

His erection grows against the crack of my arse.

Christ, he wasn't kidding about only needing a short rest.

"That's thirteen years of repressed sexuality," I gasp when he swivels his hips.

"You've really been with one man this entire time?"

"Once was enough. I didn't want anyone else. Now you're the only guy who's made me come."

He growls, and bites my shoulder. "The only guy who will *ever* make you come."

Heat flares in my core and tingles outwards, stuttering through my pulse. It wobbles my voice.

"At least the guy I picked was a little like you—same build, black hair. You went with quantity, but none of them looked like me."

Xander rolls me onto my back and kneels between my legs, his smile soft and vulnerable. "I didn't want a substitute, just a distraction. And you were so fucking tempting, I needed *a lot* of distractions."

He leans forward to kiss me and we both moan as the crown of his erection slots between my legs, cradled by the delicate petals of my body. He returns to his knees, his fingers massaging my thighs. His cock spears me another slow inch, and my eyelids flutter, my head tossed back.

He grits his teeth. "You're not too sore, are you?"

"Not yet," I smirk. "You'll have to try harder."

"Fuck, Q-tip. You'll be the death of me."

He scoops my legs over his shoulders and impales me to the hilt, his hands on my arse holding my lower half off the bed. The angle allows me to see where we're joined, see where he's sunk into my body all the way to the quivering muscles of his hips. The sight has me writhing, my fingers tangled desperately in the bed covers.

"God," he says, already ragged and breathless, "you feel like heaven."

"Tell me—describe it."

"Velvet. Slick and snug. Slippery with my cum. I want to fill you til you're so full, it dribbles down your thighs and—Jesus, I have to stop or I'm gone already." He bows his head, shoulders heaving, holding himself still, his fingers clenching on my arse. A low whimper curls in his throat. "Christ, I feel you squeezing me. Your muscles flutter when you come. Did you know that? Like hungry little kisses all along my cock."

"Xander," I breathe, dazed and throbbing, "for the love of all that's holy, *please* fuck me."

He grunts and tilts his hips, stroking deep. Nothing slow or shallow this time. He plunders between my thighs, holding me up. The position stretches my stomach muscles, tightens everything that's already tight and swollen from my belly to my knees. Tension builds to a supernova in my gut.

So close, *so good*. A scream aches in my chest, eager to escape. It's going to be loud. I can't help it. Xander makes me howl like a fox in heat.

My bedroom door rattles, and we both jump. Every muscle clenches around Xander.

"Fuck," he snarls. "Fuck, fuck, *fuck*."

A heavy fist pounds on wood, thwarted by the chair wedged under the door handle. My heart clamours in tandem.

"McTierney!" Xavier barks. "Are you in there? *McTierney!*"

A shudder runs through Xander. His pupils are so dilated, there's only a sliver of pure green around the border. He chews on his lip, his expression frantic.

"Don't move," he whispers, his voice cracking, "or my brother is definitely going to hear me come."

"Don't stop," I counter. "Please, Xander. *Please.*"

"Oh, my filthy little Q-tip. You've fucking ruined me."

He bends closer, his weight against the backs of my thighs, folding me in half. His hips thrust, his cock nailing deep inside. It's almost pain, a sensation like needing to pee. A promise that the orgasm may rip my soul from my body, anchor or no anchor.

"Yes," I gasp, sweating, shivering, teeth clenched. "Right fucking there."

"I hear you, McTierney," Xavier yells through the door. "Why have you abandoned your post? And where the hell is Xander?

How were you both seen entering my compound when I specifically forbade him to leave?"

Xander rams himself into that glorious spot over and over. My toes curl. Pleasure fizzes and sparks, swelling to a maddening peak. My pulse is beating in my freaking eyeballs.

"We'll talk soon, Captain," I grind out. "Now bugger off, unless you want to listen to your brother make me come."

Xander manages a strangled chuckle, then I'm shrieking his name and spasming on the bed. The climax rips through me, stealing everything—breath, pulse, thoughts. Everything but sensation and the sound of Xander shouting my name just as loud as he spurts inside me for what seems like hours. The orgasm sweeps me to the edge of insanity, rushing on and on and on. When it recedes like a tidal wave, leaving me licked clean and shaking, my legs ache, flopped akimbo on either side of Xander, who's sprawled on top of me, puffing hard. His heart drums a mad rhythm on my breastbone.

"Christ," he groans. "My skin is buzzing, and I can't feel my toes."

Silence from the other side of the door.

"I think we scared Xavier away," I croak.

And then we dissolve into giggles, our sweaty, sated bodies locked together.

Xander was right—this is heaven.

35

"Why is it that a day has passed since I knocked on your door, McTierney?" Xavier's disapproving glare drops to my hand linked with Xander's where we stand side by side in front of his desk. "You appear to be under the misapprehension that you can do whatever the hell you want in my compound."

His brow furrows as his glower fails to untangle our fingers. William observed us with a little more disgust, but then I *was* sitting in Xander's lap, his arms wrapped around me, while Xavier forced us to wait half an hour to be granted an audience.

In my defence, there was only one chair. And now I have Xander—*really* have him—I can't stop touching him. Won't.

"We were indisposed," Xander begins in a reasonable voice.

"We were fucking," I interrupt.

Xander coughs to hide a laugh. Xavier's eyebrows leap to his hairline, his attention flicking between us.

"All day?" he says in what I imagine is meant to be a sarcastic and disbelieving tone, but sounds closer to jealousy.

Xander meets my shocked gaze, his eyes widening.

Holy shit. I think I just overtook him in points. Lots and lots of points.

Xavier shifts in his seat, the leather creaking. He wrangles his unruly brows back to his customary scowl. A smirk tugs

217

at the corner of my lips, and I open my mouth. Xander's hand presses a warning. I swallow my inquiry into Xavier's stamina.

Damn, Xander knows me well.

"We have lost time to make up for," I say instead. At Xander's polite throat-clearing, I add, "And your brother is an insatiable stud."

Xavier waves his hand in front of his face, as if my words have solidified and attacked him. Giggles bubble in my chest. Xander's fingers shake in mine while we both grin like a couple of idiots despite the trouble we're in.

Xander is alive and himself and he loves me. He worshipped my body for hours. Nothing can bring me down.

"What—and who—you do in your own time is none of my concern, McTierney," Xavier says, jaw ticking, "but you weren't in your own time. You abandoned your post without permission. And you"—a meaty finger jabs at Xander—"disobeyed a direct order not to leave the compound."

"If he hadn't, we wouldn't have figured it out."

Xavier's cold eyes zip back to mine. "Figured what out?"

"How Rabids are made."

Xavier huffs. "I've watched the videos, McTierney, same as you. Once the torture breaks them, it happens too fast to get a read on what he does with the soul or anchor. Or his damn hunchback is in the way of the camera. I'm still leaning towards him implanting his parasitic soul."

"It wasn't too fast for one person," I say softly.

Xavier's gaze sweeps across to Xander, who stands there, beautiful and defiant, though he's still thinner than usual. The ice in Xavier's expression melts a fraction. A human emotion peeks through, something like pride, before it disappears beneath the gruff, commanding exterior.

Xavier tents his fingers against his lips. "You remembered something?"

"You could say that." Xander stares at the floor, and I give his hand a squeeze of encouragement. "He took my soul out, then put it straight back in, over and over again. Until I went mad."

"Walker!" Xavier barks, and we both jump.

William scuttles into the office, pausing short of sidling around Xavier's desk to plonk himself next to his leader. But not by much.

"Sir?"

"When did you last check Xander's soul anchor? Not including when he was Rabid."

William spares Xander a microsecond of attention. He licks his lips.

"It was, um… a year after I placed it." He mumbles the last.

"Yet what is our protocol on soul-anchor maintenance?" Xavier says, with the patience of a snake bespelling a mouse.

William's spine snaps straight. "Soul anchors must be inspected by the Anima creator after every mission and renewed at least annually. If the creator is unavailable, the anchor should be replaced by another…"

The confident recitation of a pretty fucking important policy of the Unbound trails into uncertainty. William's shoulders hunch.

"But I thought you wouldn't—"

"Are you presuming to know my own mind?" Xavier says in a deadly voice.

"But we've always—"

"*William.*"

"Ah, no. No, Sir. No presumptions here."

Xander and I watch William's verbal arse-kicking in gleeful silence. The use of his first name turns his pale skin even paler. A bead of sweat rolls from his hairline to his jaw.

"Check it again now," Xavier growls. "His soul is strong at least. Intact."

Xavier could check the anchor himself, though only the creator can tell if it's still attached and working as it should, tethering the soul to the body. Xavier would detect it even if the connection was broken, or damaged, the essence of magic lingering like cobwebs in the corner of a room.

William leaps across the office to face Xander. He's an inch or two taller, Xander's chin tipped to meet that watery-blue gaze. William masks what is no doubt a wrinkle of distaste, and places his palm on Xander's chest, right over his heart.

I don't know what his problem is. It's a fabulous chest. Attached to a fabulous body, and a fabulous person.

William scrunches his eyes shut, a frown of concentration slicing his brow. Xander's shiver transfers to my hand.

The sensation is like ice water spreading from the mystic's touch and sinking deep to enclose your heart and stomach in a chilled grasp. Essentia and Terra magic are warm in comparison.

Xavier placed my soul anchor and checks it religiously, though he was somewhat lax after the independent school fiasco. We both had a lot on our minds. He at least inspected it before I went back there to hide from Xander.

William gasps and snatches his hand away, cradling it to his chest. "It's gone."

"What do you mean 'gone'?"

William spins on his heel to address Xavier. "The chaos and deformation of the Rabidity are gone, but there's not even a hint of the anchor, either. I thought that was impossible! There's always a signature. Even if they become Revenant."

Xavier strides around his desk and slaps a hand on Xander, causing him to stagger. Xavier's eyes stay open, though his focus hazes—going beyond the earthly realm to whatever Anima mystics see when scrying for souls.

I wonder how long it's been since he voluntarily touched his brother.

Xander is patient and still beneath that broad hand, though his palm is sweaty in mine. I grip him harder. Xavier shakes his head and takes a careful step in retreat.

"Gone," he whispers. He perches on the edge of the desk, his thick arms folded. "It's the torture, of course. It must weaken or detach the anchor, then the multiple soul manipulations banish all trace. We've just never known because no one has ever recovered from Rabidity. How are you feeling?"

Xander jolts when he realises Xavier is talking to him. Asking after his wellbeing.

"Pretty goddamn vulnerable, I'll be honest," Xander says in a husky voice.

Xavier gives a sharp nod and heaves himself to his feet.

William lets out a not-so-subtle sigh. "I can replace—"

"I'll do it myself," Xavier grunts.

"But you have a meeting—"

"Thank you, William. That'll be all."

William, mouth agape, slinks from the office. Xander and I shut our own gobs.

"Lie down." Xavier gestures to the floor, then cocks a brow at me. "You'll have to keep your hands to yourself since I assume you'll be staying for this?"

"Oh, yeah, I'm not going anywhere."

"You're a piece of work, McTierney."

That might be the nicest thing Xavier's ever said to me.

Xander smirks and stretches out on his back on the carpet, the pile thick enough to emulate the softest mattress. I sit cross-legged next to him, not touching. A lock of black hair stripes across his forehead and I brush it away, leaning down to kiss his smiling lips.

Okay, not touching starting *now*.

"You finished?" Xavier kneels opposite me, Xander between us.

"I can't help it," I say. "Your brother is gorgeous, inside and out."

"Right back at you, Q-tip," Xander says softly.

Xavier makes a sound deep in his throat. "Close your eyes. No talking, no touching. I need calm and silence."

The sparkle in Xander's eye tells me he knows how desperate I am to shout, "Sir, yes, Sir!" and toss a salute.

No one ever said I was obedient, not even for the Unbound. I could never have survived in the real military.

Xander takes a deep breath in and out, then shuts his eyes. His muscles relax one by one. A slight twitch betrays him when Xavier places both hands on his chest. Xavier bows his head. The space fills with the quiet sounds of breathing.

Another Anima mystic would be able to see the soul magic, to witness the anchor forming to tether Xander's soul to the literal heart of him. Essentia and Terra mystics would feel that icy flow and prickle of power, even without contact.

I hug my knees and watch the two brothers. One blond and bulky, the other dark and slender. Sexy as hell. Strong, but not afraid to show his emotions. Loyal. Determined. Generous. Funny as shit. An absolute *rockstar* in bed.

Dammit, I want to touch him.

I rest my cheek on my knee. Xander's pulse beats steady and sure in the hollow between his collarbones. Tenderness grips my throat in a velvet fist.

My love for him has only grown sharper, more overwhelming, now that it's reciprocated. Consummated. If I didn't trust him with my life, I might be scared by how easily he could destroy me.

But the only ones getting destroyed anytime soon will be the evil bastards who dared to hurt him.

My hands clench, fingernails digging into my calves. No sound comes from beyond the closed office door, William either sulking in silence or the wood too thick for noises to penetrate.

It takes Xavier an hour to build Xander's soul anchor, about the same time he took for me. Most other Anima mystics would take two, if not three, hours.

There's more than one reason why he's the captain of our compound.

He raises his head and catches me assessing him. One blond brow ticks up. His fingers flex against Xander's chest, and Xander's eyes pop open, a rapid breath hissing through his teeth.

"Shit, I forgot how much of a rush it was," he says.

My hand grabs his and he raises it to his lips, kissing each knuckle. The mischief in his eyes and the slow, wicked smile says he has some ideas for what to do with all the extra energy zipping through his system. My body pulses in anticipation. I help him stand and he crowds in close, pressed hip to chest, all warm, solid muscle and the scent that makes me dizzy. I tilt my face up, his chin tucked down, mouth so close. He palms my arse and drags me against him.

"Xander, stop groping McTierney in my office," Xavier drawls. "You have a perfectly good bedroom for that."

Xander steals a quick kiss. "Seems we've been dismissed, Q-tip."

He tugs me towards the door, walking backwards and punctuating each step with a brush of lips to my cheekbone, my nose, my forehead. Xavier's voice stops us on the threshold.

"I expect you both to report to the surveillance team tomorrow morning. No excuses, no tardiness, no exceptions."

I glance over my shoulder, Xander's mouth curving at my temple. "Surveillance team?"

"You said you wanted to hunt the Rabid maker." Xavier's gaze flicks between us. "I assume that includes both of you."

Xander's heart thumps hard and fast under my palm.

"Fuck, yes," we say in synchrony.

"Olly, too," I add.

Xavier nods once. "*Now* you're dismissed."

We tumble from his office into the reception area, William sullen and hunched at his computer. His fingers bash the keyboard. Xander hustles me past before I can snarl something at him for being a neglectful arsehole.

Xander's soul may have been vulnerable for *months,* the anchor weakened. Any Anima mystic on the battlefield could have ripped it from his body and made him a Revenant. Though the displaced souls cling like a shadow to the meat puppet and can be returned, the longer the soul is absent, the more the body decays. Even those who have their souls replaced quickly are never quite the same.

As soon as the door to the servants' stairs shuts us into the gloom of the narrow space, I push Xander against the wall and claim his mouth, swallowing his huff of laughter. My fingers slip under his t-shirt and glide up his ribs, revelling in the silky warmth of his skin.

I get to do this whenever I want. Touch him, taste him, ride him until he's shaking and close and unravelling beneath me. Mine to tease, mine to treasure.

And, because we're blind idiots, it might never have happened if he wasn't turned Rabid.

"I have a perfectly good bedroom for this," he says while I kiss his grinning lips.

"Too far away," I pant, unbuttoning his combats. "It has to be now."

He groans. "You're going to get me in so much trouble."

"You do just fine by yourself."

He smirks. "True."

He kisses me hard, sending me reeling with one swipe of his tongue and that wicked little ball of metal. My shoulders hit the opposite wall. I shove his trousers down his thighs and squeeze the taut globes of his arse. He mirrors me, his fingers pausing to trace the banana pattern on my white cotton pants. He raises his head, his eyes dazed and tender.

"Fuck, I love you," he whispers.

His lips steal my reply. I manage to kick one leg out of my underwear and combats before Xander hooks my knee over his hip. He pins my hands above my head, holding himself away while I wriggle and pout against the wall. He slides two slim fingers inside me, and my whine of protest turns into something choked and needy.

"So wet for me, Q-tip," he purrs.

"Always," I gasp as he curls his fingers in the way that blooms heat outwards and liquefies my bones. "If you're anywhere near me, I'm wet."

"That's so goddamn hot," he growls.

He pumps his fingers until I'm trembling on the edge, then wraps his fist around his cock, coating it with my arousal. The sight sends my eyes rolling back. A gentle hand draws my thigh over his hip and he sinks inside me, our sighs mingling.

"My legs are shaking already," I moan.

His chuckle is husky. "Mine, too."

I thrust to meet him, pinned by his hands, his mouth branding my throat. Despite the risk of getting caught, Xander fucks me slow and sweet, and I shatter against the wall, my cries of his name serenading the mystics on the top floor. He comes with a shudder and a low groan, his eyes half-lidded, dark hair stuck to sweat-slick cheeks. We slump into each other, our hearts slamming against our ribs, our combats tangled around our ankles. We catch our breaths and fix our clothes, giggling and wobbly.

Xander trails a finger along my jaw, his smile soft. "There is one more thing I need to do to make it up to you. One more thing I haven't done right. If you'll let me."

He's explored every part of me with his skilled hands and lips and tongue, delighted to be the first. The only man who's made me come, hard and often enough to see galaxies, never mind stars. I'll let him do anything. Well, almost anything...

My breath catches, my pulse thrumming with nerves.

"Only if you want to," he says to my quiet panic.

"Will it hurt?"

He captures my chin and soothes me with a kiss.

"Not this time," he whispers.

36

Bare bulbs strung between wooden trusses brighten the attic lair of the surveillance team. Though can it be called a lair if it's at the apex of the house and not tucked away in a darkened basement or, god forbid, another damn cave system? Whatever the name, swept floorboards span from gable to gable, the space filled with desks and computers and white light. Most of the seats are occupied by grunts jabbing at keyboards and staring, bleary eyed, at screens. I duck under the sloping plasterboard ceiling and trail after Shaun, followed by the clomp of Xander and Olly behind me.

As well as getting to leave the compound as an errand boy, Shaun supervises the surveillance team. He's a busy little bee. But I still kick his arse at football.

"We'll get you set up on the stations over here," he says, leading us towards the furthest corner where sloping roof meets gable end.

He glances over his shoulder, and I send him a smile. He blinks, long and slow, and jerks sideways to avoid braining himself on a rafter. Skipping forward a couple of steps, he keeps his gaze on the trusses. Xander chuckles softly.

"You really are oblivious," he says to my enquiring frown.

Shaun clears his throat. "So, uh, we copied CCTV footage

right after Xander was taken and up to when the Guild fled the school. Standard protocol. Compounds 3, 9, and 15 reviewed it. Now, we're all monitoring in real time with Compounds 1 and 2."

We slide into the seats indicated, my head brushing the plasterboard ceiling. Xander sits at the station beside me, Olly claiming the one opposite.

Shaun stands at the end of our block of four desks. "We recorded a van leaving the school and mapped its progress using the historical footage. We narrowed it down to the centre of Edinburgh, where the vehicle was abandoned. We're running a tracer programme using facial images from the videos, but the quality isn't great. It might not be accurate enough to flag a match. Our best bet is finding a live sighting, and that's hoping they haven't left the region. Welcome to the team—I hope you like watching grainy videos until your eyes bleed."

"We'll do whatever it takes to find those bastards," I growl.

Xander curls his hand over mine until I relax my fist. Shaun's eyes linger on it, then rise to Xander's face.

"I didn't see the videos, but I heard about what happened in them. If that's what they did to you…" His usually gentle grey eyes harden to granite. "We'll make them fucking pay."

"Thanks, man," Xander says gruffly.

He locked the USB I gave him in a box under his bed. Turns out, it's where we all keep our secrets.

Shaun nods, then launches into a tutorial on how to use the surveillance programme and what grids we'll be assessing. An overview map on our screens shows the areas covered by CCTV cameras in a thirty-mile radius around Edinburgh. Each grid highlighted in red has a different user's name to show they're being monitored, but there are an awful lot of grey squares. An awful lot of opportunities to miss the Rabid maker and his associates. They could be anywhere now—England, Casa Blanca. The freaking moon. This could all be futile.

"How did we get access to all this footage?" I say to Shaun as he reaches the end of his spiel. "Don't tell me some mystics can manipulate electricity. Do computers even have souls?"

Shaun snorts. "We don't need mystics to do our electrical wizardry. We have grunts for that. Hackers. A bunch of them came from Compound 14."

"I always knew brute force and brainpower were better than magical hocus pocus."

Shaun grins. "Damn right."

He taps Xander's desk with his knuckle and ambles off to a computer on the other side of the attic, waylaid a few times by people with questions. Assigned a grid to the south of Edinburgh, I hunch closer to my screen and flick slowly through the cameras, Xander and Olly mirroring me with equal intensity. The feeds show the City Bypass rammed with rush-hour traffic, different angles of a supermarket car park, and several streets, residential and commercial, the cameras peering through windows or on high from street lamps. I skip the City Bypass, the footage too zoomed out to see the occupants of the vehicles, and focus on the others, scanning every person who comes into view for a familiar figure.

It's not like the Rabid maker and his pals are inconspicuous.

The morning disappears. My eyes don't bleed, but they do sting a little. I scrub my face and slump in my chair, wincing slightly at the sudden movement. I must make a sound because Xander smirks at me.

"Still a bit tender there, Q-tip?"

Heat blooms in my gut and erupts in my chest and, dammit, I'm blushing. I may have been inexperienced, but I wasn't a virgin. I like to think I'm a sexually confident woman.

I read a book. What more can anyone teach me?

Quite a lot, as it happens. For one—Xander's appetite is just as healthy as his beast's, though I knew that from all the sex bunnies. And for two—there's a right way to do anal.

But I probably should have had a rest before I demanded we do it again.

I rest my chin on my palm and send Xander a smile as smouldering as my cheeks.

"Nothing I can't handle," I purr.

Watching Xander get horny is my new favourite activity. His pupils dilate and fill with all the naughty things he's thinking about. His pulse pounds at the base of his throat. His lips tilt in a dirty little grin that begs me to rip my pants off and climb into his lap. All I have to do is breathe in his vicinity and he's ready to get naked.

I fucking love it.

He was gentle and patient with me. His tongue went places I never could have imagined. I lost count of how many times he got me to come before he decided I was relaxed enough. And *Christ* did he make up for Beast-Xander's lack of finesse.

"For god's sake," Olly sighs, breaking me from my pleasant flashback, "can you two stop making sex eyes at each other? I'm sitting right here."

"Sorry, Olls," Xander says, ducking his head and attempting to refocus on his computer.

Olly sends me a wink, and I smother a laugh behind my hand.

Xander still seems to expect Olly to wake one day and decide it's too weird or gross for his best friend to be banging his sister, and disown him. He won't, of course. He's thrilled we're both so happy. But why waste an opportunity to wind him up?

Works for me. Xander is cute when he's flustered.

"I've barely seen you in two days; you think you'd need a break," Olly continues, deadpan. "Chafing is serious, you know."

"Speaking of breaks—don't they say you should step away from the computer every couple of hours?"

I swirl my finger across Xander's exposed wrist, his hand clicking the arrow keys on the keyboard. My fingertip circles that little knob of bone. Around and around. He perks up, sliding me a sultry look from under his lashes. Then his gaze tracks to Olly, and he hunches closer to his screen.

He clears his throat. "We probably shouldn't—"

"And you say Quinn is oblivious," Olly says. "Go. Shaun said we have a pool of people to watch our grids when we need to step away. I'll get someone to cover for you."

I poke Xander in the ribs. "See? Even my brother wants us to have a sex break."

"Jesus, Q-tip," Xander chokes.

I stand and tug him to his feet, though he offers little resistance. Olly grins at us.

"We'll be fifteen minutes, tops," I tell him.

"Thirty," Xander growls, and herds me towards the stairs.

37

"I need Xavier to check my anchor again," Xander groans beside me.

He's sprawled on his back on my bed, completely naked. A sheen of sweat glistens at each heave of his ribs, highlighting planes of muscle and all his fascinating ridges and hollows.

"Why?" I manage to pant, slumped diagonally across the mattress, my legs tangled with his.

"I'm pretty sure my soul just left my body."

My laugh stirs a frazzled clump of hair that's fallen over my face. I heave myself onto my elbow and walk my fingers up Xander's chest. His heart knocks against his breastbone. Sleepy, satisfied eyes watch me.

"Well, that's not all that's left *my* body," I say.

I swipe a finger through the stickiness dribbling down my thigh and shove it in my mouth, sucking on the rich and salty taste of us both. Xander came so hard after I gave him the most vigorous ride of his life, I swear I felt it hit the back of my throat.

"*Fuck*, Q-tip," he growls. "How long do we have?"

I glance at my clock. "Five minutes."

The world spins. I blink and I'm on my back, my legs hooked over Xander's shoulders. Hot breath meets the slickness between my thighs, and goosebumps erupt at the sudden, delicious chill.

"Plenty of time to make you come," he says.

Wicked green eyes pin me while his mouth plunders. The contact on already sensitised and swollen flesh has me writhing, my stomach clenching. A garbled sound that could be his name, plus other nonsense words, spills from my mouth.

"We taste amazing together," he purrs, offering a second of reprieve before he cups my arse, tilts my hips higher, and presses me to his scorching, greedy lips.

His tongue plunges inside me. My spine attempts to curl around on itself like a party whistle. The noise I make sounds strangely similar. Xander's piercing drags on the edge of my opening. I realise it's deliberate when he does it again, and again, his tongue thrusting deep. I claw at the sheets and yowl myself hoarse. Xander sits back on his heels with a very cocky grin by the time I manage to focus on him.

"Your face is wet," I croak.

The grin widens. "That's 'cos you're fucking dripping, Q-tip."

My muscles give a valiant flutter, then ripple into a breath-stealing aftershock when Xander wipes his mouth and licks everything from his palm, his smouldering gaze burning to my core. After that display, he has to help me into my clothes since my body has gone into orgasm shock.

We stumble from my room and up the main stairs. I cling to Xander's waist, my knees as liquid as the rest of me. He chuckles at my ungraceful flailing—totally his fault—and kisses my temple. His lips freeze to my head, and his posture stiffens.

A couple pauses above us on the stairs. Blond hair and blue

eyes. The elder Dawson is a balding version of Xavier, the frown lines deep between his brows. Xander's mother has the cold beauty of an icicle. Lovely to look at, but you're liable to lose a layer of skin if you dare to touch. A delicate sneer twists her lips.

I stop myself in the act of patting my hair. Her gaze rakes to my toes, and she sniffs. Her nose wrinkles. I imagine I smell like I've been rolling around on top of her son. Which I have.

"Mrs Dawson," I squeak, then clear my throat. "Mr Dawson. Nice to bump into you."

I earn a minuscule nod from Mr Dawson, then he sweeps his wife past us and continues down. Hurt flickers across Xander's face before he schools his expression.

"I'm okay, thanks for asking," he says.

Mr Dawson tenses, then spins on his heel, head tilted to glare up at us. His blue eyes flash a warning.

"You got yourself captured and endangered the entire compound," he barks. Just like Xavier. "You are an *embarrassment.*"

Xander flinches. My hackles rise at his parents' dismissal as they glide down the stairs.

"He is a *miracle,*" I yell at their retreating backs. "And he doesn't need to be a mystic to be pretty fucking magical."

Neither Dawson deigns to reply. They scurry out of sight. The only Dawson that matters gives me a squeeze.

"Thanks, Q-tip. I think you're pretty fucking magical, too."

Olly greets us in the attic with an eye roll and fond, "My god, you two reek of sex."

Xander ducks his head, his blush adorable. I, as the only mature adult, stick my tongue out at Olly. We take our places opposite him and reclaim our grids, flicking through our camera feeds.

Days pass like this. My eyes may actually bleed. I become so familiar with my square of bypass, car park, and streets, I recognise vehicles and people as they go about their routine. Nomags content to labour under the yoke of their magical overlords, as long as it doesn't interfere with their pub and TV time.

Xavier sanctioned the release of footage from the torture videos on social media and internet forums. Snippets of the rapes, the beatings. Zoomed images of Neck-tattoo and Eyebrow-piercing and the cowled visage of the Rabid maker himself. Xavier hoped it might flush them from wherever they're hiding.

The nomags were outraged, but the Unbound were blamed, of course. The videos were removed. And social media returned to its trolling and shit-posting about gender identity and snowflakes.

Xander and I don't take anymore unsanctioned breaks, intent on catching the bastards. We save our energy for the evening. People have started to complain that Xander howls louder than when he was Rabid.

I slump in my seat. My vertebrae crunch when I straighten my spine and roll my shoulders. Xander's warm hand rubs my knee under the table, his gaze on his screen. The blue-white light makes the angles of his face even more stark and beautiful. Olly's cheek is pillowed on his fist, his eyes half-lidded and glazed. I return my focus to my monitor.

A woman in a pink, zebra-striped onesie shuffles through the supermarket car park. She never seems to shop in normal clothes, but appears three times a week dressed in her pyjamas. Once in the morning, twice in the evening. She'll spend an hour in the store, then come out heaving a trolley laden with enough food to feed a family of fifty.

On the bypass, Bentley-prick does his usual weaving in and out of the gathering rush-hour traffic. There's no audio, but I imagine a chorus of honks follows him. He gives me Anima mystic vibes. Perfect and untouchable arrogance, not to mention the ostentatious wealth.

The residential streets are quiet. I dig a thumb into my tired eye socket. Movement catches my attention. A black figure and a stoop-shouldered gait. I jerk forwards, my nose an inch from the screen. My heart kicks.

"Q-tip? You having a seizure?"

The person on the screen has their hood drawn—not unusual given the drizzly weather. They stride towards the camera mounted on the lamppost. I peer closer.

"Maybe you should take a break, Quinn," Olly says while I whisper, "Look up. Look *up,* you fucker."

The man pauses on the edge of the camera's field of view. I hold my breath. Slowly, so goddamn slowly I can count every heartbeat, the shrouded figure raises his head. Dark, deep-set eyes stare right into mine, as if he can feel me watching him. My soul quivers in protest.

The Rabid maker hunches his shoulders and disappears down the street.

38

"I can't believe you talked me into this, McTierney," Xavier growls in my earpiece. "You three are a nightmare for my stress levels."

"Aww, we love you, too, Captain," I say.

Xavier grunts.

Xander pats my leg, and mouths, "Twenty points."

I slide him a grin where he's sitting next to me, pressed shoulder to thigh in the passenger seats of the nondescript van, his Bluetooth earpiece half-hidden by the fall of his dark hair. On his other side, Olly grips the steering wheel and smoothly overtakes a lorry on the City Bypass. The wipers smear greasy drizzle across the windscreen.

"Well, you should find it comforting that if this all goes tits up like our last mission, you'll finally be rid of us."

Xavier makes a noncommittal, "Hmm," to my statement.

"Or we'll all be sent back Rabid," Olly says, bending closer to the wheel.

His voice echoes in my ear as it's picked up by his microphone and relayed through the radio app we're using on our mobiles. Xander shivers beside me. I thread my fingers through his and squeeze his hand.

"That only confirms the recklessness of my decision, other

McTierney," Xavier barks.

"How am *I* the other McTierney?" Olly grumbles, slowing for the traffic lights at Sheriffhall roundabout, then taking the exit onto the A7. "I'm the eldest."

I trace a finger around the shape of my phone in my pocket. "You know this makes sense, Xavier. If we waited to mobilise an attack team, we'd risk losing the Rabid maker. If we haven't lost him already. Plus, it minimises the time our mystics are out of the compound, and vulnerable."

"And remind me of my orders, McTierney. Just so *your* task is explicitly clear."

I sigh. "We've to scout the area and attempt to pinpoint the douchebag's evil, hidey lair, then monitor and wait for proper reinforcements."

"And what are you not to do under any circumstances?"

Another, gustier sigh. "Approach or engage with the Rabid maker."

Xavier took a hell of a lot of convincing to let us out the compound, so I guess I should be pleased. We can track the bastard, confirm he's in one place, then wait for the informed support of our mystics before we storm that castle. It's less dangerous for grunts to scout than it is for our mystics to wander around and risk detection by the enemy.

The waiting will be the hard part—if we even find him. It's been two hours since I saw his grim-reaper stoop on the CCTV. We tried to track him on different cameras, but he was spotted in a satellite town to Edinburgh. If he was in the centre of the city, there would have been way more CCTV options to monitor him. He could be anywhere now. The Highlands. Even England. All he needed to do was jump in a car.

But my gut says he's here. He's close. I bet it chafed his balls to be driven from the caves near the private school. He had a pretty sweet setup, if you're into torture and rape. At least he won't have another victim, unless he's paired up with more Rabid makers. Maybe they share their videos and coo over what sadistic fuckers they all are.

"I'm glad you're finally listening to me, McTierney," Xavier says, "though the night is young."

We're on a smaller road. Hedges and fields. Streetlights flicker on as walls and houses replace the countryside.

"I always listen. I don't always agree."

Teeth grind through my earpiece. "You don't need to agree. You just need to obey."

"Aye, aye, *El Capitan*," I say cheerfully.

Olly drives a little further, then parks opposite a bus stop on Straiton High Street. The misty drizzle and darkening light turn the surrounding tenements oppressive and murky. A red scrawl of graffiti on the bus stop reads 'Burn the Unbound.'

"We're here." Olly twists the keys and the engine dies. He nods at a road forking off from the main street. "That's where the camera was looking."

Xander scrubs his face. Since I'm still holding his hand, I end up skimming his eyelashes and cheekbones.

"Are you sure I can't come? I hate the thought of staying in the van while you're both out there." He kisses my knuckles. "Especially you."

"Favouritism," Olly mutters, and Xander manages a weak smile.

"Remain in the vehicle," Xavier barks.

I ignore his voice, and cup Xander's face. "They know what you look like. Who you are. Olly and I are strangers. We can find and follow them without tipping them off."

"Maybe it'll lure them out if they see me. They won't be able to resist."

"You will remain in the vehicle, *as ordered,*" Xavier growls. "McTierneys—get your butts out there. You will monitor and report. There will be no luring."

My thumbs stroke Xander's pouty bottom lip. "See—your big brother really cares about you."

Xavier's frustrated huff coaxes a smirk from Xander.

Xavier didn't want Xander to come at all. It takes a lot to rile Xander up, but ordering him to stay in the compound had him yelling at Xavier, much to the ever-present William's affront and disgust. Words like 'love of my life' and 'no fucking way' and 'I'm going, you insufferable dick-hole.' His cheeks were flushed, fists clenched, his green eyes sparking with menace and defiance while he squared off against his much bulkier brother.

He was goddamn beautiful.

He traps my hands to his face, and leans down to kiss me. A gentle graze of lips.

"Be careful," he says softly.

"I will."

He clears his throat. "And, uh, you, too, Olls."

"Yeah, I know I'm the afterthought here," Olly says, though his voice is teasing.

I kiss Xander harder. He opens his lips to the press of my tongue, sucking it into his mouth and teasing me with his piercing. It never fails to curl heat low in my belly. I hook a leg over his thighs, hampered from climbing into his lap by the constriction of my seatbelt. I devour his mouth and he matches my hunger, his jaw working under my palms. A delicious little groan rumbles in his throat.

"McTierney, would you stop sucking my bro—Xander's face and get on with it. You were the one desperate to drive up there without proper planning or support."

Xander slumps in his seat, blinking and panting. "Did he almost call me...?"

"I think this means I win," I say, betrayed by my heartbeat wobbling through my voice.

Kissing Xander should come with a label. Warning: may cause rapid dysfunction of limbs and brain, fever, and a loss of underwear.

Screw it. I kiss him again, then flop out of the van. The cold drizzle feels wonderful on my cheeks. My hair immediately frizzes into a red cloud around my head. Olly joins me on the pavement, tugging the hood of his black jacket up. I copy him, and tuck my already bedraggled hair into the collar. Cold air licks into the half-open zip, lowered so I can reach my silenced Glock in its shoulder holster. I check the radio app is still working on my phone and that the tracker function is engaged.

Xander rolls down the window. "Keep her safe, Olls."

Olly snorts. "You know you'd be dead now if I hadn't knocked her gun away when they captured you, right? She would've shot you before they'd dragged you into the van."

"That's why I love her." Xander grins.

I blow him a kiss. Xavier coughs his impatience in my earpiece.

"We're moving onto Clerk Street," I say.

Olly and I hustle down the road as darkness falls. The streets are quiet. Drizzle eddies in the headlights of passing cars. The narrow avenue hems us in between businesses and ancient-bricked residential flats above, leaving only a tiny slice of cloudy sky. I scan each window and store front for a glimpse of the Rabid maker's creepy face. Skeletal trees dot the route, which finally opens out at a used-car lot and the first patch of grass I've seen.

Olly nods at a lamppost. "There's the camera."

A black globe follows our progress. Is anyone watching us back in the attic?

We pause on the corner beneath the all-seeing eye. The Rabid maker headed the way we just came, deeper into the drab and narrow street, and back towards Xander in the van. We turn to retrace the path.

"Let's take a side each," I say. "Check he's not in any of the shops or restaurants."

Olly nods, and crosses the road. I stroll down the pavement, hands at my sides, ignoring all the worn and battered doors to the houses above, and the shuttered businesses closed for the night.

"Xander?" I say.

"Yeah, Q-tip?"

"I love you."

"I love you, too," he says, and I can hear the smile in his voice.

A red, glowing T sign juts from the side of a building. I push open the fogged-glass door into a humid heat smelling of hops and the sweat of drunk men. A couple of patrons swivel on the stools at the bar to peruse my entrance. The music is low and folksy. A slot machine flashes brightly in the corner.

"Hey, Xavier?" Xander says in my ear.

"What?" Xavier says gruffly. "I'm not going to tell you I love you."

I chuckle, and earn myself a suspicious glare from a bleary-eyed man in a booth on his own. He takes a noisy slurp of his pint as I mosey past, scanning the people scattered about.

"I left you a present in your drawer."

A pregnant pause, then, "Did you take a dump in my desk?"

Xander laughs. "No, darling brother, I did not shit in your drawer. But it's funny that's where your mind went."

I scope out the pub's bathrooms, earning a disgruntled squawk from a man pissing haphazardly into a urinal in the men's. I hustle outside and gulp a lungful of blessed fresh air. Olly waits for me on his side of the pavement, and we continue our hunt in tandem.

"How did you get into my office?" Xavier growls. Without waiting for a response, he barks, "*Walker!*"

I jump, catching Olly's flinch out of the corner of my eye. No doubt Xander leapt in his seat in the van.

It's hard not to crap yourself at that commanding tone.

William mumbles in the background.

"Search my desk drawers for something out of place," Xavier says.

The doors of a Scotmid convenience store slide open into a bright interior. I circle the aisles, ignoring the produce and focusing on the people.

More mumbling from William. The bang of drawers being shut.

"There's a USB," Xavier says slowly.

Olly catches my gaze from across the street. One corner of his mouth twitches into a grim smile.

Xander played him the video of his descent into Rabidity. Olly took it about as well as I did, though the audio was muted from the start. He was the one who suggested showing it to Xavier.

"It's my video," Xander says.

"You told me there was no Xander video, McTierney."

I shrug, though Xavier can't see me. "I lied. Given the contents, it's up to Xander if he wants anyone to see it."

"So why are you sharing this with me now?"

Xander stays quiet. I picture him sitting in the van, staring at his hands clasped between his knees. Is he regretting giving it to his brother? I told him he was brave for even thinking about it, and that it didn't matter what Xavier thought, one way or the other. But, despite everything Xavier has done to him, Xander still hopes his brother will look at him with something other than irritation and shame.

If he doesn't after he's watched it, I'm going to punch him in the nose.

"So you can see what a badass your brother is," I say into the silence. "And realise how lucky you are to have him."

"No," Xander gasps.

I stop beside a bakery, the lights off. The scent of bread and yeast somehow lingers through the glass.

I press a finger to my earpiece. "Xander? You okay?"

"Don't fucking touch me!" he yelps.

There's a scuffle. The harsh rasp of fabric. A clatter, and everything becomes muffled behind a burst of static.

My heart and stomach drop to my feet.

There are only three people who could make his voice that high and ragged with fear.

And not a single fucking one of them gets to touch him ever again.

39

My boots slap the pavement, the force vibrating up my shinbones. Businesses and streetlights blur past, helped by the drizzle swirling in my eyeballs. My breaths rip from my chest, but I pump my arms harder, forcing my legs to run faster. Olly is a dark streak on his side of the road. We launch across the street at the junction and sprint for the van.

Two dark figures tussle by the passenger door. The healthier, non-evil one shoves the taller man in the chest, forcing him to stumble a step. The Rabid maker's teeth flash in the gloomy cavern of his hood. He swipes a baton through the air. Xander ducks, then pops straight up, his shoulder dropping to deliver a solid hook on the Rabid maker's pointy chin. The douchebag's head snaps back, and he lands on his arse.

Olly and I clatter around the nose of the van. The Rabid maker scrambles to his feet and takes off down the pavement, his spine more hunched than usual. Xander slumps against the passenger door, cradling his left arm. His gun lies in the gutter.

"Fucker came out of nowhere," he pants.

I grip his face and kiss his pale, trembling lips while Olly updates a rather shouty Xavier. My hands explore Xander's injured arm, but my eyes dart to the retreating Rabid maker as he scuttles into a side street and out of sight. Rage boils in my chest.

"Is it broken?" I say without looking at Xander.

I twitch from foot to foot, my muscles screaming at me to pursue. The sound of the bastard's footfalls have already faded.

"Bruised, I think. He got me with his bat, then knocked the gun—"

I plant a sloppy, ungraceful kiss on him while he's still speaking, our teeth clashing together. He smells of rain and bergamot.

"I'll be right back."

I launch myself down the pavement before the pressure in my chest makes me explode.

"Quinn, no! *Wait.*"

"Keep him safe!" I yell at Olly.

My hood has fallen down at some point during my mad dash to Xander. My wet hair flops against my jacket with each bouncing step. The tension in my muscles releases as I give chase. Everything narrows to my pounding heart and pounding feet.

I round the corner into the side street, catching a glimpse of a stooped, black figure vanishing between buildings.

"What the hell are you doing, McTierney?" Xavier growls. "I ordered you not to engage under *any* circumstances."

"I'm not letting this arsehole get away," I say through gritted teeth.

I pivot into an alley between tenements, my boot crunching on loose gravel. A shadow swells and shrinks on the wall at the far end. I dash past stinking, overflowing bins.

"*McTierney.*" Xavier's voice somehow goes deeper in warning. "I order you to stop."

"He hurt Xander. *Again.* He's going to fucking pay for all of it." My own voice drops to a level I don't recognise.

I'm running so fast, I almost miss the enclosed tunnel branching out of the alleyway, the roof formed by the flats above. I bounce off the wall and careen into the tunnel, scraping my palms on rough brick. My harsh breaths echo in the narrow space. I burst out into an open street of terraced and semi-detached houses. A black shape jumps over a wall about fifty metres further down. I snarl, and urge my limbs after him.

Xavier continues to bark in my ear, but I can no longer decipher the words over the rushing of my blood.

My stinging palms slap the top of the wall and boost me over. My boots flatten a floral display next to a weather-bitten headstone. The scent of lily pollen and mulch fill my nose. A small, triangular cemetery separates me and the rabbiting Rabid maker. He pauses on the wooded edge of the opposite side. His head swivels slowly. A smirk tilts his lips in the shadow of his hood. Then the fucker flicks his fingers in a 'come get me' gesture, and hops into the trees.

I pelt across the grass, dodging gravestones. Drizzle and sweat puff from my lips on each breath. I leap the fence like an Olympic hurdler and crash into the undergrowth. Metal rattles somewhere ahead. I aim towards it, carving a path through the vegetation. Brambles tug at my clothes. A chain-link barrier prevents access onto a footpath cut into an embankment. The Rabid maker vaults the second, parallel fence with another shiver of metal.

I bruise my fingers scrabbling over the barrier. I dart across the concrete path and flop over the second fence, landing on my face in a biting patch of nettles. Cursing, I stagger upright and lurch out of the trees, dogging the Rabid maker into another residential street.

Despite his cadaverous frame, he seems to be showing no ill effect from our little chase, while my muscles burn and wobble. My throat and chest ache from sucking gulps of cold air. Scrapes and stings clamour for my attention.

The Rabid maker zig-zags through a gate into a park, and his long legs spirit him over the mown grass. I huff along in his wake. Water stipples the lawn. His footprints form dark marks in the dampness where they aim diagonally across the park. I lose sight of him when he easily scales a green wooden fence surrounding the grounds of a church, disappearing in a flap of his long, black coat.

Splinters prick my fingers. I land on my feet, but collapse to my knees in the dirt, taking a few seconds to catch my breath and calm the spots flaring in my vision. I shuffle down the side of the church like a Revenant, and stutter to a halt on a main road. Possibly the one we started on, though my sense of direction has gone to shit.

The street is empty.

My heart kicks.

No! I can't have lost the bastard. That kind of evil doesn't deserve to be free.

Behind me, a heavy door clicks closed.

I whirl around. The red entrance to the church stares placidly back at me. Off to the side, a yellow defibrillator box is fixed to the sandstone. I creep up the steps and press an ear to the wood.

"Shut *up*, Xavier," I wheeze. "I need to listen."

Xavier's belligerent voice ceases mid-threat. I'm kind of impressed he's kept up the tirade for this long. It feels like I've been running for hours, but it's probably only been about ten minutes. My gangly frame is built for long distance, not manic sprinting. The defibrillator may come in handy soon.

No noises come from inside the church. I glance around, but I'm alone on the steps, the street empty apart from a fine mist. I draw my gun and keep it pressed to my side.

"I'm going into a church," I whisper.

"Don't you *dare*—"

"Shush," I say, and ease open the door.

I wince at the screech of rusted hinges. In the silence that follows, I can hear Xavier's lips flapping.

"Did you just *shush me*, McTierney?" he growls.

I slip through the red door. A narrow vestibule and narthex lead straight into the central aisle of the nave, flanked by rows of pews. A hooded figure stands on the altar, swathed in black, his back to me. Candles flicker, the soft glow struggling to banish the dark. Shadows pool in the clerestory.

My shoes squeak on the polished floor. The figure turns. I raise my gun. A wide smile stretches sallow cheeks.

"You soulblind little fool," says the Rabid maker.

Arms grab me from behind and pin my weapon to my side.

40

"Did you really think I ran because I was *scared?*" The Rabid maker sneers. "I simply separated you from the herd. And now you're mine."

The grip around me tightens, clamping my arms to my sides, my Glock pointed at the ground in my white-knuckled hold. Eyebrow-piercing leers at me over my shoulder while he attempts to crush the air from my lungs. I bare my teeth at him, and he laughs. Sour breath fans my cheek. Neck-tattoo stands beside Eyebrow-piercing, both of them blocking the aisle with their overly muscled carcasses.

"It's just you and your two rapists," I say for Xavier's benefit, "and you won't have enough juice left to make me Rabid for a long while. Longer than you'll be allowed to live."

Eyebrow-piercing and Neck-tattoo could be Anima mystics, but their builds suggest they're grunts. They definitely don't have the gauntness of pure evil.

The Rabid maker raises an unimpressed brow and descends the steps from the altar. "Turning you into a mindless Revenant to chomp on your friends will be almost as satisfying."

"Good luck with that," I spit.

His pitted eyes focus on my chest. I steel myself, but can't

250

help a gasp when he tugs on my soul. It's a horrible sensation—as if someone's plucking my abdominal aorta like a harp string.

Instead of frustration, a slow smile curves his lips. "What a shame for you. My associates will have to weaken your soul anchor. I'm sure you know how that works."

Degradation, rape, and beatings. Yup, I'm familiar.

Eyebrow-piercing and Neck-tattoo continue to leer. The Rabid maker tilts my chin with a finger, snatching his hand back when I try to bite him. His slap rocks my head to the side and throws my damp hair across my face. Fire radiates from my cheek to my jaw.

"At least we'll have more time together," he says, his voice placid despite his actions. "You can tell me how you worthless rebels managed to cure one of my Rabids."

"Again," I say, "good luck with that."

The Rabid maker draws the baton from a voluminous sleeve. "Now, drop the weapon or I break your arm."

I kick my leg out, not with any real force, but my toe hits the Rabid maker in the shin and he dances back a step. I wrench my head to the side to look down past Eyebrow-piercing's bulging bicep. I squeeze the trigger. My first bullet gouges the wooden floor. The muffled *phut* flutters around the clerestory. My second bullet slams into Eyebrow-piercing's boot before he can react to the first. His squeal rings in my ears, and his grip loosens.

I shrug free from his limp arms, ducking Neck-tattoo's wild swing. My shoulder ploughs into the Rabid maker's bony chest and knocks him on his arse in a tangle of skinny limbs and long, black coat. The bat clatters under a pew. I vault his body, using the benches on either side for leverage, my gun scraping on the wood. I raise the Glock and spin around.

Eyebrow-piercing is on the floor with the Rabid maker, clutching his dripping foot, and howling. Neck-tattoo bunches a massive fist. A rough yank on my soul doubles me over. Heavy boots thunder on wood.

The red door of the church crashes open. Yelling and footsteps form a cacophony in the dome of the clerestory. I stagger backwards, clutching my chest. Neck-tattoo blocks my view, facing the new threat. Eyebrow-piercing's snivels weave between his legs.

Honestly, these big guys—they can dish out the pain, but can never take it. The fucking babies.

The Rabid maker claws himself upright using the pews. His hood has fallen down to bare his balding scalp. I sidle into a gap between the benches until I can see Xander and Olly, shoulder to shoulder where narthex meets aisle. Their guns aim at the Rabid maker and his grunts.

Another cruel smile stretches that haggard face.

I'm beginning to think this guy is one bird short of a cuckoo clock.

"How wonderful," the Rabid maker says. "My cured pet has returned to his master. I wanted another chance to rip out that beautiful soul."

Xander shudders, but keeps his gun steady on Neck-tattoo. I point my weapon at the bedraggled-crow shape of the Rabid maker. He flexes his fingers towards Olly and Xander.

"Hey, arsehole," I growl. "You're awfully smug for someone who brought magic to a gun fight."

The Rabid maker blinks at me. Eyebrow-piercing finally wobbles onto one leg, leaving a slick of blood on the floor.

Neck-tattoo glares at Xander and claims a step towards him. "Pull that trigger and it'll be the last thing you do."

"Okay," Xander says.

The barrel drops. Xander fires. I wince at Neck-tattoo's shriek. He staggers against the pews, blood already blooming around a charred hole in his sweatpants.

I thought Xander aimed at Neck-tattoo's gut, but he's gone for something lower and much more, ahem, *precious*.

Eyebrow-piercing manages a strangled bleat of, "Wait!" before the *thuck* of a second bullet ripples through the church. Eyebrow-piercing folds around himself and collapses to the floor. The Rabid maker sprints for the altar, his coat flapping.

I don't even have to think about it.

The crack of a shot joins mine a split second after I squeeze the trigger. The Rabid maker disappears from view in a flail of limbs and cloth. I meet Xander in the aisle. Olly guards the keening Neck-tattoo and the silent Eyebrow-piercing, which doesn't bode well for Eyebrow-piercing's general wellbeing.

Such a shame.

The Rabid maker claws at the floor, painfully dragging himself towards the altar. The bullet holes are difficult to see in the material of his coat, but two neat circles pierce the blackness, one high between his shoulder blades and the other centred perfectly on his lumbar spine.

Xander toes him onto his back. The Rabid maker's groan rattles in his throat. His chest hitches, and a bead of red gathers in the corner of his mouth. His teeth flash in a bloody smile.

"You may be cured, but you will always be *mine*," the Rabid maker snarls. "What I did to you will taint your soul forever."

"Don't flatter yourself," Xander says, and shoots him between the eyes.

41

"McTierney, my office!" Xavier barks as soon as my boot kisses the tiles of the hall. "All three of you."

His voice crackles through a hidden speaker. He rarely uses the PA system of the compound—I often forget it's there—but we'd silenced our radio apps on the journey back from Straiton, cutting him off mid-tirade.

Probably a mistake on our part.

Slouching, we head for the stairs and the long climb to the third floor. Xander squeezes my hand, his skin warm against mine. His other arm is still cradled across his chest.

The clinical wing will be our next stop, as soon as Xavier has finished yelling at us.

"Do you think he's watched the video?" Xander says quietly, his gaze on his feet.

Olly trots ahead of us. "What if he has?"

Xander shrugs his uninjured shoulder.

"He's probably not had a chance," I say. "Between monitoring our op and snarling in my ear about what a liability I am, he's been preoccupied."

The third floor is hushed, most of the mystics enjoying their evening downtime. William greets us with a sneer that reminds me of the Rabid maker's henchmen. He aims his nose so high in the air, I'm surprised he doesn't tip over. He marches to Xavier's office door and swings it wide, herding us through.

"Your assistance will not be needed, Walker," Xavier says before the smug William can perch on his desk to witness our scolding. "You can clock off for the night."

Xavier stands at his window, staring out into the dark, and misses William's sulky expression as he trudges from the room and shuts the door. Olly, Xander, and I stand at attention.

Silence descends on the office.

The urge to speak tickles my throat. Xander catches my eye and shakes his head. I press my lips together. A smirk tugs at the corner of his mouth.

Xavier's sigh mists the glass. "What the hell am I going to do with you, McTierney?"

"Um… say thank you?"

Xavier spins on his heel, his brows disappearing into his hairline. "*Thank* you?!"

"You're welcome, Captain," I say.

His mouth hangs agape for two glorious seconds, then his focus drops to Xander's arm cuddled around his middle. Xavier's unruly brows scrumple into a serious line.

"Is it broken?" he says, his voice gruff.

"I…" Xander clears his throat. "I don't think so."

Xavier circles his desk and reaches for Xander, but his broad hands pause before completing the movement.

"May I?"

Xander blinks, and manages a nod. Olly leans back on Xander's other side, his wide eyes catching mine.

Xavier has watched the video. He must have. There's no other reason for this hesitant compassion towards his brother.

Xavier cradles Xander's forearm. Thick fingers carefully

palpate muscle and bone. Icy-blue eyes catalogue Xander's wince, and remain lasered in on his face.

"I would've done the same," Xavier murmurs.

"You're not angry they're all dead?"

Xavier keeps holding Xander's arm, though his fingers have stilled. His gaze slides to me. A muscle in his cheek twitches suspiciously close to a smirk.

"You weren't the only one who put a few holes in them."

Neck-tattoo bled out in a puddle not long after Eyebrow-piercing fell silent. We left their bodies in the church, since it had already been desecrated. No doubt the massacre will be spun so that they're the innocent victims slaughtered by the evil villains of the Unbound.

But we know the truth. Someday, everyone else will.

I notch my chin higher. "They deserved a few more holes, in my opinion."

Xavier releases Xander, and pats his shoulder. "I don't think it's broken, either, but get it checked by the medic."

"Uh, sure… Captain."

Xavier perches on the edge of his desk and crosses his arms. "You want to explain to me again, McTierney, why you disobeyed my orders?"

"You saw why," I say.

His gaze flits to Xander, then back. He shoves to his feet and stomps behind his desk. The chair shrieks when he lowers himself into it.

"Nevertheless, I'll come up with an appropriate punishment. Until then, you're all dismissed."

"One more thing," I say, eliciting a weary sigh. I slip a phone from my pocket and place it on Xavier's blotter in front of his clasped hands. "This might inspire some leniency. Also,

Xander and Olly didn't do anything wrong."

"I'm well aware of who needs the punishment here, McTierney." Xavier aims an arched brow from me to the mobile on his desk. "What's this?"

"We got it off the Rabid maker. Xander was smart enough to use the arsehole's fingerprint to unlock it before we left, and he changed the passcode so we'll always have access."

"And?"

"*And* there's a list on there. Names and addresses." I wait until Xavier raises his eyes from the screen to me. "We think it's *all* their Rabid makers."

Xavier snatches the device in one meaty paw, and peers at it. Before he can do more than tap at the screen, the door opens behind us. Mr and Mrs Dawson sweep into the office without knocking. I guess it's their house, but still—rude.

"We didn't realise you had"—frosty eyes catalogue Xander from head to toe—"company."

"They were just leaving."

"Good," Mrs Dawson sniffs. "I still don't understand why you won't reassign him to another compound."

"Mother, we've talked about this…"

"He murdered two of your soldiers with his bare hands," Mr Dawson growls, in perfect imitation of his bulkier son.

Xander flinches, hunching around his injured arm. Olly's affronted expression matches the indignation bristling across my shoulders.

"He wasn't himself," I spit. "Xander would never—"

"Be quiet, McTierney."

"But—"

I shut my mouth at the sight of Xavier's thunderous brows crashing together. Mrs Dawson gives me a pinched-mouthed little smile.

"I believe you three have been dismissed."

Of course Xavier won't defend his own brother from his parents. No wonder he sent William away. He didn't want anyone he respected enough to witness him being anything but a hardass to Xander.

We crowd the door in our haste to leave the stuffy office, Olly popping out first. I spare one last glare over my shoulder, my hand on Xander's back.

"Dawson."

Xavier's low voice rumbles through the room. Xander spins around, and I walk into his chest. I grab his hips to steady myself.

"Do not use that name for him," Mrs Dawson honks, like a startled goose. "He is not—"

"Mother," Xavier barks. "You should also be quiet."

I turn in time to catch Mrs Dawson all agog. Mr Dawson scowls, but a raised hand keeps his trap shut.

"Dawson," Xavier repeats with his usual gravitas, looking right at Xander. Unflinching. The perfect captain.

The proud older brother.

"You did good out there," he says.

42

Six Months Later

Sunset burnishes the pine needles in orange and gold and filters into shadows at the base of the trunks. Warmth lingers in the autumn air, though there's a crispness as the night draws closer. Xander blows a puff of steam at the darkening sky and passes me the vape. I still get a thrill from putting my lips where his have so recently been, though those lips have been everywhere on me.

And I mean *everywhere*.

I suck a lungful of earthy weed, then send it towards the first hint of stars, reaching across Xander to give the pen to Olly on his other side. I wriggle closer to Xander on the bench in the tiny garden of the cottage. His arm tightens across my shoulders. The water feature tinkles in the background, cleared of the clogging leaves.

It's not the only change from when we last hung out here. Now, I have one leg hooked over Xander's, his warm hand on my thigh, a fingertip tracing tiny, tickling swirls on my knee. The tingles merge with the pleasant buzz in my veins from all the weed we've been huffing.

It's been an exhausting few months. But we finally get to celebrate.

"Do you think they'll get more?" Olly says, making sloppy circles with his mouthful of steam. His head lolls on the bench back, his eyes half-lidded.

"I guess evil little babies could be born at any time," I say. "Their flavour of poison is rare, though. That list was short, despite them being the arsehole majority."

Olly snorts. "Evil little baby makers. *Rabid* makers. Little baby Rabid makers."

"Okay, that's enough for you." Xander swipes the vape pen and tucks it into his combat jacket. His hand returns to my knee, and all the happy buzzing and tingling.

Olly pouts, then seems to forget why he's pouting. "Do you think Xavier will stop punishing you now that we've executed the last name on the list? The list he never would have gotten without you. He never would have gotten his brother back without you, either. Have we told him that? We should tell him that."

Olly tries to sit up, pedals his arms and legs like a dying fly, then slumps against the bench.

"Remind me tomorrow. Let's do that tomorrow."

"Thanks, bro." I grin at him. "But I think *El Capitan* likes having me around. And William gets in a tizzy whenever it's my turn with him."

Xavier, in his mystical wisdom, decided that my punishment for ignoring his orders and chasing after the Rabid maker was to make me his part-time personal assistant, so he could 'keep an eye on me'. He also said it would give Walker a well-earned break from being at his constant beck and call, much to William's chagrin.

Turns out I'm good at being his assistant. And I enjoy having more opportunity to snark at Xavier. Teasing out his long-suffering sighs is almost as satisfying as ending the evil majority's use of Rabid warfare. If Xavier really couldn't stand it, he'd send me away. He is the captain, after all. But he secretly loves it.

Just like he not-so-secretly loves his little brother.

I had a little sniffle after he dismissed us from his office the day we killed the first, and worst, Rabid maker. Okay, I howled like a wounded fox and Xander had to comfort me instead of the other way around, though he had a tear in his eye and a husk in his voice for a few hours after.

Xavier has been nicer to him ever since. Calling him by his proper surname in front of everyone. Joining in our football matches with Shaun and the others. He convinced us to try rugby, but made the mistake of putting Xander and me on different teams. All it took was one tackle, Xander panting and muddy underneath me, and I forgot what we were playing. We had to take a time-out. A *private* time-out.

My bedsheets have never been so filthy.

"What are you thinking, Q-tip?" Xander purrs in my ear.

His fingertip swirls higher, caressing along the inseam of my combat trousers. The tingly buzzes turn to a heady throbbing, and I open my legs wider. Xander's chuckle flushes heat through my skin.

"What do you suppose they'll do now?" Olly mumbles, his eyes shut, his body sunk into the fold of the bench. "We've dealt them a massive blow, but there're still so many of them. Stupid Guild. Big fat liars."

Olly's huff of breath stirs the auburn hair flopped over his forehead. The dying light of sunset highlights the freckles on his sleepy face.

Xander's wicked fingers reach the sensitive curve of my inner thigh, right below the crease where leg meets molten core. He traces that little swell of muscle, and I gasp. My heart and tongue feel too big for their respective cavities.

"Quinn?"

"Hmm?"

"What do you think they'll do?" Olly says, his voice drifting off into the dusk.

His putty-limbed relaxation is at odds with my trembling anticipation. With the *thud-thud-thud* of the pulse between my thighs.

Honestly, six months of bunny sex and I still can't get enough. One touch from Xander, and I'm a puddle. Totally soaking.

He twists his body closer to me, his hot mouth nibbling on my ear.

"Answer him, Q-tip," Xander whispers. He flicks my lobe with the ball of his piercing, and I almost melt through the bench.

He likes to do that to the piece of my anatomy only millimetres from his fingers, until I scream his name and hump his face.

"They'll, uh…" I squeak, then clear my throat. And clear my throat again. "They'll still hate us. They'll still lie and manipulate. They're still world-leading dicks. But…"

Xander pulls back to give me a smile that's both soft and hungry, his pupils dilated and as dark as the night falling around us. I try to turn a whimper into a cough, though I'm not fooling anyone.

"But who gives a fuck what they do?" I say in a rush. "I'm with my two best friends. I've got a good buzz on. Life is perfect." I slide to my feet while I still can, and hold a hand out to Xander. "And I'm about to make my soulmate come until he finds oblivion."

"I'm so glad you made your sister miss that shot," Xander sighs. "She is the best."

And he hustles me into the cottage, buoyed by the sound of Olly's chuckle.

Free Stuff!

Sign up to my mailing list by scanning one of the QR codes on the next few pages. Or all of them. Go nuts.

Free prequel to *The Faction War Chronicles:*

Character sheet from *Who the Monsters Are*:

Bonus epilogue from *The Warrior Angels:*

Bonus scene from *Better the Devil You Know:*

As always, thank you for reading my book! If *Soulblind* stole your soul or made you wonder if you're dating a Rabid—leave a review! Every review sends a little spark into the bookish ether, guiding lost readers to this enchanted mess of romantic chaos.

Can't wait to hear from you!

About the Author

Nadine Little lives in Scotland and is an ecologist who specialises in sitting at her desk because she has a gammy knee. And hip. And foot…

This book is technically the first standalone she's written (yes, she will finish the *Verdana* series at some point), but will not be the last. The next has sexy butterfly men. Make of that what you will.

When she's not writing (and when she is), Nadine can be found ignoring most self-publishing advice.

For more on her books and a peek behind the scenes, sign up to her mailing list and follow her on social media.

You can connect with me on:
- https://nadinelittle.com
- https://twitter.com/Nadine_Little_
- https://www.facebook.com/nadinelittleauthor